CARNIVAL OF CHAOS

The Basilica Diaries
Book Four

Richard Kurti

SAPERE
BOOKS

CARNIVAL OF CHAOS

Published by Sapere Books.

24 Trafalgar Road, Ilkley, LS29 8HH

saperebooks.com

ISBN:

Money is like fire, we cannot live without it,
but we should never get too close to it.
16th-century Rabbi

1: STRANGER

Papal States, 1508

If he stopped, he would die. Just like all the others. But the boy wasn't ready for death. He didn't want to meet Allah. Not today. So his arms thrashed with desperation, clawing at the water as it tried to drag him into the terrifying depths of its cold heart.

The waves slapped his face, driving water into his mouth and up his nose until he was choking more than breathing.

But still his arms tore at the sea, refusing to give up. He craned his neck. Through salt-stung eyes, he glimpsed the outline of a building on the clifftop. *Focus on that. Just that. Forget everything else. Forget all the dead bodies chained on the ship...*

But how could he forget?

Flashbacks of horror flooded his mind — contorted bodies chained in the ship's hold, screams of agony, images of blood and vomit and fear cutting down everyone it touched ... his uncles ... his cousins ... his father.

Grief ballooned inside the boy's skinny body. He opened his mouth and howled, trying to let the pain out before its leaden weight dragged him under.

The building on the cliff. Focus on that.

The boy paralysed his mind so that his body could do its work. One arm after the other, pulling at the water, inching forward ... until he was within touching distance of some jagged rocks that punctured the undulating surface.

He reached out, fingers touching the cold rocks, but they were wet with slime and moss, and he couldn't grab hold.

Suddenly the undertow clasped his feet and sucked him away from land.

The boy thrashed forward again, so close, if only he could grasp onto the jags.

Without warning, the capricious waves pushed him from behind, driving him onto the rocks. He screamed in agony as his face was dragged across a cluster of barnacles. The boy's hands flew out, reaching to grab hold, but waves wrapped around his small body and hauled him back into the foaming water.

Three times the sea drove him into the rocks, and three times it snatched him away again, like a monster toying with its prey. Until finally the waves overplayed their hand, and the boy was able to jam his fingers into a crack in the rockface and haul himself up.

Somehow, he managed to slither over the boulders, barnacles slicing his palms and knees, then roll down onto the wet sand. He landed with a thump.

The boy closed his eyes and gulped in a lungful of air. He could hear the sea snarling behind him. Furious at being outwitted, it sent waves chasing up the beach to reclaim its prize, but the boy was no longer within reach. He had cheated death. Yet it was a pyrrhic victory, for now he remembered — there was nothing left to live for, because everyone was dead.

So the boy closed his eyes and let go.

A dog's wet nose snuffled into the boy's neck and nudged him awake. He licked the boy's face and started barking urgently for his master.

Feet hurried across the sand. A man bent down and gently lifted the boy up. He was an old man with a kind face and barely any teeth, but he cradled the boy with such tenderness, reassuring him in a strange language that he was safe now, that the ordeal was over. As the man carried him up the beach, the dog circling them excitedly, he called up to the clifftop, urgently summoning help.

The boy must have passed out again, because barely a moment later he was in a small hut, the air thick with pungent woodsmoke that caught the back of his throat. Two women were wrapping him in a warm, dry blanket that smelled of straw. The old man was standing in the shadows, watching as the women tended the cuts on the boy's body, wincing in empathy at every touch of the vinegar-cloth.

Soup was the next thing he remembered. A bowl of steaming broth with herbs and onions. A young woman was feeding him sips with a wooden spoon, urging him to keep eating, smiling encouragement at every drop he swallowed. The boy glanced up — the little hut was now full of people, as if the whole village had crowded inside to gaze at this strange boy who had been washed up on their shore.

Suddenly an excited voice started shouting outside. "*Pronto! Pronto! Il battello!*"

A girl rushed into the hut. She was about twelve years old, the same age as the boy. "*Il battello! Vieni!*" She grabbed the old man's hand and hauled him out of the hut. The other men followed, and the boy sensed this was something to do with him. He tried to stand up, but the woman with the soup held him tightly. She was trying to protect him, but he didn't want protection, he wanted the truth.

The boy wriggled to free himself until the woman relented, took his hand in hers and led him outside.

The boy squinted in the bright sunlight. There were a dozen shacks clustered around some animal pens, a donkey was harnessed to a rickety cart that was creaking under the weight of a large barrel, and a handful of scrawny goats nibbled their way around the village. But all the people had left their huts and were now standing on the edge of the cliff, staring out to sea.

With a growing sense of dread, the boy pushed through the villagers until he stood on the very edge of the cliff.

And then he saw it.

A ship was drifting towards the beach. It was a merchant ship, a carrack, but all the sails were down and there was no sign of the crew. No-one in the rigging, no-one at the helm, no-one in the lookout.

Dreadful memories assaulted the boy's mind — bodies twisted in death, blood and vomit swilling across the deck. Now that he was safe on land, there was nothing he could do to keep the harrowing images at bay. He screamed, trying to shatter their power, but the visions fed off his fear.

He remembered crouching in the salty darkness, trying to hide from rampaging Death.

He remembered listening to his family crying out to Allah, begging for mercy.

He remembered the sound of death rattling in the throats of young men.

Overwhelmed, the boy's legs gave way and he collapsed to the ground, fists clamped against his ears, his hands trembling uncontrollably.

Women crouched next to him, trying to comfort him, but every gentle touch triggered another harrowing memory. The boy lashed out with his feet, driving everyone away, until he was curled up in a tight ball, alone and howling like a stricken animal.

2: ADRIFT

It was not the interruption Deputato Tomasso of the Guardia Apostolica del Vaticano wanted.

He had been undercover in the port of Civitavecchia for a month, painstakingly gathering evidence against a criminal gang suspected of running a sophisticated racket to avoid paying import duties to the Vatican, effectively stealing from the Pope. Tomasso was now just days away from making arrests, when the harbourmaster burst into the observation post hidden in one of the lantern houses that studded the walls of the port.

"Drop everything! You have to come with me!"

"I don't exist, remember?" Tomasso said irritably.

"This is different."

"Covert means no interruptions."

"Deputato! This can't wait!"

Tomasso turned to look at the harbourmaster, a lean man in his fifties with the tanned, weather-beaten skin of someone who spent most of his time on the water; yet the silver hair and beard made him look as if he should perhaps be sitting in some village square playing chess and enjoying his retirement. "You do realise that when you barged in here, you alerted the whole port to my reconnaissance operation?"

"This is more important!"

"Then send word to Rome! There's a guardhouse full of soldiers waiting for a mission."

"No!" Panic tensed the harbourmaster's face. "An abandoned carrack has been spotted. It could drift into the shipping lanes at any moment and cause havoc."

"The Tyrrhenian Sea is quite big. I don't think a collision is likely."

"Do I tell you how to do your job?" the harbourmaster growled.

"No. You just interrupt me when I'm trying to do it."

"Deputato, this is my harbour. My responsibility. My authority."

Tomasso closed his eyes and counted to five. At thirty-three years old, he was hungry for promotion, but if he was ever going to make it beyond *Deputato* he needed to solve a big case on his own, and this was supposed to be it. But it was clear the harbourmaster wasn't going to give up; he had the quiet stubbornness of a seasoned bureaucrat. "Very well." Tomasso stood up and stretched his back. "Where is it?"

"Off the coast of Santa Severa, ten miles south of here. A caravel is being rigged to take us."

As they strode along the wide stone jetty, Tomasso tried to cling to what was left of his anonymity by sticking to the shadows, which were still littered with stinking fish debris from that morning's catch. But the harbourmaster was not one for the shadows; his uniform was designed to advertise authority, the red breeches and blue doublet adorned with gold brocade warning would-be smugglers to think twice.

The port was busy this morning, with a dozen ships already unloading and more at anchor, waiting for a berth. If Civitavecchia were ever put under siege, the Papal States would grind to a halt within weeks.

"You're sure these villagers who reported the ship hadn't been drinking?"

"There was a survivor," the harbourmaster said with a grim face. "A boy who got washed ashore."

"So, we're doing all this on the word of a young boy?"

"We're doing this because it's your job to protect Vatican interests. On land and at sea." The harbourmaster stopped by a sleek caravel with twin masts and lateen sails, flying the official flag of the port of Civitavecchia. "How soon can we leave?" he called out to the boatswain.

"All rigged and ready, sir," the sailor replied.

The harbourmaster hopped onto the small ship with well-practised ease and took his place on the quarterdeck, leaving Tomasso to clamber aboard and perch on a bench at the base of the main mast.

The moment the ship cast off, Tomasso realised why the port authorities had chosen a caravel for their official business. The ship was fast and incredibly manoeuvrable; it made light work of weaving between the anchored ships, and in a few minutes was cutting through the heavy swell of the sea.

As he watched the harbourmaster take control of the vessel, Tomasso wondered if he had underestimated the man. Far from being a petty bureaucrat, the harbourmaster understood every inch of the rigging; he made sure the sails were perfectly trimmed, and that they always held the shortest line to Santa Severa, regardless of the tidal currents that were trying to pull them to the west.

As soon as they rounded the Marinella headland, they saw the outline of a ship in the distance; an hour later, they were pulling alongside the carrack. Immediately, Tomasso could see the gravity of the situation: the ship had drifted sideways and was being washed closer to the shore with every undulating wave; if it grounded on the beach and tipped over, it would be very difficult to refloat, and if it drifted further south onto the rocks, the carrack would be wrecked. All the villagers had gathered on the clifftop to watch the spectacle unfold.

"As soon as we're on board, secure lines to the hull and pull it away from the rocks," the harbourmaster called out to the boatswain.

"Aye, aye, sir."

"And when you've got some depth, we'll drop its anchor."

The harbourmaster spun the ship's wheel and steered the caravel under the bowsprit so they could board it on the leeward side. As they crossed the keel, Tomasso looked up and saw the name of the ship painted in gold letters: *Speranza*.

But there was nothing hopeful about the stench that was seeping out of the abandoned vessel — it was the cloying, sickly smell of decay.

As the caravel nudged alongside the larger ship, the boatswain reached out and lashed a rope around one of the iron loops hanging from the hull, tying the two boats together. The harbourmaster grabbed a rigging-rope hanging from the deck rail and started scaling the side of the ship.

Tomasso smiled. "You're as nimble as a mountain goat!" he called up.

"Plenty of practice boarding smuggling ships," the harbourmaster replied. Then he looked down and quietly enjoyed the spectacle of Tomasso scrambling up the same ropes with all the poise of a drunken octopus.

But once on deck, a heavy atmosphere of doom crushed all humour out of the two men. The silent emptiness of the ship was unnerving: the rigging was empty, the ropes unmanned, and the lookouts gone. There was no crude banter, no barked orders from a grumpy chief mate, no sounds of scrubbing brushes cleaning the decks; there was just a gentle creak as the ship rocked in the swell.

"What is that stench?" Tomasso said, tying a scarf around his mouth and nose to block it out.

But the harbourmaster drew a deep breath like a wine connoisseur studying a vintage bouquet. "The cargo is rotting livestock," he concluded. "Maybe it's diseased."

"So how long has the ship been adrift?"

"Too long." The harbourmaster walked to the stern, pushed open the door to the captain's cabin and rummaged through the desk, looking for charts and logs, but everything had been removed.

"What does that mean?" Tomasso asked, peering through the door.

"That the ship was deliberately abandoned. And the crew didn't want to be traced."

"That doesn't make sense. How far do you think it's come?"

The harbourmaster shrugged. "There are thousands of these caravels trading around the Mediterranean. Probably heading up the coast."

"Until something went wrong."

"Very wrong, judging by that stench."

Tomasso followed the harbourmaster as he slid down the ladder to the lower deck and approached the main hatch leading deeper into the darkness of the hold. With every footstep, the foul smell became more pungent, until even the harbourmaster was forced to cover his face. They stood either side of the lowest hatch, steeling themselves.

"Should we wait for reinforcements?" Tomasso suggested.

The harbourmaster shook his head. "Whatever animals were down there are long dead."

Tomasso took a lantern from the wall and struck a tinderbox to light it, then the harbourmaster slid back the iron bolts and swung open the hatch.

Immediately the sound of a thousand buzzing flies ballooned up from the darkness.

The harbourmaster cursed.

Holding the lantern in front of him, Tomasso picked his way down the steps and edged into the gloom. As his eyes adjusted, he was hit by the horror — a tangle of human corpses filled the hold, hundreds of them, chained together and twisted in frozen contortions of agony. Their dark skins were covered in strange tattoos and pus-filled blisters. Blood had burst from their noses and mouths and was smeared down their bodies. What hadn't been spewed from their mouths had erupted from their bowels, covering the deck in blood and faeces.

Tomasso felt the strength draining from his legs. He clung to one of the chain hooks hanging from the ceiling, desperately trying not to pass out. He had seen plenty of death in the line of duty, but never anything on this scale. Sweat broke out across his forehead and he could feel his stomach start to heave.

"Deputato! Get outside!" the harbourmaster yelled.

Tomasso peered through the gloom, but his vision was swimming and all he could see was a blurred shape looming towards him.

"Deputato Tomasso!"

His head lolled forward and he started to keel over, when suddenly two hands gripped his torso. "You need air!"

With a single heave, the harbourmaster threw Tomasso over his shoulder and scrambled out of the hold. He ran through the deserted crew quarters and up the next ladder, then threw the deputy out into the fresh air of the top deck.

"Breathe!" he commanded.

Tomasso opened his mouth and vomited profusely.

The harbourmaster dodged out of the way just in time. "Well, that's one way to do it."

Tomasso looked up at the harbourmaster, incredulous at his composure; he really had underestimated this man. "A boy survived that?"

"He must have flung himself into the water and swam."

"How could anyone survive such horror?"

"I doubt his mind will ever be the same again."

Tomasso looked down at his own trembling hands — his skin was grey and clammy. "What devil walked here?"

The harbourmaster looked out to sea with weary cynicism. "No devil. Just the evil of men."

3: DENIALS

It was just the two of them in the Vatican's Council Chamber. Domenico Falchoni and Pope Julius II. Countless millions of Christians would have given anything to be alone with His Holiness Pope Julius, Supreme Pontiff, Bishop of Rome, and Leader of the Papal States. But Domenico knew the furious temper of the man behind the pious titles; he could feel it now, like a physical force boiling inside the grand chamber, terrifying even the delicate frescoes which clung to the walls.

Domenico had been through many difficult moments in his twelve years as Captain of the Apostolic Guard and was now on his third pope; but in the fraught politics of the Vatican, survival meant walking a never-ending tightrope.

As soon as the report came in from his deputy, Domenico told the Pope about the terrible discovery near Civitavecchia. The Holy Father had taken the news badly, dropping to his knees and offering earnest prayers for all the lost souls.

Then his mind turned to vengeance, and he summoned the heads of the great dynastic families to appear before him.

The ornate, gilt-inlaid doors of the Council Chamber swung open, and a sombre-faced Cardinal Riario led in four of the most powerful men in the Italian peninsula: Medici, Sforza, Colonna and Orsini. Their ages ranged from mid-thirties to mid-fifties, but they all shared the arrogant demeanour of the wealthy. All were well-nourished, and all had dressed to impress in heavy velvets, fur trims and gold chains of office.

But the Holy Father was not interested in fripperies. He glared at the four oligarchs. "The good ship *Speranza*. Speak!" he commanded.

The aristocrats remained the picture of innocence. Medici and Sforza exchanged a baffled glance, Colonna's brow creased as if he was wracking his memory, and Orsini's large eyes widened like a young child.

"Let me refresh your failing memories," said the Holy Father, adding a dash of sarcasm to his words. "An abandoned ship was found drifting off the coast yesterday. It contained the bodies of two hundred and seventy-nine men and fourteen boys. They died in the most appalling circumstances, diseased and chained like lost souls in purgatory."

Orsini crossed himself. "Our thoughts and prayers are with them, Holy Father."

"And with their poor families," Colonna added, not wanting to be out-pioused by his rival.

"I don't give a damn about your thoughts and prayers!" Pope Julius thundered. "I want to know the truth about what happened. What led to this appalling loss of life?"

"Surely you cannot think *we* would in any way be involved in such a tragedy, Holy Father?" Giovanni de Medici looked shocked at the suggestion.

"The dynasties that you lead run all the major construction contracts in Rome. The creation of the greatest basilica in history is in your hands. You charter hundreds of ships; you employ thousands of men to shape millions of tons of stone. Nothing happens in Rome without your knowledge, and yet the name *Speranza* means nothing to you?"

Medici shook his head slowly. "Truly, Your Holiness, I have no recollection of that name."

"I am sorry if we have offended you, Holy Father," Colonna concurred, "but you have summoned the wrong men to account for this terrible tragedy."

Orsini couldn't let his rival have the last word. "If there is anything my family can do to help bring those responsible to justice, we are at your disposal, Your Holiness."

Pope Julius studied the aristocrats with his penetrating gaze. "One of you is lying. And those who lie to me are damned in the hereafter."

The oligarchs looked down at their finely cut leather boots in a synchronised display of humility. They were old hands at dealing with difficult moments and knew that silence had a power all of its own.

Pope Julius turned to Domenico. "Perhaps some details will stimulate their memories, Capitano Falchoni."

"We have yet to determine the exact cause of death, Holy Father, but even before disease took hold, the conditions on the ship would have been atrocious." Domenico glanced at the oligarchs. "There were far too many bodies in the hold. They were chained together, forced to relieve themselves where they lay. The water buckets were all empty. The absence of women suggests they were to be used as manual labour. One thing is certain: given the unbearable suffering they endured in the darkness of that ship, death would have been a relief."

Giulio Orsini cleared his throat to speak. "Holy Father, Capitano Falchoni's account only serves to exonerate us. Our families are honoured to be part of the greatest building project in all Christendom, and it is out of respect for St Peter that we *only* employ the finest craftsmen. To use slave labour would tarnish the sanctity of the new basilica. And since these unfortunate souls you describe were clearly enslaved, that proves they are nothing to do with us."

The other oligarchs nodded sagely, relieved to have found a flaw in the logic of their accuser.

"Perhaps they were being shipped north, to join the mercenary armies of the barbarous Germans," Fabrizio Colonna suggested.

Which prompted Medici to add his half-ducat of wisdom. "Much as we are rivals in business, Orsini speaks the truth. Craftsmen are building St Peter's. The work is hard and demanding, but one must never conflate manual labour with slave labour."

"We all abhor slavery, Holy Father, as do you," Colonna concluded.

"Do you presume to lecture me?" Pope Julius hissed with rage. "Do you dare lecture God's anointed representative on Earth?"

Again, the oligarchs looked down.

"St Peter's is a basilica to glorify God, not heap misery on the least fortunate." The Pope's steely gaze moved from one aristocrat to the next. "Almost three hundred souls perished in torment barely thirty miles from this very room. Yet you, some of the most powerful men in Rome, have no knowledge of the atrocity."

Silence.

"Get your houses in order," Pope Julius warned. "Moral order. For I will not have sin built into the fabric of my basilica. Now get out!"

The Holy Father watched as the oligarchs retreated from the chamber in silence, then he turned his deep-set eyes on Cardinal Riario. "You think I'm mistaken."

The cardinal hesitated, running his fingers through the curly hair of his tonsure as he tried to compose a diplomatic answer. "Not at all, Holy Father. Your wisdom comes from God."

Pope Julius scoffed. "And your candied words are precisely what I would expect from a talented camerlengo. But your eyes betray your true thoughts, Riario."

"Forgive me, Holy Father."

Julius stood up and paced to the window which looked out over the Belvedere Courtyard, where groundsmen were hard at work shaping the new gardens. "Does anyone believe the dynastic families' protestations of innocence? 'Thoughts and prayers' indeed. The only people they think about are themselves. And the only thing they pray for is further enrichment."

"Yet there are many different construction projects on the peninsula," Riario ventured. "And the point about mercenary armies in the German states is valid."

"Plausibility does not imply truth."

"Yet it would be imprudent to dismiss all other explanations."

Domenico cleared his throat to remind the two men that he was still in the room. Pope Julius lifted his gaze from the toiling gardeners and turned to face him. "A summer cough? Or you wish to speak?"

"Holy Father, it is my firm belief that the *Speranza* tragedy is directly linked to the construction of St Peter's."

"Because?"

"The dynastic families claim they only use skilled craftsmen, but in reality, there is a huge demand for brute strength. Digging the massive foundation pits, moving mountains of earth and stone… Skilled craftsmen can only start work once unskilled labour has put the elements in place."

Pope Julius smoothed his long silver beard, considering the captain's words. Cardinal Riario was less indulgent. "Do not speculate unless you have firm knowledge, Falchoni. We cannot act on rumour."

"The oligarchs are lying. I can sense it," Julius muttered with frustration. "They know what is going on and who is responsible, yet they dare to come here and lie to my face, whilst I must be held to a more exacting standard of proof."

"Because you occupy the moral high ground," the cardinal replied. "That is why the world respects you and looks up to you. Whereas everyone despises the oligarchs, even though they fear them and grovel to them."

Domenico was losing patience with the political manoeuvring. "Forgive me, Holy Father, but you must take swift action to punish those responsible. And punish them harshly."

Riario glared at Domenico. "Do not presume to tell the Holy Father what needs to be done!"

"Your Eminence, if this atrocity goes unpunished, it will happen again."

"Silence!"

"It's all very well telling the oligarchs to get their houses in order, but if they are left to regulate their own behaviour, we will have another atrocity on our hands before the year is out."

"Leave, Falchoni!" It was rare to see Cardinal Riario lose his temper, which made it more shocking.

Domenico drew a breath to calm down, then bowed. "Forgive me."

But as he turned to leave, Pope Julius raised his hand. "Stay!"

Domenico froze, caught between the Cardinal and the Pope.

"Actually, I like the fact that Capitano Falchoni speaks his mind. That is what a good servant does. Go on."

"I do not wish to speak above my rank, Holy Father, but I know how these oligarchs think. I have seen them on the battlefield and at various times interrogated them about other crimes. Their only concern is to enrich their dynasties. If that involves breaking the law, then they will do it, and continue doing it for as long as they can get away with it. They will not stop of their own accord. They have to be stopped. By force."

"Force?" Julius raised his eyebrows as he considered what that might mean.

"By the force of the law, Holy Father. By using the power of truth to expose their crimes."

Pope Julius nodded. "Then I order you to get to the truth, Capitano Falchoni. Marshal all the resources of the Apostolic Guard to investigate this atrocity. If there is a connection between the *Speranza* deaths and the construction of St Peter's, it must be exposed, and those responsible punished." Julius turned to Cardinal Riario and saw the displeasure in his eyes. "That is not the look of an obedient servant of the Church."

"An investigation will not bring back the lives of two hundred and ninety-three poor souls, Holy Father."

"Cardinal, you speak as if you are trying to protect the interests of the aristocracy," Pope Julius said in a barbed tone. "Perhaps your loyalties are torn?"

"My loyalties are only to you and the Church, Holy Father. But going to war with the oligarchs will benefit no-one."

"Justice benefits everyone. Which is why justice is the bedrock of Christianity." Julius crossed the room and sat at the head of the great table that dominated the council chamber. "Whichever of the dynastic families has lied to me will pay a heavy price. They will be barred from all future construction contracts for St Peter's Basilica and struck from the tender list for any other work undertaken by the Vatican. There will be no more enrichment for liars and those who sacrifice innocent lives on the altar of greed."

4: CLOISTERED

"For Castro!" he exclaimed one last time. Then with an agonised cry, he succumbed to the flames.

The last drop of ink drained from her quill just as Cristina Falchoni reached the end of the page. She picked up a small wooden scoop and sprinkled some blotting sand across the paper. As she waited for the excess ink to be soaked up, she rolled her shoulders to ease the stiffness that always set in after a few hours at the desk. Then Cristina picked up the paper, shook the sand into a metal bucket, and placed the sheet on top of the pile of pages she'd already completed that week.

When she had first started writing these diaries recounting the various crimes and misdemeanours surrounding the construction of the new St Peter's Basilica, Cristina had felt daunted by the enormous task. After writing from dawn until dusk, she was dismayed to have only produced three sheets of paper. But she kept going regardless, head down, writing something every day without fail until it became a habit. After a month, she was pleasantly surprised to discover that the pile of completed sheets was starting to feel more substantial.

It was at this point that she created a set of rituals to stop herself getting overwhelmed by the scale of the undertaking. Whenever she had completed a quire of twenty-five sheets, she would move the papers from her desk to the bookshelf. When twenty quires were stacked on the shelf, she would collect them into a ream secured with some string. Two reams combined to make a bundle (a thousand sheets!) which she would carefully secure in a large leather pouch.

Cristina glanced at the three completed pouches that nestled under the simple iron bed in the convent cell; pride may be a sin, but how could she not feel satisfaction at the progress she had made?

A tolling from the convent's belltower prompted Cristina to stand up from the desk. She had discovered the hard way that the secret to prolonged periods of concentrated writing was to take a short break every two pages. So she opened the door to her small cell, entered the cloisters and gazed across the cobbled courtyard, where the sisters of the House of Eternal Grace were hurrying about their duties.

It had been nearly two years since the terrible events surrounding Sister Ysabella's death had shattered the peace of the convent. Some of the sisters had found it hard to forgive Cristina for her role in the scandal, and were unhappy about her being part of their community, even as a guest. But Abbess Beatrice understood that forgiveness did not come with caveats; she knew that Cristina needed time to heal and had given her refuge here to pour her thoughts onto paper. Both women believed that if she could write everything down, God would understand what Cristina had done and forgive her.

But this wasn't solely about God; Cristina had to learn how to forgive herself. Her confidence had been badly damaged by the unforeseen consequences of her 'Bones of St Peter' campaign of disinformation, and she needed time to start trusting her own judgement again.

By the time the bell had stopped tolling, all the sisters had settled at the tasks that would carry them through to lunch. It intrigued Cristina how much she had come to like the 'tyranny of the bell'. At first, she had resented the way it held the sisters in servitude, but over time she had come to realise that there was solace and reassurance in the rigid routines of convent life.

The repetition and ritual relieved her of the need to wrestle with reality, which in turn freed up her mind to untangle itself. That she now occupied the room where Sister Ysabella had lived and died was a sombre warning about what happened when a mind veered off course.

"Cristina! You have a visitor."

Cristina turned to see one of the young postulants hurrying towards her along the cloisters.

"Can't they just leave a message?"

"He was most insistent."

"He? Did he give a name?"

"He said if you knew who he was, you would make an excuse to avoid him."

Cristina felt suddenly anxious. The few people who were close to her all knew that she didn't want to be disturbed. This must be unwelcome news; perhaps someone was seriously ill. Her fears were compounded when she entered the gatehouse and saw her brother standing there.

"Domenico, what's wrong? Is it our parents? Has something happened?" she demanded.

"Their last letter was as robust as ever," Domenico replied with a casual shrug. "A little too obsessed with strange details, but that seems to go with old age."

"How many times have I told you about making sweeping generalisations, Domenico?"

"It was an observation. Not a judgement."

"Well, you might feel differently when you get to their age. You know there are some sisters in this convent who regard me as old?"

"At thirty-six? That's a bit of a stretch."

"Some of the postulants here are barely out of childhood."

Domenico drew up a chair for Cristina, but she shook her head. "I have another page to complete before lunch. So, if this isn't bad news, why the visit?"

"Maybe it's just nice to see you."

"Come on, don't pretend this is a social visit. I know you too well."

"Hypothetically, if there was an investigation to be undertaken," Domenico said, tiptoeing around the point, "would you be interested?"

"No. Absolutely not."

"You don't even know what it's about."

"I need to keep the world at bay until I've unravelled how I got to this point."

"Just because you're no longer winding your clocks, it doesn't mean that time has stopped. The world won't wait forever."

"Please, don't take away the peace I have found here."

Domenico hesitated as he tried to think of a way through his sister's defences. "Can I at least introduce you to someone?"

Cristina sensed she was being lured into a trap.

"It'll only take a few minutes," Domenico insisted.

"Maybe next week. I'll have completed another ream by then."

"The thing is … he's actually waiting in the convent library."

"That was very presumptuous."

"Cristina, if you knew what he'd been through, you would not refuse."

She saw her brother glance down and knew that this must be serious.

As Domenico swung open the door to the convent library, Cristina felt the boy's large brown eyes lock onto her. But his face didn't crease into a smile, and his mouth didn't utter a sound. He didn't show joy or anticipation the way many children might; there was just an immense aura of sadness surrounding him, and the epicentre of sorrow was his eyes. It was as if they belonged to another person, perhaps some old man who had seen a lifetime of suffering and betrayal, or a fading general who had witnessed too much bloodshed on the battlefield. And yet there was no rage or bitterness in the boy's gaze, just a desperate, silent plea for help.

"He was found washed up on the beach at Santa Severa, barely alive," Domenico explained. "The villagers rescued him and sent word to the magistrates in Civitavecchia."

Cristina looked at the boy's mop of curly brown hair, and the worry lines that creased his young forehead. "How did he get washed up? From where?"

"He escaped from a ship."

"What?" Cristina turned to her brother in confusion. "Why would anyone jump from a ship?"

"Because everyone on board was dead."

"What are you talking about, Domenico?"

"Deputy Tomasso boarded the vessel with the harbourmaster. The crew had abandoned the ship. In the hold were two hundred and ninety-three dead bodies."

"Dear God," Cristina whispered.

"It's impossible to imagine what this boy has endured."

"What's his name?"

"We don't know. He hasn't uttered a word since he was rescued."

Cristina drew up a stool and sat opposite the boy so that their faces were level. Gently she reached out to take his hand, but he flinched and pulled away.

"It's all right. I won't hurt you," she whispered. Slowly she reached out again, and this time he let her hold his right hand. She looked at the thin fingers and felt the callouses on his palm from some sort of manual labour; on the back of both his hands were geometrical tattoos that looked like cuneiform symbols.

"And he's spoken to no-one?"

"We don't even know which language he speaks. Or where all the victims were from."

Cristina studied the boy's complexion. "Judging from his skin tone, I'd guess the North African coast."

"So Arabic is worth a try?"

Cristina looked directly into the boy's eyes. "*Min 'ayn 'ant?*"

There was no response.

"What did you ask?"

"Where he comes from. The problem is most of the North African countries practise diglossia."

Domenico looked at her blankly.

"It's when ordinary people use two languages side by side. That was classical Arabic I just tried, the language of learning." Cristina turned to her brother. "All the texts I've read from the Islamic Golden Age are written in it. If he doesn't understand, he probably has no education."

"How about trying some other dialects?"

"I know a few phrases in Egyptian Arabic. A little more of Levantine."

"Then try those."

Cristina rummaged a few phrases from her memory and repeated them to the boy, but there was no flicker of recognition on his face.

"Maybe…" Cristina stood up and strode across the library, plucked an atlas of maps from one of the shelves and opened it on a lectern. She studied the most recent charts of the Mediterranean. "That would make sense…"

Domenico peered over her shoulder. "From Santa Severa, the shortest route to Africa takes you directly south."

"Right into the Hafsid Kingdom," Cristina agreed. "Where Arabic is widely spoken, but ordinary people speak Berber."

"Are they similar?"

"No. Not at all. And each of the scattered tribes has a different Berber language, so those from the west of the kingdom can't even understand those from the east. Unless we can find out exactly where he's from, we'll never be able to talk to him."

They both turned and looked at the boy, who was now gazing at a small robin that had perched on the window ledge and was chirruping gaily.

"One thing's for sure," Domenico said, "he's a very long way from home."

"Did his family all die on the ship?" Cristina whispered.

"We don't know."

"Was it illness?"

"I don't have any answers for you, Cristina."

"It's an appalling tragedy."

"And that's why I'm here. To ask for your help in unravelling this horror."

Cristina shook her head and stepped away from her brother. "You know I am committed to writing the diaries. In full."

"Look at him." Domenico pointed to the boy who had tiptoed closer to the robin, as if this were the only living creature in the world who understood him. "All I'm asking is that you use your formidable intelligence to help the most vulnerable."

"Is that how the Pope expressed it?"

Domenico hesitated. "The Holy Father has many agendas. But I'm asking you as a human being. If nothing else, help me get this boy back to his home and family."

Cristina watched as the boy slowly extended his hand and waited … until the robin hopped onto his fingers. The faintest glimmer of a smile crossed the boy's face.

"You don't need to ask my permission," Abbess Beatrice said as she pressed a fresh log onto the fire glowing in the hearth. "You are a guest here, Cristina, not one of the sisters."

"But I respect your wisdom, Reverend Mother." Cristina gazed at the fire, watching the flames try to find a vulnerability in the newly arrived log. It was only on the very hottest of days that the abbess let the fire in her office go out, for she had reached that age when her bones seemed to hold the cold better than the warmth.

"I vowed not to reengage with life until I had unravelled the tangle of my past mistakes," Cristina continued. "And I am still engaged in that battle, yet now the outside world is trying to pull me back into the maelstrom."

"I have a suspicion that most of us are still trying to untangle the meaning of our lives on the day we draw our final breaths," Abbess Beatrice said with a smile. "Perhaps only God can complete that task."

"I feel weak for not persevering with my writing. But when I look into the eyes of that boy…"

"A cloistered life is a rich one, Cristina, yet it is not the whole of life. Perhaps God is calling you through that lost child?"

"Perhaps." Cristina gazed at the log, whose bark had now started to singe under the attack of the flames. "If I do leave the convent, will you still accept me back in a few weeks to finish my writing?"

"I will make sure the room is untouched. As you leave it, so shall you find it. No matter how long you take."

"Thank you, Reverend Mother. Perhaps this will help me understand where my destiny lies."

The abbess nodded. "The poor and defenceless need justice. God is asking you to rejoin the fray. If that isn't destiny, I don't know what is."

5: HOME

The moment she heard footsteps in the entrance hall, Isra Sahin knew her mistress had returned. The way Cristina entered the house was unique: keys turned decisively in the lock without a fumble; the door swung open so that it bounced off the iron stop. Four steps in then a momentary pause as she turned on the spot to take in the space, checking to see what had changed. It couldn't be anyone else.

Isra hurried from the kitchen at the back of the house and arrived in the hall to see Cristina standing on her own, illuminated by a shaft of sunlight that burst through the high window. She wanted to run over and hug her, but Isra knew that would make Cristina feel awkward. "You're back!" she laughed. "So nice to have you home!"

Isra plucked the small bag from Cristina's hand and took the woollen cloak from her shoulders. "Are you hungry? Do you need a fresh set of clothes? The laundry is all aired and pressed. The house is waiting for you."

"And it all looks wonderful, Isra. Thank you for taking care of everything." Cristina glanced up the stairs to the library doors.

"I've kept all the bedrooms cleaned and ready for your return," Isra said, leading the way. "But I'm the only person who's been in the library, and then only to keep the clock wound." She pushed open the double doors and Cristina drew a deep breath, savouring the smell of leather and paper.

"Did you miss its tick?" Isra pointed to the verge-and-foliot clock dominating one wall.

"Is it keeping good time?"

"Perfect. I haven't had to call the clockmaker out once."

Cristina nodded. "It makes sense. Unused room, stable temperature, no vibrations from footsteps or the doors opening and closing. Some things thrive in isolation."

Isra fluttered around the room in a domestic whirl, throwing open window shutters and letting sunlight back into a room that had only been half-alive for the past two years. Cristina could almost feel the one thousand, eight hundred and seventy-nine volumes flinching at the sudden brightness.

Her eyes roamed across the bookshelves. Everything was so familiar … and yet also a little strange, as if this was someone else's library. She craned her neck to read some of the titles, and memories of how and why she had acquired each book flooded back. It was like a reunion of old friends, so why did it feel disorientating? If nothing had changed in the library, perhaps the only explanation was that Cristina herself had changed. All that time she had spent immersed in reflection and writing must have subtly reshaped her mind.

"You're sure you're not hungry?" Isra repeated, enjoying the feeling of Cristina's presence in the library once again. "I can rustle you something up in no time."

"I couldn't eat a thing, Isra."

"And what about your writing? Have you finished all the diaries? Are you looking for a publisher yet?"

Cristina scoffed. "I'm not even a quarter of the way through."

"After all this time?"

"Writing is a slow business."

"You need a deadline," Isra smiled. "You have always worked best under pressure."

Cristina turned and looked at Isra. How she'd missed those large, brown eyes, the easy-going smile and the unwavering loyalty. "I'm so glad you're still here, Isra."

The housekeeper was puzzled. "Why wouldn't I be?"

"I thought maybe some dashing young man might have swept you off your feet."

"I know it sounds strange, but even looking after an empty house, there are barely enough hours in the day."

Cristina smiled. "Are you on course?"

"Ahead!"

"Show me."

Isra thought for a moment, then said, "*Missio latina per tricesimum diem natalem meum discere potuit. Successit mihi tres annos primo.*"

Cristina clapped her hands with joy. "*The mission was to learn Latin by my thirtieth birthday. I have succeeded three years early.* Bravo, Isra. Impressive."

"Is that why you've come home? To check on my progress?"

Cristina laughed.

"And how long are you staying?" Isra added.

Suddenly there was a loud knock on the main door downstairs.

"I think that will answer all your questions."

"Who is it?"

The fist hammered on the door again, and Isra led the way, hurrying down the stairs. When she swung open the front door, she saw Domenico standing there with a young boy.

Isra glanced warily at Cristina. "What exactly have you been doing in that convent?"

Domenico ushered the boy into the house. "There was an abandoned ship found floating off the coast."

"I heard talk of that at the market," Isra replied.

"Well, this boy is the only survivor."

Isra looked at the skinny figure. "What exactly did he survive?"

"We don't know yet. But everyone on board was found dead. Somehow, he escaped. And even then, he nearly drowned."

Isra crouched down so that she could look at him properly. Immediately she sensed that he had known profound fear and sadness. She reached out, folded her arms around the boy and hugged him tightly. As she felt his heart beating next to hers, a wave of compassion welled up inside her; she knew what it meant to be an abandoned child.

"You're safe now," Isra whispered, tears pricking her eyes. "We'll look after you." But when she relaxed her hug to look into the boy's face, he seemed unmoved and unreachable, as if he was locked far away inside his own mind.

Suddenly the clock in the library started chiming twelve. The tuneless metallic clang seemed to penetrate the boy's defences.

"Do you want to see it?" Isra asked.

No response.

Isra took the boy's hand and led him up the stairs, Cristina and Domenico following in their wake. They entered the library just as the clock struck the final three chimes. The boy stood in front of the clock and gazed at it, watching the small weights swing back and forth in a perfect rhythm.

"It's a clock," Cristina said.

No response.

"For telling the time of day."

Silence.

"Perhaps he's hungry," Isra suggested.

"Food isn't always the answer."

"It is with boys." Isra took his hand to lead him to the kitchen, but the boy pulled away. All he wanted was to gaze at the clock.

Cristina drew up a stool and set it next to him. Then she reached up and slid the protective hood off the clock, revealing the intricate mechanism of interlocking cogs and coiled springs.

It was mesmerising to see the strange connection between the boy and the clock. He reached out and gently touched the lead drop-weights, intuitively realising that these were somehow the key to driving everything.

Cristina could see that in some inexplicable way, the boy was drawing strength from the beating mechanical heart.

6: ALNAAJI

How could they build on the clock moment to connect with this lost boy?

Isra was convinced that home was the key. "Make him feel safe and loved, and he will start to trust again." To this end, she selected one of the empty rooms on the second floor of the house and set about turning it into the boy's bedroom. It had windows overlooking Piazza Navona, which provided entertainment in the form of an endless bustle of people and traders coming and going; perhaps all that restless energy would help distract the boy from his own trauma.

Then Isra went to one of the fashionable decorating studios that were springing up across the city, and selected some huge wall hangings that were printed with different depictions of the Tree of Life. Once hung, they gave the room a Garden of Eden feel, and the boy spent hours running his fingers over the printed branches and curling vines, tracing the links between all the living and mythological Beasts of Creation.

Next, Isra moved some spare furniture into the room: a small washstand, a desk and bench, a wooden chest, an armchair and a large mirror. She piled it all in the centre of the room, then stared at it and shook her head, not knowing where to start. She lifted the washstand and walked to various parts of the room, alternately smiling and frowning, then glancing back at the boy.

At first the boy was puzzled by her indecision, but then he realised that Isra wanted his approval in arranging the room. He thought for a moment, then walked to the spot where he wanted the washstand. Isra placed it next to him, stood back and smiled. Then they both returned to the pile of furniture and started on the next piece.

It wasn't the quickest way of setting up a room, but it gave the boy some control over his life, and working together, even without language, they started to build a rapport.

The same thinking took them both to the market at Campo de' Fiori, where Isra helped the boy pick out a new set of clothes. After much browsing, they finally settled on a white linen shift, a red tunic, grey breeches, and a bright green velvet cap.

Gazing in the mirror, he looked more like a prince from one of the wealthy palazzos on the Tiber than a refugee who had been washed ashore just days earlier.

"What do you think?" Isra asked as she adjusted his cap to a jauntier angle. "Do you like it?"

He didn't understand her words, but he could feel Isra's kindness, and he put his arms around her waist and hugged her.

"It's all right," she whispered, stroking his hair. "Everything will be all right. I promise."

Yet Cristina knew that all this progress was pointless if they couldn't actually talk to the boy, so she spent hours in her library researching the different languages of the Hafsid Kingdom.

Fortunately, the ruling dynasty had been a generous patron of culture and education ever since they had come to power over two hundred years earlier and had established numerous madrasas across the region. Cristina found a set of journals written by a Sicilian scholar who had travelled across the Maghreb, and from these she was able to piece together a sketchy map of the Berber languages. It was even more complicated than she had expected.

There were seven main subdivisions of language: Zenaga, Tetserret, Tuareg, Zenatic, Kabyle, Ghadames, and Awjila; but there were radical differences between these, and the Sicilian scholar hadn't recorded any lists of vocabulary that she could try out on the boy. The only way to get to grips with the different languages would be to actually go to the North African kingdom.

In the end, Cristina reverted to using classical Arabic, the language of scholars across the region, and even though the boy was uneducated, maybe a few words would be similar enough for him to understand. Most urgent of all was to give him a new name.

As the three of them sat round the table in the kitchen eating one of Isra's signature *ribollitas*, Cristina pointed to herself. "Cristina. My name is Cristina."

The boy blinked.

"Can you say it? 'Cristina'."

No response.

She pointed at Isra. "This is Isra. Her name is Isra."

The boy's lips fluttered silently — was he trying out her name?

Then Cristina touched the boy's shoulder. "And you are called Alnaaji. Alnaaji."

"What does it mean?" Isra asked.

"It's Arabic for survivor."

"I like it. It's a strong name."

Isra touched the boy's cheek. "Alnaaji."

The boy nodded. His lips moved, and slowly he whispered, "Alnaaji."

Encouraged by this progress, Cristina decided to try an experiment. The next morning, she took Alnaaji up to the top floor of the house and guided him into the camera obscura room that she used to record the progress of St Peter's. She approached the shuttered windows and slid back a small hatch in the central panel. Immediately a beam of light rushed through the hole and cast an image of Vatican Hill onto the far wall. In the centre of the projection was the huge, scaffolded construction site of the new basilica, with four massive pillars rising above the clutter of rooftops. The strong morning light created a vivid image, and you could even make out construction workers clambering over the scaffold towers.

"This is St Peter's. Or it will be," Cristina explained. But when she turned to look at Alnaaji, she saw fear crumple his face.

"What is it? What's wrong?"

Suddenly the boy started to cry out.

"It's all right!" Cristina ran back across the room to close the shutter and cut off the image, but it was too late. With tears streaming down his face, Alnaaji yanked open the door and bolted from the room.

"I'm sorry! Wait!" She heard his footsteps thundering down the stairs and chased after him.

At the same time, Isra ran up from the kitchens. "What's wrong? What's happened?"

Both women converged outside Alnaaji's room, but when they entered, they saw that he had curled up tightly on the bed, blanket wrapped around him, sobbing.

Isra sat next to him and gently kissed the top of his head. "Calm now. Be calm," she whispered. Then she turned accusingly to Cristina.

"I didn't mean… It was the only way of finding out."

"What exactly did you do to him?"

"I showed him the projection of St Peter's. In the obscura."

Isra was puzzled. "A picture filled him with terror?"

"It can't have been just a picture to him. It must have been a memory." Cristina sat on the edge of the desk. "Those men who perished on the *Speranza*, they must have been coming to work on the basilica. And the people who trafficked them … maybe they used pictures to describe the building. A grand project to lure the men from their homes." She looked at the trembling figure under the blanket. "But now we know for sure — the horrors on that ship are inextricably linked to the new St Peter's."

"So who is responsible? Who is going to be punished for all this cruelty?"

"That's where things are going to get difficult," Cristina said darkly. "Domenico was in the meeting when the Holy Father confronted the oligarchs. They swore blind that they knew nothing of the *Speranza*, yet between them, the dynastic families control nearly all the construction in Rome."

"So they lied to the Pope?" Isra whispered. "Do they not fear for their souls?"

"The only thing oligarchs fear is losing their wealth."

Isra winced. "You certainly know how to choose your enemies."

7: GHOSTS

Evidence. That was the key. Gather enough evidence to piece together a trail, then follow that trail using logic as your only compass, and you would inevitably arrive at the truth.

Cristina smiled to herself as she rode along the coastal road leading northwest from Rome. Much as she enjoyed writing, it felt good to put introspection to one side and re-engage with the world. She had read the official report about the *Speranza* but felt confident that if she saw the ship with her own eyes, she would pick up clues that everyone else had missed. Domenico rode a short distance ahead; Deputy Tomasso was supposed be riding behind, but he was so pleased to see Cristina after all this time that he kept catching up to ask her questions.

He wanted to know about her routine in the convent, and how she was tackling the huge task of recording all the investigations they had undertaken. He was particularly keen to know how Cristina had portrayed his own role in the events.

"Am I heroic?"

"You have your moments, Tomasso."

"Presumably you don't write about all the dead-ends we pursued?"

"Everything goes onto the page. Right and wrong."

Tomasso frowned. "But that might give the impression we don't always know what we are doing."

"We learn more from our mistakes than our triumphs."

"But who wants to read about mistakes?"

"Oh, you don't have to worry about that. These accounts will never be read by anyone."

"So ... what's the point in writing them?"

"To help me make sense of the world."

"Huh. Curious. But I do think other people might be interested to read about how we solve crimes."

Now it was Cristina's turn to frown. "It's not a very ennobling subject for a book, is it?"

"But it's intriguing. Imagine, a book that's all about 'who did the crime?' The reader could walk in the footsteps of the investigators for a few hours each evening."

"Surely people would just turn to the last page to discover the solution?"

"Where's the fun in that, Cristina? The joy is in the journey."

Cristina was surprised by how much she enjoyed casual conversation; it made the silence of the convent seem very austere.

But the closer they got to Civitavecchia, the more Deputy Tomasso sank into his own silence. He rode his horse more slowly and kept finding excuses to stop for a few moments. When they crested a hill and caught sight of the port, rather than celebrating their arrival, Tomasso looked as if he had seen a ghost. It was clear to Cristina that he was still deeply troubled by the memories of what he'd witnessed when he boarded the *Speranza*.

They stopped at a tavern to rest their horses and have some lunch, but when it was time to go, Tomasso remained in his seat. "Actually, I'm still hungry. I think I'll order something else."

Cristina glanced at Domenico, silently urging him not to object. Domenico put a reassuring hand on his deputy's shoulder. "If you don't want to come on board, you don't have to."

"No, no. It's not that." Tomasso turned to look at the menu that was chalked on a board over the kitchen counter. "It's just ... the ride made me hungry."

"When you're ready, wait for us on the dock."

"I'll see you there." Tomasso watched them leave the tavern, then ordered a fresh jug of wine.

Cristina and Domenico gazed up at the silent hulk of the *Speranza*.

"The bodies have all been removed to a temporary mortuary," Domenico said, trying to steel his resolve. "They'll be buried first thing tomorrow."

"It should have been within three days of death," Cristina replied. "That's what Sharia law demands."

"It was never going to happen. They'd been dead at least two days when the ship was discovered."

"I'll need to examine the bodies before they're buried."

Domenico winced at the thought. "You'll need some smelling salts. And an empty stomach."

"Well ... let's do the ship first." Cristina led the way up the gangplank.

They checked the upper decks, but the logs, charts and any paperwork that might have given a clue to the ownership of the vessel had been removed, just as the harbourmaster had indicated in his report.

"The captain knew what he was doing when he abandoned ship," Domenico said. "He didn't want anyone to track him down."

All that remained in the crew quarters were a few hammocks, some tin plates and cutlery, and a dozen empty bottles. The food had gone, most likely pilfered by the sailors as they left.

"How did they get it off the ship?" Cristina asked. "They couldn't have swum with all those provisions."

"This type of ship often has a tender in tow. They could have used that to escape."

With no more cabins left to search, they had little choice but to make their way down into the gloom of the hold. Whoever had been assigned the grim task of removing the bodies had been very thorough. All that was left to see were the tangle of chains and manacles, and the dried stains of bodily fluids. Even though several days had passed, the stench of vomit and faeces was overpowering.

"It looks to me as if disease moved through this ship at great speed," Cristina said.

"Was it disease? Or suffocation?"

Cristina looked at the small wooden shutters high up in the hold walls — they were still latched open. "Unlikely. And death by suffocation wouldn't have led to all this." She pointed at the ugly stains under their feet. "Chained together in such cramped conditions, disease would have run rampant."

"So how did Alnaaji escape?" Domenico asked. "Why didn't he fall sick?"

"That's a very good question."

"Has he shown any symptoms since you took him in?"

"No. But maybe he's somehow immune."

"The only one out of nearly three hundred?" Domenico gazed around the gruesome deck. "And if whatever killed them is infectious, should we even be standing here?" Instinctively he pulled up his neck scarf to cover his mouth.

"It's a bit late for that," Cristina said. "Either we've got it, or we haven't. Whatever 'it' is. Were any crew found among the bodies?"

"No. They must have abandoned ship to save their own lives."

"So they could be out there now, spreading disease though the Papal States?"

"There have been no reports of plague-type illnesses in the last few days," Domenico replied. "But I'll get Tomasso to send out messengers."

"Good idea. Especially as we don't know how long it takes to incubate." Cristina started to make her way back towards the steps leading out of the gloom — she desperately needed some fresh air. "You have to track that crew down."

"We'll try. But I fear they'll be long gone," Domenico said, following Cristina up the steps.

"Are there no crew registers lodged with the port authorities?"

Domenico laughed. "Half the ships sailing the Mediterranean are manned by convicts dragged from gaols. Whoever crewed this ship will have vanished into the cracks or joined another ship to get as far away from Rome as possible."

They clambered onto the main deck and breathed in lungfuls of fresh air to drive out the miasma of the hold.

"Someone is responsible for the deaths of those men," Cristina said. "And they need to be brought to justice."

Domenico gazed across the harbour; on the surface it looked civilised and welcoming, with ships loading and unloading, and boys running up and down the quays selling food and trinkets to the sailors. "Do you really think we can get to the truth?"

Cristina nodded. "It's impossible that such a terrible crime hasn't left a trail of incriminating evidence. Impossible."

8: BURIALS

The bodies had been swilled down with buckets of water to try and quench the smell, but in this heat, it was all but ineffective. Before they stepped into the customs warehouse, Cristina and Domenico wrapped several layers of scarf around their mouth and nose.

Great shafts of sunlight drove in through the high windows, throwing a heavy lattice of shadows from the ceiling beams onto the crumbling plaster on the far wall. It would have made an interesting oil painting, were it not for the naked corpses laid out in lines on the stone floor.

Cristina saw Domenico close his eyes. "You don't have to stay," she said. "I can examine the bodies on my own."

"I've encountered worse on the battlefield." Technically that was true. He had seen plenty of bodies ravaged by violent conflict, horrifically deconstructed by sword and cannonball, but it was the calmness inside this warehouse that was so chilling. Death had passed over these unfortunate souls and moved on, leaving them in grotesque attitudes, limbs twisted at odd angles, faces pulled out of shape by gaping mouths and bulging eyes. Thank God the mesh screens across the windows had prevented the degradation of flies.

Cristina coped by shuttering her mind until it was just a narrow shaft of concentration searching for physical evidence.

Her eyes roamed across the floor. The skin tones of the victims were not so different to the Mediterranean complexion, but a quarter of the men had very dark sub-Saharan skin. Around half of them had tattoos on their arms in a similar geometric style to those on Alnaaji's hands.

She walked down the rows of bodies, studying them intently. The natural processes of decay were already underway, making it difficult to isolate symptoms of the disease that had destroyed these men. Yet she did notice a distinctive blistering on all the bodies and made a detailed sketch of one so that she could check it against her medical encyclopaedias back in Rome, although she suspected there were many illnesses that could cause this type of lesion. At least half the victims had dried blood around their noses and mouths, and it was possible the others may have had similar traces before they were swilled with water.

Cristina stood up and stretched. She could have spent hours here, hunting for clues, but she wasn't convinced the bodies would yield any more secrets, and every minute she spent in the warehouse increased the risk of becoming infected herself. So she beckoned to Domenico, and they made their way back out to the fresh sea breeze of the harbour.

"If there's anything else you need from the bodies, look for it now, Cristina. We're burying them today."

"There can't be a graveyard big enough around here," Cristina said, untying her scarf and folding it up.

"The harbourmaster's guards have dug a pit up on the clifftop, away from the town. They'll be buried there."

Cristina nodded. "They perished in our waters. The least we can do is help them reach their afterlife."

Deputy Tomasso was dispatched to Rome on an urgent mission to find an imam and bring him back. Meanwhile, the harbourmaster's long-suffering guards started the grim task of wrapping the bodies in winding sheets, loading them onto carts and transporting them to the top of the cliff.

Cristina was struck by how the simple act of shrouding restored dignity to the victims. As their agonised faces and terrified eyes were hidden, you could almost imagine they had died peacefully in their sleep.

By the time the sombre procession of carts reached the clifftop, Tomasso had arrived with an elderly imam who ran the small faculty of Arabian Scholarship at Sapienza University. Under his direction, the bodies were laid in the mass grave on their right side, with each victim's head facing towards Mecca. When the grave was full, the imam began to recite the *Salat-al-Janazah*.

The guards and Domenico stood in respectful silence. Cristina used her knowledge of Arabic to try and follow the prayers, translating in her head.

O Allah, forgive our living and our dead, those present and those absent, our young and our old, our males and our females. O Allah, whom among us You keep alive, then let such a life be upon Islam, and whom among us You take unto Yourself, then let such a death be upon faith. O Allah, do not deprive us of his reward and do not let us stray after him.

When the imam had finished, Domenico accompanied him back down to the port, while Tomasso supervised the teams of guards backfilling the mass grave with soil.

Cristina walked to the edge of the cliff and looked down at the sea. The water looked particularly beautiful in the late afternoon sunlight. Swirls of vivid blue and luminous green danced tirelessly around the rocks, churning up spume that drifted away on the breeze.

Where was the Speranza *heading?* Cristina wondered. Everyone had assumed it was trying to reach one of the ports close by, but was that true? No captain would dare land a cargo of chained men in the Papal States after so many popes had issued decrees condemning slavery. Yet if the victims were free men, why were they chained in the hold? Perhaps it was just a coincidence that the ship was abandoned in this stretch of sea. What if its destination was somewhere else altogether?

Fired with the conviction that they had missed something on their search of the ship, Cristina rode back down to the port and persuaded Domenico to accompany her on board the *Speranza*. This time she had no interest in the hold but wanted to see the officers' quarters. Two previous searches had found no charts or logs, but if the *Speranza*'s cargo was illegal, perhaps their destination was secret ... and where would you hide secret navigation charts?

She got down on her hands and knees and started tapping the floor planks, listening for a change of tone. From there she moved to the cabin walls, and then tried the ceiling.

"This is all solid timber," Domenico said. "And no-one cuts into an oak frame without special tools."

Cristina said nothing, but she knew her brother was right — ships weren't like buildings; every inch of them was engineered to withstand gale-force storms, so modifying them was not for the fainthearted.

But if the fabric of the ship wasn't a hiding place, then...

Her eyes fell on the captain's desk. It was unassuming: a sloping writing surface that hinged up to reveal a storage compartment, with four drawers built into the body of the desk. Was it fixed to the wall, or had it been brought in later?

"Give me a hand with this," she said to Domenico. They each gripped an end and dragged the desk into the middle of the cabin. Cristina crouched down and ran her hands over the thin panel of wood that formed the desk's backing, pressing gently along the edges until...

Click.

The panel swung open to reveal a shallow cavity. Cristina reached in and withdrew a nautical chart. "Someone forgot to take this when they abandoned ship."

"Or maybe they were planning to come back and retrieve it later."

Cristina unfolded the chart on the desk — it showed the coastline of the Papal States, on which someone had plotted a course to an inlet just north of the Fiora River.

"That's inhospitable marshland," Domenico said. "Perfect terrain for people smuggling."

9: COVES

The harbourmaster put his caravel at Domenico's disposal, and because the crew knew precisely how to pick up the best winds and coastal currents, it took just over two hours to sail to the marshlands around the Fiora River.

"Can't sail up the river, mind," the boatswain warned. "Too shallow. Mudbanks everywhere."

"But we need to get closer," Cristina said, peering into the small, muddy mouth of the river.

"Then you'll have to row."

The crew prepared the tender, then Cristina and Domenico clambered down the rigging ropes and boarded the rowing boat. They used the oars to push themselves away from the caravel, then started rowing directly into the mouth of the Fiora.

It was like journeying into a primeval swamp — long grasses grew in wild abundance on both banks, reaching out across the water as if to prevent anyone from entering. Clouds of blood-hungry mosquitoes swirled above the murky waters, and strange birds cried out in sorrow from their hiding places. Darting splashes reminded everyone that predators stalked this gloomy place, and that if you paused too long, you might perish.

"This is where the *Speranza* was heading," Cristina whispered, even though no-one was there to hear them. "They must have been planning to moor off the coast, then transfer the men using a tender."

"Or maybe someone was waiting for them with longboats." Domenico's oar became tangled in some reeds, forcing him to lift it clear of the water and bang it on the hull. The boat drifted closer to the bank, and just as Cristina reached out for a tree to push them away, she saw a four-lined snake lying on the branch and pulled her hand away quickly.

Domenico plunged his oar back into the water and rowed them away from the bank. As they navigated round the next bend, the river widened to reveal a long, shallow mudflat on the left; debris was scattered across it.

As the boat squelched into the bank, a rotting smell erupted from the mud. Cristina clambered out and immediately her foot sank a few inches.

"Get higher up, or you'll lose your boots," Domenico warned as he hauled the boat out of the water, but Cristina ignored him and squelched her way towards the debris instead. As she got closer, she could make out abandoned shoes, a few leather caps and scraps of torn clothing, some empty wine bottles, odd lengths of rope and broken manacles. Picking her way towards the drier ground, she saw numerous tracks cutting through the dense grass, along with the charred leftovers of campfires. Cristina heard the plop-and-suck of boots in mud and turned to see Domenico approaching.

"The *Speranza* wasn't the first," she said. "People have been smuggled in here before."

Domenico counted six scorched circles in the grass. "This is a big operation. It must have been going on for weeks. Months, maybe. Look how they've hacked back the vegetation."

"So once the men are landed here, they're probably taken away on carts," Cristina said. "It's slavery in all but name. And the Church has decreed against slavery."

"That's why all this is being done in secret."

"You need to set up an ambush right here. Catch the people-traffickers red-handed."

Domenico shook his head. "Too late. The minute the *Speranza* was found, they would have abandoned this landing site."

"You can't be sure of that."

"They'd be terrified of getting caught. Why take the risk when there are hundreds of coves and creeks dotted along the coastline?"

"Then you need to organise a systematic search."

"Will you stop telling me how to do my job?" Domenico was getting frustrated.

"I'm trying to help!"

"Well, you're not!"

Brother and sister glared at each other, then Domenico sighed heavily.

"We just don't have the manpower to search the entire coastline, Cristina. And they'll have bribed the local villagers to stay silent."

Cristina waded back down to the waterline and plucked a belt from the sucking mud. She rinsed it in the water to reveal a carved ivory buckle.

"The demand for cheap labour is being driven by the construction of St Peter's," Domenico continued. "The trafficking won't stop until the basilica is complete."

"That's not good enough." Cristina slid the buckle from the belt and put it in her pocket.

"You've seen how many cart tracks there are. Fixers are more than likely going to North Africa every month, to remote villages like Alnaaji's, to get slave labour."

"You can't just kidnap people in another country and ship them abroad. Someone would raise the alarm."

"Perhaps they're lied to. Promised good wages. Maybe paid an advance. Then once they're at sea, they're put in chains."

Cristina nodded pensively. "All across North Africa, women are waiting for husbands and sons who will never return."

"It's the cruelty of greed."

"But that's where this doesn't make sense." Cristina squelched back towards Domenico, an idea forming. "If slave labour is so important for boosting profits, why were all the men allowed to die?"

"Disease took hold," Domenico replied. "You saw it for yourself."

"But they made no attempt to isolate the illness. When the first man falls sick, you separate him. Maybe even throw him overboard. But there was no sign of that. The crew abandoned everyone."

"Maybe they feared for their own lives."

Cristina shook her head. "You go to all that trouble to ship people over, you're nearly at the landing site, and then you just abandon an entire cargo? It doesn't make sense. There's something else going on here — something we can't yet see."

Domenico looked back to the boat and saw that it was starting to bob loose on the currents. "Come on, let's get to the caravel before we're stuck here."

Cristina followed in her brother's muddy footprints. "What if we approach the problem from the other direction? If we can't search the coastline, then we should look at the basilica workforce. The trafficked men have tribal tattoos; they should be easy to spot. We find them, question them, and discover who's behind all this."

Domenico helped Cristina back into the boat. "You've been shut away in that convent for too long. The construction project is now vast. The supply chains touch every town in the

Papal States. It's not just the workers you can see on Vatican Hill; there are thousands more hidden away."

"Then let's get to work." Cristina handed the oars to her brother.

"You do know this means going to war with the oligarchs?" Domenico warned.

"They may be powerful, but we have God on our side," Cristina replied, undaunted.

10: IL RUINANTE

It was one thing to see an image projected on the wall of the camera obscura, quite another to actually walk among the colossal pillars that rose from the ground. The sheer scale of the new St Peter's made Cristina feel dizzy.

At ninety feet high and thirty feet thick, the northwest pier was almost complete, and as Cristina paced around its vast base, she estimated its circumference to be over two hundred feet. The southwest pier was hard on its heels, while the other two had just emerged above ground level. The chief architect, Donato Bramante, was building from the centre out, and these pillars would soon be linked by huge barrel vaults soaring one hundred and fifty feet into the air. Sitting on top of those would ultimately be the tallest dome in the world, the heart of St Peter's Basilica.

But not everyone was happy, because now the collateral damage had begun. To make room for the two eastern piers, Bramante had started to pull down the thousand-year-old church that had stood on Vatican Hill since Roman times. The roof above the high altar had been removed and the surrounding walls demolished, condemning ancient mosaics and frescoes to oblivion.

"It's earned Bramante a new nickname," Domenico said discreetly, so that none of the workmen would overhear. "*Il Ruinante*. The wrecker."

"A bit harsh," Cristina replied, looking at the now open-air altar where the Pope still conducted Mass every Sunday. "The old basilica was falling down. Something had to be done."

"Bramante brushes off the criticism. He says Rome will have to get used to it. But Pope Julius is so worried for his own safety, he's sent a cardinal to Switzerland to recruit a team of bodyguards."

"Has anyone built on this scale since the ancient Egyptians?" Cristina asked in wonder.

"There are two and a half thousand men on this site alone. And no-one's even counted the mules." Domenico led his sister deeper into the cacophony of construction.

Wherever possible, machinery had been deployed to amplify the muscle of men. Winches, elaborate rigs of block and tackle, levers, gears and mechanical screws all transmitted energy through a web of wheels and cables that criss-crossed the building site. The variety of trades focussed on this project was astonishing: draughtsmen, groundsmen, foremen, pulley-men, masons, bricklayers, carpenters and carvers; animal wranglers, scaffolders, furnacemen, cutters, ropemakers, tool-sharpeners and cement-men were all feeding the beast of Bramante's conjuring.

Cristina sat on a windlass that was temporarily idle and enjoyed the restless energy surrounding her. "How is all this managed? It's so complex, yet it isn't chaotic."

"Everything is broken down into manageable units. Thousands of them, all co-ordinated by teams of foremen. But here's the thing." Domenico sat down next to his sister. "Each of those units is put out to tender, so contracts are awarded for everything from the supply of rope to the carting away of donkey dung. And each of those contracts is subject to a bidding war. It's the only way to stop costs from spiralling out of control."

"Does it work?"

"So far. It gets the lowest price by setting the oligarchs at each other's throats."

"Are they really the only ones bidding for contracts?"

"On paper, no. But in practice all the smaller companies are just subsidiaries of subsidiaries, and in the end, it always comes back to the big four."

Cristina's brow furrowed. "But what if the oligarchs colluded to inflate the costs?"

"They won't, because they hate each other too much. The feud between the Colonna and Orsini families has been festering for centuries."

"There can't be many things worth arguing about for that long."

"Control of Rome. At its worst, their thugs fight street battles with each other over who extorts protection money from who. Now it's been elevated to a fight for lucrative commercial contracts. Both families have their eye on the Papal Crown, and they're using the construction of St Peter's to build themselves into the very fabric of the Vatican."

Cristina looked crestfallen. "This cathedral was supposed to be about inspiring ordinary people. A symbol of enlightenment and Christian values."

"And when it's finished, it will be," Domenico replied. "But until then, it's a feeding frenzy for the rich."

"Only if we let them get away with it."

"Oi!" One of the under-foremen was striding towards them with a scowl on his face. "You can't sit there!"

Cristina and Domenico jumped up from the windlass.

"We didn't touch anything," Cristina said.

"You were sitting on the winch! I saw you. If you're not in the guild, you can't touch the machinery."

"Sorry."

"What are you even doing here?"

"Leaving." Domenico took Cristina's arm, and they hurried back into the relative safety of the old basilica.

"And that's why the build doesn't descend into chaos," Domenico whispered. "Because men like that keep everyone in their place."

Cristina stopped halfway down the nave and turned back to look at the bustling construction site. "Who decides which oligarch gets what contract? Or does it just go to the cheapest bidder?"

Domenico laughed. "That would be far too simple. And too transparent."

"Don't tell me they've set up a special committee?"

"The Building Committee of St Peter's, no less."

"Bureaucrats," Cristina said with a weary sigh. "They seem to get everywhere."

"Like mould," Domenico smiled.

11: GATEKEEPERS

Cristina couldn't believe the irony. "Of all the rooms in the Vatican, *this* is where the committee meets?"

She and Domenico had been shown into a well-appointed chamber that was dominated by a long, deeply polished table with thirteen chairs lined up along one side, obliging all applicants to stand on the opposite side. But it wasn't the blatant powerplay of the seating that had caught Cristina's eye, it was the large tapestry on the wall depicting Christ in the temple, overturning the tables of the moneychangers. "'My house shall be called the house of prayer; but you have made it a den of thieves.'"

Domenico studied the tapestry. "I suppose it could be read in two ways."

"Seems pretty unequivocal to me."

"Either the Building Committee are the corrupt moneychangers, or they're Christ throwing thieves out of the tendering process."

"You're becoming quite the diplomat, Domenico."

The side door clicked open, and Cristina braced herself for the committee's entrance, but it was just a workman carrying a leather satchel of tools and a small stepladder. He looked momentarily confused. "Oh. They told me this room wasn't being used."

"The committee will be here in a minute," Cristina said.

"It's not them I want." The workman pointed to a bank of leaded windows on the far side of the room. "One of the panes needs repairing."

Cristina turned to the windows and saw that several small glass circles at the bottom of the central panel had broken, leaving a jagged hole.

"It'll get worse the longer it's left," said the man.

"Don't mind us," Domenico said.

They watched as the workman crossed the room, examined the damage, then laid out his tools and started removing pieces of broken glass.

"Do you think that job was put out to tender as well?" Cristina whispered to Domenico.

Domenico chuckled. "Maybe it was a failed bidder who punched the hole with his fist."

Thinking that they were laughing at him, the workman turned and glared at them. "Problem?"

"No," Cristina assured him. "No problem at all."

The workman gave a derisive snort, took out a sharp knife and started cutting away one of the lead seams. They were spared an escalation of awkwardness when the double doors swung open, and the thirteen esteemed members of the Building Committee of St Peter's processed into the room.

Cristina studied them as they took their seats and adjusted their paperwork. She had done her homework on these men and knew that they were all middle-ranking priests plucked from deep within the Vatican. None of them were architects, as that might call into question their impartiality; there were no cardinals, as most of those had links to the four dynastic families; and there was no-one who had any experience of supervising a major construction project, as that might mean they already had preferred suppliers. The result was that this committee, which wielded such enormous power, was comprised of amateurs, men who had achieved nothing but survival within a hierarchy, men who had risen by perfecting the art of offending no-one.

Finally, the committee chairman, Father Fringuello, deigned to look up. "Proceed."

Domenico gave a small, respectful bow. "First, can I thank the committee for agreeing to this meeting."

Father Fringuello waved his hand dismissively. "We were going to meet in any case, to decide who shall be awarded the contract to acquire unwanted material from the Roman ruins. You have merely been added to the agenda." The priest's reptilian manner matched his face perfectly.

"Wait. You're going to pillage Capitoline Hill?" Cristina exclaimed.

The members of the committee all turned their gaze on her. "Pillage is an emotive term," Fringuello replied in an icy tone.

"How about vandalise?"

"Cristina, please!" Domenico interrupted. "That's not why we're here." He turned back to the committee with an apologetic smile. "We simply want to understand more fully how the decision-making process of this committee works."

"That is confidential," said Fringuello.

"On a need-to-know basis," the deputy chair, Father Vigliacco added.

Cristina could see what was going on. The deputy chair had one job: to agree with Fringuello. All the other committee members were expected to remain silent and compliant. It angered her to see men build successful careers on the back of timidity.

"We ask these questions with the direct authority of the Holy Father," Cristina said. "Pope Julius wants answers."

Fringuello went into a hushed consultation with Vigliacco, and after much muttering turned back to Domenico. "Very well. But please, be brief."

Domenico turned to Cristina and whispered, "Try to be respectful."

Cristina had no papers to refer to, but she didn't need them, as she had committed all her research to memory. "Perhaps we could start by focusing on three particular contracts. First: five hundred miles of rope were commissioned from a company that had only ever made silk scarves. Was there not a bidder with more suitable experience?"

Cristina locked eyes with Father Fringuello, but he remained glacial. "Go on."

"Second: four thousand two hundred pulley blocks were ordered from a company that six weeks earlier had lost a contract to supply the Papal Navy. When the blocks were delivered, it was discovered that two thousand, seven hundred and five of them were faulty and unusable, yet the contract was never rescinded."

A high-pitched scraping sound cut across the tense atmosphere. All eyes turned to the man working on the window, who was now cleaning the lead calmes in preparation for dressing in some new glass.

"Do you have to do that *now*?" Father Fringuello thundered.

The workman froze.

"Wait outside." Father Vigliacco beckoned to the door.

The workman hurried out of the room, grateful for an excuse to leave.

"There was a third?" Fringuello said, turning back to Cristina.

"Yes, the contract for the groundsmen digging the pit for the northeast pier. It seems there are large discrepancies between how much the workers are paid, and how much the tender submission said they would be paid. In all three cases, what concerns us is that the tendering process does not seem to deliver what is best for the basilica."

Fringuello adjusted his papers carefully. "I see from your line of questioning that you have one aim: to discredit the work of this committee."

"Nothing could be further from the truth," Domenico interjected. "We are merely trying to help perfect what is clearly a very complex process."

Father Vigliacco picked up the defence. "These specific contracts to which you refer have all been transferred to the Audit and Accounting Committee. In theory it might be possible to retrieve the documents, but the committee is quite overwhelmed and it could take several months. You've seen for yourself the pace of the build."

"But you can rest assured," Fringuello added, "that our first and only loyalty is to the Church."

Cristina realised this was going to be their standard response to all her questions. "Many in Rome believe that for the dynastic families, these contracts are actually about choosing the next pope."

Fringuello raised an eyebrow. "The Pope is chosen by God. That is beyond the remit of the Building Committee."

"Indeed," Vigliacco said with a nod. "We do not have a smoking chimney."

"And under precisely which contract was the *Speranza* chartered?" Cristina had hoped to ambush them with the question, but the chairman had been expecting it.

"I speak for everyone on this committee when I say that we would never award even the smallest contract to any company or consortium that had such a callous attitude towards human life. Our thoughts and prayers go out to the victims."

The rest of the committee all nodded their heartfelt agreement.

"But how could you possibly know the *Speranza* didn't sail on basilica work?"

"Because that is our job."

"You said yourself, Father Fringuello, there are thousands of contracts. It is surely inevitable that some crimes are hidden amongst those."

"We have highly specialised skills in this area. That is why we are on the committee, and you are not."

Father Vigliacco stifled a smile at what he thought was a decisive blow.

"And is it *open* tendering?" Cristina persisted.

"It is competitive."

"But is it open? Can anyone bid for the contracts?"

There was an awkward glance between Fringuello and his deputy.

"No," Fringuello conceded.

Cristina looked puzzled. "But if you want to hire the best people, surely the tendering process should be open to everyone?"

"We cannot have the whole of Christendom knocking on our door," Vigliacco replied, sensing that his superior was struggling. "That would be anarchy."

"So how do you get onto the tender list?" Cristina asked.

"We are not at liberty to disclose all the protocols," Fringuello said.

"Remember," Domenico interjected, "we are asking on behalf of Pope Julius himself."

Fringuello fidgeted.

"We use our judgement and experience," Vigliacco said, coming to the rescue again.

"Hypothetically, could I bribe my way onto the tender list?" Cristina asked with faux innocence.

Indignation rippled down the long table.

"How dare you? That is a most serious accusation," Fringuello said with menace. "Serious, ill-judged and libellous. Either particularise your allegation or be prepared to face the repercussions in a court of law."

"You misunderstand," Cristina said. "I made no allegation; I simply asked a question."

"Which was defamatory and insulting! You are attempting to suppress the legitimate business of this committee and smear the professional reputations of everyone on it. We do this job not for the glorification of ourselves, but for the greater good of the Church. Each one of us makes considerable sacrifices to serve St Peter's. We give our time and energy and ask for nothing in return."

There were grave nods around the table.

"Perhaps I should rephrase the question," Cristina ventured.

"Perhaps." Father Vigliacco offered a chilly smile. "But if I were you, I would apologise and leave. Immediately."

12: CRONIES

Cristina and Domenico escaped into the anonymity of the labyrinthine Vatican corridors. As they approached the eastern stairs, they saw the workman who had been repairing the glass, leaning on a marble balustrade. He was idly cleaning his fingernails with a small chisel. "Can I go in there now?"

"I'd give it a few minutes if I were you," Domenico replied, and the workman went back to cleaning his nails.

"They can't just stonewall us with denials," Cristina said as she followed her brother down the steps.

"That's exactly what they're going to do."

"And they know more than they're saying about the *Speranza*," Cristina grumbled.

"Of course they do, but as long as they all stick together, we won't be able to get any purchase."

Domenico reached the bottom of the staircase, turned hard right and opened a modest oak door that led to a back staircase.

"All that rubbish about making sacrifices to serve St Peter's," Cristina scoffed. "As if anyone believes that. The very mediocrity of those men leaves them open to corruption. They have no talent, so the only way they're going to prosper is by accepting bribes."

"The fact is, Cristina, they can just keep denying everything until the last stone of St Peter's is laid." Domenico ushered her into a corridor that ran along the upper service floor.

"We just need one of them to talk. To break rank. Then we can get access to the committee's files. It's the only way we're going to dismantle the people-trafficking network."

"Why don't we ask Pope Julius to order the immediate release of all the contracts?" Domenico suggested.

"Because if we back the committee into a corner, they may well start destroying documents, and the evidence will be lost forever."

Finally, they arrived at the inner courtyard of the Vatican complex that was home to the barracks of the Apostolic Guard. Domenico led Cristina into his office and poured them both a small glass of wine, but Cristina put hers on the desk, untouched.

"We have to take a leaf from Caesar's book," she said. "*Divide et Impera*. Set the members of the committee against each other to destroy their unity."

"Good luck with that," Domenico replied. "You saw them. They're all terrified of Fringuello and Vigliacco."

Cristina's eyes flashed as an idea formed. "The great thing about timid men is that they're easy to frighten."

"Please, not another of your fake apparitions. I thought you'd turned your back on deliberately misinforming people."

"Domenico, can you put all thirteen members of the committee under round-the-clock surveillance?"

"We're a bit short of men at the moment." Domenico glanced at the rotas hanging on the wall. "Let me ask Tomasso."

"If we can get hard evidence that one of the committee is taking bribes, it will make him vulnerable. Then we can threaten to expose him to Pope Julius unless he cooperates with our investigation."

"But everyone takes bribes in this city."

"I'm not talking about the odd sweetener; I mean huge backhanders. Bribes on a massive scale."

Domenico looked sceptical. "Getting reprimanded by the Pope seems like a small price to pay for amassing a fortune."

"But it won't just be a reprimand. He will be threatened with expulsion from the Church, losing his positions. Julius even has the power to confiscate all his wealth."

"So … it's cooperate or be destroyed?"

"In a nutshell."

"When did you get so hard, Cristina?"

She smiled at him. "I prefer the word 'efficient'."

Domenico opened the door to his office and called across the barracks. "Tomasso! How do you fancy setting up an operation to catch corrupt bureaucrats?"

The deputy hurried over, sword and polishing cloth still in his hands. "I'd love to. But there probably won't be many people left in Rome by the time we've finished."

"I'll drink to that." Cristina picked up her wine and slugged it back.

Tomasso excelled at this type of thing. Before the day was out, covert tails had been placed on each member of the Building Committee of St Peter's. The aim was to discover what they owned, what they spent, who they met, and whether there were any glaring discrepancies between their lifestyles and the money they earned.

The results were shocking. Every single member of the committee was living far beyond his means. These were priests from solid families, yet they lived like princes.

It wasn't just the properties they owned (a palazzo in the city and a villa in the country were de rigueur), it was the extravagance of their hospitality. Not content with obscene amounts of the finest food and rarest wines, one committee member had brought Sandro Botticelli over from Florence simply to draw sketches of all the guests at his *Giovedì Grasso* banquet. Another had marked the start of Christmas festivities by flooding three of his downstairs salons to create a miniature Venice for the amusement of his guests. Still another had indulged his illegitimate son by bringing over five elephants from Africa to liven up the child's birthday party.

And the extravagance wasn't confined to special occasions. Father Fringuello was attempting to build the largest collection of clothing in Rome. Much to the delight of the city's tailors, he had commissioned three hundred and sixty-five different versions of every item of clothing, so that he would never have to wear each piece more than once a year.

Yet the sheer scale of corruption became problematic in an unexpected way.

"We cannot threaten to expose what is already in plain sight," Cristina lamented as she flicked through the weighty dossiers that Tomasso had compiled. "The committee members are all utterly without shame. They make no attempt to hide their ill-gotten wealth."

"I suppose as long as they're all *equally* corrupt, no-one will speak out against the others," Tomasso ventured.

"It's just business as usual in Rome," Domenico agreed.

Cristina slammed the dossier shut. "What about the two hundred and ninety-three souls who perished on the *Speranza*? Is that business as usual?"

"I don't mean it's right. I just mean —"

"How many thousands of people are illegally enslaved across the Papal States? Locked away, leading lives of fear and misery?"

"There's no point lecturing me!" Domenico snapped. "You and I are on the same side. But unless one of the committee members is using bribes to finance some shameful secret, I don't see how we can force anyone to cooperate."

The room fell silent. Banter from the barracks outside filtered into Domenico's office.

Suddenly Tomasso started rummaging in the folios. "Actually, there may be something…" He pulled out a report sheet and quickly read it. "Yes. Father Volpe. He is spending his money in a strange way."

He handed the sheet to Cristina. "A subterranean building? Dug *underneath* his palazzo?"

"Show me." Domenico took the report sheet from his sister.

"The rumours are it's four storeys deep," Tomasso added. "Which is a bit excessive for something like a wine cellar."

Cristina's brow furrowed. "Whatever Volpe intends to do down there, he wants to keep it out of sight. And secrets are the key to successful blackmail."

"Just think of the manpower needed to dig a pit that deep."

Cristina immediately caught onto Domenico's logic. "Which makes it the perfect job for slave labour."

13: UNDERWORLD

From the surveillance dossiers, they deduced the best time to visit Palazzo Volpe without accidentally running into its owner. But just to be safe, Cristina and Domenico went along with a Vatican building superintendent called Ispettore Biscotto.

On the outside, the palazzo looked like many other grand houses nestled on the banks of the Tiber.

"A substantial dwelling in an imposing location," Biscotto observed. "It would make an ideal family residence."

"But don't the darkest secrets often hide behind the most respectable facades?" Cristina replied.

Biscotto looked confused. "Was that a rhetorical question, or are you seeking my professional opinion?"

Cristina stared at the superintendent. "I don't think we're looking for dry rot, Ispettore, if that's what you mean."

"Strange that there are no builders actually working on it," Domenico said. "Given the scale of the construction, you'd think a small army would be hard at work."

He led the way into the property through some gates in the walled garden, which gave access to the construction works without having to enter the palazzo itself, but as soon as they drew back the canvas awnings, they were confronted by a surly foreman.

"This is private property. You have to leave."

"We're here on official business." Domenico flourished his Vatican credentials. "This is Ispettore Biscotto, and he needs to check that your building permits are in order."

The foreman shook his head. "It's a private build. We don't need Vatican permits."

"But we need to check the work is structurally sound," Domenico insisted.

"No-one is allowed on site who isn't working on the construction." The foreman folded his arms and puffed out his chest.

"Poor Ispettore Biscotto has carried his tools all this way." Domenico took the leather satchel from the superintendent's shoulder and opened it to reveal a plumbline, some setsquares, a small hammer, and a folding measuring rod. "And in this heat, please don't tell us his journey's been in vain?"

"Go back the way you came," the foreman said irritably.

"The thing is, we've actually come to help you." Cristina stepped forward. "You see, the church across the road has reported cracks in their walls."

"Cracks?"

It was the worst thing you could say to a builder.

"They suspect it's caused by the work you're doing here, on this basement."

"Impossible," the foreman said. "It's nothing to do with us."

"I agree," Cristina soothed. "It's a ludicrous suggestion, but the priest is an awkward man, threatening to make a fuss."

"And you *are* digging out the foundations," Domenico said with a hint of accusation.

"We're only going under this building! We're staying within the perimeter."

"I believe you," Cristina said, "but the priest thinks his precious church is going to collapse. Along with half the street."

"Idiot!" the foreman scoffed.

"The city is full of them," Cristina sympathised. "But if you let us inspect the building work and measure what you've done, we'll be able to confirm that you are completely blameless in all this."

The foreman teetered on the edge of a decision. Hoping to nudge him across the line, Domenico leaned forward and whispered, "You know what architects are like. If something goes wrong, it's *you* who will get the blame, not him."

It was just enough. Reluctantly the foreman handed them each a lantern, unlocked the gates that led to the excavation works and let them through. "If anyone asks, we never spoke," he warned.

It was astonishing how far the workmen had dug down: there were five floors below ground level, each one beautifully lined with stone slabs and dotted with carefully positioned pillars to support massive wooden ceiling beams.

By the time they reached the lowest floor, Ispettore Biscotto was wide-eyed. "A surprising and accomplished piece of engineering. They certainly know what they're doing."

"But what's it for?" Domenico asked.

Biscotto peered up into a small shaft on one side of the ceiling that stretched all the way to the surface. "That, I assume, is for ventilation. Which means this space isn't just for storage."

"Why don't you take some measurements?" Cristina suggested. "It'll keep our cover story intact."

While Biscotto got busy with his instruments, Cristina and Domenico climbed up a level, where the walls were still only half-clad.

"What the hell is Volpe going to do down here?" Domenico whispered. He began pacing the room.

Cristina ran her hands along the cool travertine slabs that lined the walls. "This is very odd. All these floors with no windows ... what is he so desperate to hide from the world?"

Suddenly Domenico stopped pacing. "You know, I've been somewhere like this before. The Vatican's Deep Vaults go underground. It's where all the most precious treasures of the Church are kept."

"But what treasures does Father Volpe have to justify the cost of all this building work?"

"Perhaps *that's* the real secret."

Domenico peered up into the ventilation shaft. "The air supply makes sense if Volpe intended to spend time down here, admiring his collection of ... God knows what."

"Or is the air supply to keep whoever's down here alive?"

They heard footsteps thumping down the stone steps and moments later the foreman appeared. "How much longer will you be?"

"We're nearly done."

"I can't have anyone seeing you here."

"What is the purpose of all this?" Cristina asked, waving her hand around the room.

The foreman shrugged. "Like they tell us anything."

"Do you have any idea at all? Have you overheard speculation?"

"We just do our jobs and keep our mouths shut."

Ispettore Biscotto emerged from the lower level. "And a very good job you've done, too. Beautifully built, and all within the perimeter of the palazzo grounds."

"I did say, but you wouldn't believe me."

Biscotto patted his leather satchel. "I only believe the measuring rod."

Though he tried not to show it, the foreman was relieved to have been vindicated, and he started trudging back up the steps towards daylight.

"We'll be up in a minute," Domenico called after him.

When the foreman was out of earshot, Cristina turned to her brother. "I think you should put a round-the-clock watch on this building."

Domenico nodded. "We can do it from the other side of the river. No-one will know we're there."

"Perfect. We have to discover exactly what comes in and goes out of this building. Meanwhile, I'll tap into my contacts in the art world. Let's see if Father Volpe has been secretly hoarding stolen treasures."

14: LEGACY

"Just tell her I'm not in."

"She already knows you're here, sir."

"Then lie!"

"I don't think she'll believe me."

"That's what I pay you for, isn't it?"

Cristina was alone in the reception room, so she was the only one able to enjoy the argument playing out behind the doors to the inner sanctum. She had come unannounced to the offices of the art manager, Ludovico Labirinto, because she knew he would try to avoid her. And not without reason — Labirinto had been making a small fortune from the paintings of Vito Visconti before Cristina had exposed him as one of the biggest frauds in the history of art.

The unseen argument raged on.

"Do you have any idea how much money that woman has cost me?"

"Please, sir. I don't think she'll go away, no matter what I say."

"Just take a message. Fob her off. Anything!"

"But she has letters of authority from the Apostolic Guard."

Labirinto cursed. Cristina heard footsteps, then the office doors swung open and the man himself appeared, beaming a warm smile. "Signorina Falchoni. What a charming surprise! Won't you come through?"

"There's really no need to pretend," Cristina replied as she stood up. "I know you hate me."

Labirinto looked genuinely shocked. "What on earth gave you that impression?"

"You speak too loudly, and your walls are too thin." She strode past Labirinto and entered his private office.

As Cristina took a seat, Labirinto poured them both a glass of sherry. "Just so that you know: all those things I said about you — they're absolutely true."

"So much for time healing all wounds." Cristina raised her glass and took a sip.

"When I think about all the commissions that were cancelled, the masterpieces never painted … frankly, it breaks my heart."

"Perhaps you're looking at it the wrong way," Cristina suggested. "I saved you from being dragged through the courts as an accomplice to fraud and obtaining money by deception. It actually suited you to sweep the whole affair aside as a 'tragic accident'."

"But vast wealth would have suited me better."

Cristina glanced around the room with its gilt panelling and fine oil paintings. "You're not exactly poor."

"It's all relative." Labirinto topped up their glasses. "So, to what do I owe this dubious pleasure?"

"The Holy Father, Pope Julius, needs your help."

Labirinto's brows rose hopefully. "He asked for me? By name?"

Cristina hesitated. "In a way."

"Ah. You're playing games."

"The fact is, the Holy Father needs to root out a terrible darkness that is weaving itself into the fabric of the new St Peter's. You can help him, or you can shun him."

Labirinto gave an indifferent shrug. "How will it profit me?"

"You have heard stories of his temper?"

"Wild exaggerations, I'm sure. Anger is one of the deadly sins. A bad look for a pope."

"Actually, wrath is the deadly sin, not anger."

"Same thing."

"Not at all. Wrath is anger accompanied by an overwhelming desire for revenge. Whereas righteous anger is something Christ experienced many times in his own life."

"I had forgotten what a pedant you are, signorina."

"Either way, Ludovico, you wouldn't want to find yourself on a list of the Pope's enemies. Especially given how much patronage the Vatican gives to artists."

Labirinto leant forward. "As long as whatever is discussed here remains confidential."

"Of course. Strictly between you, me, and whoever is standing on the other side of that wall."

Labirinto chuckled. "We will have it soundproofed as a matter of urgency."

"I want to know if Father Volpe, who sits on the Building Committee of St Peter's, is secretly accumulating a large collection of art."

"Secretly?"

"This art is not for public display in churches or official buildings, but for Volpe's enjoyment alone. It's a collection the world will never see."

"It's true," Labirinto conceded. "He is acquiring some of the finest pieces being produced in Europe. I have personally sold him seven paintings and shipped another three from the Low Countries."

"And he's doing it anonymously?"

"Ostensibly. But everyone knows. It's made him very unpopular."

"Not with artists."

"With rival collectors. His greed has driven prices up."

Cristina slugged back the last of the sherry, then started examining the art hanging on the walls. "Surely collecting art is all about vanity. Why doesn't Volpe want his name all over Rome as a great patron of culture?"

"Because a true collector does just that: collects."

"To what end? If the paintings never see the light of day, they might as well not exist. Art is created to be gazed upon."

"Not if you're rich. For the wealthy, art is about creating a legacy. Volpe wants to establish his own dynasty, and to do that he needs more than gold, because gold can be squandered. But paintings — great paintings — become more valuable as they age. That is how new money becomes old money. That is how dynasties are born."

"It's a very grand ambition for a very middle-ranking priest."

"Your grandfather built a thriving cloth business. Your father turned it into the biggest supplier of velvet in Italy. Wealth has given you freedom and privilege, Signorina Falchoni, and that will ripple down the generations. But a man like Volpe is talentless, so he must resort to collecting the talent of others. The construction of St Peter's is injecting so much money into the lifeblood of Rome, it gives men like Volpe a chance to secure his family's wealth for generations."

Cristina turned to face Labirinto. "You speak as if you admire him."

"He is only doing what any of us would do, given the chance."

"Not me," Cristina replied. "Money is vastly overrated. It distorts everything."

Labirinto roared with laughter.

"What is so funny?" Cristina glared at him. "I'm being serious."

Labirinto poured himself another drink. "Those who come from money are always dismissive of it. They can afford to be." He pointed an accusing finger at Cristina. "Rich people like you cannot even imagine what ordinary people have to do just to make it through each day. You will never understand."

15: INSOMNIA

The brothers Marco and Paolo Bottero were inseparable. Born within minutes of each other, they had enlisted in the *Guardia Apostolica* on the same day and loved nothing more than working joint shifts. Deputy Tomasso always tried to accommodate this in the rotas, because their instinctive understanding of each other made the twins so much more than the sum of their parts, and he felt confident they would do an excellent job of setting up the overnight reconnaissance of Palazzo Volpe. His plan was to grab some sleep and return first thing in the morning for a debriefing.

Yet as the deputy turned right off Via del Corso, unease started to catch up with him again. It had been like this ever since he'd set foot on the *Speranza*; as long as his mind was occupied with the busyness of work, he was fine, but as soon as there was space to reflect, ghastly images from that ship of death crawled out of their hiding places in his mind.

Tomasso's rooms were close to the artists' district, where he rented the whole first floor of a grand (if faded) building on the south side of Via della Fontanella. He slipped his key into the heavy iron lock of the front door, crept inside, and eased the latch shut again so as not to wake the landlady. But as he tiptoed along the hallway, a voice barked out from somewhere at the back of the house.

"Have you wiped your feet?"

"Yes, Padrona," Tomasso replied. Then he tiptoed back to the entrance and wiped his boots on the rush mat.

"I don't want the filth of the streets on my clean floors." It was the voice of misery, moaning from the depths of Purgatory.

"No, Padrona." Tomasso had learned long ago not to argue with his landlady. He just had to get past her as quickly as possible and say as little as necessary. He was halfway up the stairs when her voice barked out again.

"Rent's due on Friday."

"Yes, Padrona."

"Don't forget. My life is hard enough without you forgetting your rent all the time."

Once. In all the years he'd lived here, he'd been late with the rent just once, yet she would never forgive him.

Tomasso made it to his rooms and locked the door behind him. The problem was, now he had to deal with the silence. Quickly he poured a large tumbler of wine and slugged it back; fortified, he set about lighting the four oil lamps dotted around the lounge.

He plonked himself in one of the battered leather armchairs and waited for the numbing power of the wine to take effect; only then would it be safe to risk sleep. As he waited, Tomasso's eyes wandered around the room.

Why did this place never feel like home? During the previous Christmas holidays, he had made a point of studying the houses of his married friends. Their rooms seemed to be full of bits and pieces that made no sense but did make a difference: ornaments, cushions, flowers, lengths of fabric draped across furniture, plates painted with pastoral scenes propped on window ledges. Tomasso had tried to emulate this in his own rooms, but the result was a disaster — it looked as if a violent storm had blown through the apartment and deposited debris from across Rome.

He noticed a bunch of dead flowers in a vase on the washstand. They had looked nice for a few days, before suddenly dying. Then he noticed that the vase was bone-dry because he had forgotten to replenish the water. Maybe flowers weren't the answer for a man who spent so many hours at work.

Tomasso poured himself another tumbler of wine and crossed the room to close the shutters, but as he stood at the window, he paused. In the apartment on the opposite side of the street, two young children were giggling hysterically and refusing to go to bed. They danced joyously across the floor as their mother tried to scold them and their father tried to suppress his laughter. There was so much chaotic energy, it was impossible not to smile.

Tomasso remembered when these toddlers had been little babies, helpless and hungry; now they were playing up with wild abandon like street acrobats. He decided to leave the shutters open in the vague hope that some of the family warmth might spill across the street into his own dwelling.

He turned and gazed into the darkness of his bedroom, wondering what nightmares were lying in wait to ambush his sleep … when suddenly there was an urgent pounding on the front door downstairs.

Tomasso hurried from his room and bolted down the stairs, desperate to reach the door before the padrona awoke, but he wasn't quick enough.

"Can't a woman sleep in her own house?" the voice moaned from the back of the hall.

"Apologies, Padrona," he called out.

"Every week!"

"Won't happen again."

"Every week you bring some new chaos into my home."

Tomasso flung open the door and saw a breathless Marco standing there.

"What's happened?"

"It's best you see for yourself, sir."

Grateful for an excuse to avoid closing his eyes for a while longer, Tomasso grabbed his cloak and followed Marco out into the dark streets of Rome.

The twins had set up their surveillance post in an abandoned boat shed directly opposite Palazzo Volpe, which gave them a commanding view of everything that moved on this section of the river.

"They started arriving an hour ago," Paolo explained as Tomasso and Marco clambered into the hide. "One small boat after another, each one packed with workmen."

Tomasso peered through the slats in the boathouse and saw a team of about fifty builders milling on the landing jetty adjacent to the palazzo. "This is strange. During the day, not a workman in sight. Now it's mobbed."

"Do you think they're moonlighting from St Peter's?" Marco asked.

"They could be, but even builders have to sleep sometime."

"I think *that's* what they're waiting for." Paolo pointed upriver to a huge barge that was edging towards the far bank; the crew were clambering across the deck wrangling mooring ropes.

The three Apostolic Guards watched in silence as the barge tied off and the crew hoisted an unloading crane into position. One by one they winched great slabs of stone from the hold and swung them onto the jetty, where the workmen started hauling them by hand into the palazzo. It was striking how quiet the builders were; no-one whistled or shouted instructions or told lewd jokes. They all just worked in clandestine silence.

"Should we arrest them, sir?" Marco asked.

"For what?" Tomasso replied.

"Creeping around like that… They must be doing something illegal."

"Maybe we should just observe," Paolo suggested.

Tomasso was torn, unsure which course of action would get them closer to the truth. "We need Capitano Falchoni. I'll go and report to him."

"And in the meantime?" Paolo asked.

"Gather as much information as you can."

The twins exchanged a sceptical glance. "We're not going to see anything new from this distance," Paolo grumbled.

"Unless…" Marco suggested.

Paolo laughed. "I like your thinking."

"What?" But Tomasso was locked out of their silent understanding. He could only watch as the brothers scrambled into the darkness at one end of the shed, rummaged around under some torn oilskin sheets, then emerged dragging a small coracle.

"This feels like a bad idea," Tomasso whispered.

"No, it's brilliant," Paolo replied. "This is how we can get really close."

"And discover the name of the barge," Marco added.

"Listen to their accents."

"Work out where they're from."

"And who sent them."

"Wait, wait!" Tomasso interrupted. He looked at the coracle. "You won't both fit in there."

"One goes, one waits here," Marco replied.

"And there's no oar," Tomasso objected.

"But the current's with us." Paolo's mind had dealt with all objections. "I cast off from here, Marco gives me a strong push, I drift past the barge, then hit the shore at the bend under Ponte Fabricio."

"Where I'll be waiting to pull him to safety," Marco concluded.

Tomasso looked from the boat to the twins and realised that argument was futile. "Just be careful."

The twins gave a mocking laugh. "*Si, Mamma!*"

16: RESILIENCE

It was later than Cristina realised. She had planned to get home early enough to have supper with Isra and Alnaaji, but had become so absorbed in combing through Vatican customs and shipping records that time had slipped away from her.

She was trying to build a picture of the *Speranza*'s movements in and out of the Papal States over the past five years, but it was painstaking work. Line after line in ledger after ledger, detailing shipments of just about everything under the sun, from peppers to pearls, ebony to eggplants, and salt to cement. So far, all her efforts had yielded no useful insights, leaving her tired but with nothing to show for it. During the months spent writing her diaries in the convent cloisters, it had felt like Cristina was taking a step forward every day. Running an active investigation, however, was like stumbling through a maze backwards.

She turned her key in the lock as quietly as she could, then crept across the hallway and into the kitchen, where she found Isra dozing in an armchair in front of the dying embers of the fire. A very tempting aroma filled the kitchen, and Cristina started lifting the lids of various saucepans that sat on the stove.

"Bread soup," Isra said, stirring. "It should still be warm."

"Sorry, I didn't mean to wake you."

"I wasn't asleep." Isra stood up and stretched. "Just resting my eyes." She reached for a bowl and ladled some thick soup into it.

"Thank you." Cristina started to eat enthusiastically, wondering why she never felt hungry until food was actually in front of her, when she suddenly became ravenous.

"Any progress?"

"It's slow. But we'll get there."

"You really think you'll catch whoever is smuggling those poor people?"

"We have to." Cristina tore off a chunk of bread and started mopping up the soup. "What about Alnaaji? Any progress there? Is he coming out of his shell?"

"No. But he's starting to feel safer."

"How can you tell if he won't talk?"

"I'll show you."

Cristina popped the last piece of bread into her mouth, then followed Isra up the stairs. They paused on the landing outside the boy's room to dim the lantern, then Isra quietly opened the door.

They tiptoed into the gloom and saw Alnaaji fast asleep; his left hand was touching his ear, and his right was stretched above his head.

"Any more nightmares?" Cristina whispered.

Isra shook her head. "And it's the first time he's slept this long."

"He looks like the picture of innocence. If you didn't know, you'd never guess what he's been through."

The two women crept back out into the hall and entered Cristina's bedroom, where Isra started to turn down the bed.

"Do you think he'll ever forget?" Cristina asked as she started to unbutton her jacket.

"I hope not."

"Why would you say something like that?"

Isra plumped up the pillows. "You never forget suffering, but you can either let it destroy you, or you can grow from it. With help, Alnaaji will learn to draw strength from the trauma. It's like a knife being sharpened on a grindstone."

Cristina hung up her clothes and slipped on a cotton nightdress as she thought about Isra's own suffering: a child refugee wandering the wild lands of the south, then orphaned as she turned thirteen. "What good did *you* take from suffering?"

"Resilience. And an appreciation of what I have." Isra picked up a brush and began to draw it through Cristina's hair. "A home. Friendship. And an understanding that material things are just trifles. Money is nothing without happiness."

"Try telling that to the oligarchs."

"Exactly. They're men who have never suffered, so they have no appreciation of true value." She finished Cristina's hair and put the brush down. "All done."

"Thank you." Cristina hurried over to the bed and slid between the clean sheets with an appreciative sigh. "You make such a comfortable bed, Isra."

"The secret's in the iron. It has to be really hot to get the sheets smooth."

Cristina wriggled lower under the sheets until she was just a head on a pillow. "You know the thing that really concerns me? The construction of St Peter's has unleashed a flood of avarice. The more the dynastic families have, the more they want. And their greed cascades down through every level of Rome, until all anyone can think about is money."

"Then the Pope needs to speak out. Only he has the authority to stop the madness."

"His head issues proclamations and warnings, but his hand continues to give out lucrative contracts, so nothing changes.

At this rate, by the time the basilica is finished, there won't be an innocent soul left in the city."

"Just as well St Peter's will be so big, then. We can all fit inside it to repent." Isra snuffed out the lamp. "Now stop thinking and get some sleep."

Cristina listened to Isra's footsteps as she padded out of the room. But rather than close her eyes, she waited for them to adjust to the darkness; one by one, the familiar objects in the room started to become visible. She decided to run through the various fragments of evidence one last time so that her mind could work on the investigation as she slept, but she had barely started when her eyelids drooped and she fell into a deep sleep.

"Wake up!" Isra burst through the door.

"What?"

"Cristina! Wake up!" Isra flung open the shutters, blasting sunshine into the bedroom.

"What time is it?" Cristina squinted and struggled to get her bearings.

"Your brother has sent a message. You have to go to the Ponte Fabricio immediately."

"Why? What's happened?"

"Just get up and get dressed!"

Cristina looked at Isra and saw worry etched on her face. "Tell me — what's happened?"

"There's been a murder. One of the Apostolic Guards is dead."

17: WARNING

The horror lay on the mudbank under Ponte Fabricio, where the River Tiber veered south. Cristina arrived to find a handful of Apostolic Guards milling aimlessly in a state of shock. One of them crouched in the mud, clasping his head in disbelief. Down by the waterline, Domenico and Tomasso were standing on either side of a corpse that had been dragged from the river.

Cristina pushed forward until she was standing next to the body. It was horrific. A chisel had been hammered into the soldier's skull until just an inch remained visible above the blood-matted hair. His hands had been tied behind his back with a plumbline, and a muslin sack filled with something heavy had been lashed to his feet.

"What in God's name happened here?" Cristina whispered.

"I-I told them to be careful," Tomasso stuttered. "I told them!"

"It's not your fault," Domenico said.

"I should have ordered them to stay put. I should have —" He stopped talking to swallow back his tears.

Cristina put a hand on his shoulder. "Just tell me what you know."

"The twins found a coracle and wanted to cross the river. I told them it was dangerous, but Paolo..." He glanced down at the corpse. "Paolo wouldn't take no for an answer."

"Why cross the river at all? They could see everything from the observation post."

"A barge had arrived, unloading stone from upriver. The twins..." Tomasso glanced over to Marco, who was now rocking back and forth, struggling to process what had happened. "They wanted to get the name of the barge. Overhear what the workmen were saying. Afterwards, Marco was going to meet him here, where the currents would wash the boat ashore. But when he got here…" He trailed off, overcome with emotion.

"In your own time," Cristina soothed.

Tomasso took a deep breath, trying to wrestle back control of his grief. "The coracle was smashed up on the mud." He pointed to the broken wreckage a few feet away. "And Paolo … his body was floating in the weeds, his legs weighted down. Marco pulled him out, but … it was too late." Tomasso lowered his head and sobbed. "Imagine finding your own brother like that…"

Cristina looked across to Marco, crouched in the stinking mud. The man was so overwhelmed, his mind seemed to have shut down.

"Do you think he'll be able to identify any of the builders?" Cristina asked her brother.

Domenico shook his head. "It was dark. They were on the other side of the river. Thousands of men are working on St Peter's. It could have been any of a hundred labouring gangs."

"If only I'd stopped them!" Tomasso cried out, clenching his fists. "I should have forbidden them. Ordered them to stay put!"

Cristina reached out to comfort him, but he turned away.

"It's not your fault, Tomasso."

"It is! It is my fault. It was on my watch." He walked over to Marco and slumped down next to him.

Cristina exchanged a glance with Domenico. "I'm worried about him."

"Tomasso's stronger than you think."

"But he's been through a lot. He was first to board the *Speranza*. Now this. It would break most men."

"The best healing is revenge." Domenico turned his gaze back to the violated body at his feet. "Whoever did this must be caught and punished. That's what my men need. Retribution."

Cristina knelt down next to Paolo's body and gently rocked his head towards her. His eyes were bloodshot, and his mouth and nose clogged with congealing blood. Cristina shuddered. His young life had ended in horror, and the evil of this act would savage the lives of everyone who had known and loved him.

Part of Cristina wanted to recoil from this darkness. To turn and run back to the convent, where she could hide from the horrors of the world. And yet there was another part of her that was angry, that demanded justice.

She drew a breath, gripped Paolo's chin with her left hand, then clamped her right around the handle of the chisel that protruded from the top of his skull.

"No, Cristina," Domenico warned. "Don't do that!"

She braced herself, then pulled on the chisel, which emerged from Paolo's head with a ghastly slither.

Domenico turned away. "That was not necessary."

"Sometimes workers mark their tools to stop them getting mixed up." Cristina wiped the blood and brains from the chisel, then studied the metal shaft. There were plenty of nicks and scratches from cutting stone, but no stamped letters or personalised markings. She placed the chisel gently on the soldier's body. "The violence of this murder... It shows we're on the right lines, Domenico. Someone is trying to warn us off. Which means we must be getting closer to the truth."

Cristina untied the rope that held the muslin sack to Paolo's feet, pulled it open and peered inside. "And *that* completes the message."

Domenico bent down and put his hand into the sack. He had been expecting smooth stones gathered from the riverbed, but instead found jagged chunks of travertine rock.

Cristina stood up, stretched her back and gazed across the river to Palazzo Volpe. "Everything about this murder is designed to intimidate us. Paolo was killed with a stonecutter's tools — the chisel, the plumbline, the travertine. So the killers aren't trying to hide; they're saying they're above the law. Too powerful to touch."

"No-one is above Pope Julius," Domenico said grimly. "And we act with his authority."

"Given what was weighing down the body, it's more than likely that travertine was being unloaded from that barge."

"It must have come downriver from the quarries at Tivoli."

"But did Volpe pay for it? Or was the stone ordered for St Peter's then diverted to his own palazzo?"

"If it was a legitimate shipment, why would it be delivered in the middle of the night?" Domenico replied.

"Exactly."

"So, let's say the travertine was stolen, and the workers are moonlighting. Which means Volpe's palazzo is effectively being paid for by the Pope."

"Which is fraud on a massive scale."

Domenico looked down at the corpse. "And this is a warning of what will happen to anyone who tries to expose it."

"But in trying to scare us, they have overplayed their hand." Cristina plucked a chunk of travertine from the wet sack and held it up. "This shows that someone in the quarries is playing a key role in the construction black markets. Only someone quite high up could steal an entire shipment of stone." Cristina gazed upriver. "That's where we need to investigate — the quarries."

Domenico looked thoughtful. "Have you ever been to a stone quarry, Cristina?"

She shook her head.

"They have a handful of skilled cutters and quarrymen who can read the rockface, but the rest are just brute force. Those places need an army of strong labourers. No skills or language required."

Cristina's mind circled the same thought as her brother. "The *Speranza*."

"Exactly. Maybe that's where all those men were being shipped to."

Cristina dropped the chunk of travertine back into the sack. "I'll go upriver with Tomasso. We'll try to infiltrate the quarries."

"What? No."

"We'll be undercover."

"It's too dangerous. I need to send a squad of men up there."

"And alert everyone that we're onto them?" She looked down at Paolo's body. "We don't want any more 'warnings'."

"But Tomasso needs to take some time off."

Cristina looked over to the deputy, his arm now around Marco's shoulders. "Sitting at home on his own is that last thing Tomasso needs. If revenge is the best medicine, he should focus on that."

"Then I will stay in Rome and launch the investigation into Paolo's murder." Domenico picked up the chisel from the soldier's body.

"That's a good strategy," Cristina replied. "Whoever is responsible for Paolo's death is also involved with the *Speranza*. I'm convinced of it. Solve one crime, solve them both."

Domenico looked at the gruesome chisel. "If they think they can kill with impunity, it'll only be a matter of time until the streets of Rome are awash with blood."

18: VOLPE

Father Volpe made his regular confession at *Basilica di Santa Pudenziana*, the oldest place of Christian worship in Rome. Perhaps a part of him believed that the antiquity of the church would add spiritual heft to his words, or perhaps it was just habit. Either way, it made him easier to track down.

Domenico sat patiently on a bench halfway down the arched nave, listening to the faint murmur of voices drifting from the confessional. They had already been in there quite a while, giving Domenico plenty of time to study the thousand-year-old apse mosaic depicting an enthroned Christ surrounded by his adoring Apostles. Was that how Father Volpe saw himself? An apostle of the all-powerful Building Committee of St Peter's, handing out contracts rather than salvation?

The burble of voices finished. Domenico heard the curtain being drawn open, footsteps on the stone floor, then Father Volpe strode down the nave, head bowed as if meditating on his spiritual purification.

Domenico stepped in front of the priest. "Feeling cleansed?"

Volpe was startled, then recognition came with a frown. "Capitano Falchoni. You were told to leave us alone."

"It's you who have overstepped the mark," Domenico replied.

"I really don't have time for this." Volpe tried to walk past, but Domenico grabbed his arm.

"How dare you?" Father Volpe thundered. Angrily he shook his arm free.

"Did you order one of my men to be murdered?"

Shock registered on Volpe's face. "Have you lost your mind?"

"He was on a surveillance team, watching the construction work on your palazzo."

Indignation replaced surprise. "Are you spying on me, Capitano?"

"I need the names of all the builders working on your basement rooms. As well as details of the contractors who supplied all that beautiful travertine stone. It's a remarkable coincidence that it's the same stone being used in St Peter's."

The two men eyed each other. Then Volpe gave a shrug. "Honestly? I have no idea who is working on the palazzo. As far as I am concerned, they are nameless labourers."

"How convenient."

"But you haven't answered my question, Capitano. Are you spying on me?"

"We're investigating fraudulent contracts, theft of building materials, the illegal use of slave labour —" he paused — "and murder. One of my men was killed."

"Everyone knows the streets of Rome are unsafe after curfew," Father Volpe replied. "In future, your men should take more care." He walked confidently towards the doors.

"A chisel was driven through the top of his skull."

The violence of the image stopped Volpe in his tracks.

"His hands were tied with a plumbline," Domenico continued. "And his body was drowned with the weight of travertine stone. This was not the work of a common cutpurse."

Father Volpe drew himself up to his full height. "I am sorry to hear about your colleague. But I am undertaking vital work for both the Church and this city. The last thing I need is to be harassed by the Apostolic Guard."

"Then tell me the truth, Father, and I might leave you alone."

"The truth is, I have no idea what happens in the grubby lower reaches of the building process. I commissioned the work on my palazzo. I discussed the project with my architect. How they execute my ideas is of no concern to me."

"Well, it was of great concern to my murdered officer."

The priest didn't flinch. "Perhaps the builders thought your man was a thief. Perhaps he insulted them. Or threatened them. Builders are easily provoked, you know."

"How typical," Domenico said with contempt. "Blame always falls onto those at the bottom. Whereas we both know that it's those at the top who take the bribes and skim off whatever they can."

"I really have no idea what you're talking about." Father Volpe turned and strode out into the sharp sunlight, but he was not even halfway across the courtyard when he heard Domenico's voice behind him.

"I am not a fool, Volpe!"

"I beg to differ." Volpe turned to face Domenico. "This is how ambitious building projects are accomplished."

"With the blood of others?"

"Everything has a cost."

"Pope Julius has ordered me to root out corruption."

"And he has ordered *me* to build the greatest basilica in Christendom. You would be well advised not to interfere."

Domenico chased across the grey mosaic tiles, eyes locked on Father Volpe. "One of my men was brutally murdered while doing his duty. Two hundred and ninety-three innocent souls died in the most horrendous circumstances on the *Speranza*. I swear, these crimes will not go unpunished."

Volpe crossed himself in a show of piety. "Alas, tragedies happen at sea all the time."

Domenico clenched his fists. He wanted to grab Volpe's beautiful silk cassock and shake the truth out of him. He wanted to drag him to the morgue and force him to look at Paolo's corpse and witness the grief of his twin brother.

But then what?

The Vatican bureaucrats would close ranks and manoeuvre against him; they would brief cardinals who owed them favours and pour poisonous gossip into the ears of those who had the trust of the Holy Father. By the end of the week, Domenico would be isolated and friendless, and his career would effectively be over.

Volpe saw the rage in Domenico's face and smiled. He raised his hand and made a sign of the cross on Domenico's forehead. "In the name of the Father, and of the Son, and of the Holy Spirit. Go in peace, my child."

Then Father Volpe strode confidently back onto the street and turned right, heading towards the Vatican.

19: BLAME

Cristina and Tomasso set out from Rome just after dawn, riding straight into the rising sun towards the travertine quarries near Tivoli.

They had made a conscious effort to look as anonymous as possible: no uniforms, all weapons concealed, Vatican livery removed from their saddles. They encountered no difficulties on the road and made timely progress, so that by early afternoon they were on the high track that overlooked the flat farmlands of the Aniene Valley.

Cristina pulled her horse to a stop and gazed at the tranquil landscape. She had mixed memories of Tivoli — the dark secrets in the orphanage ... Geometra Castano, who had abused his position of trust ... her own intellectual arrogance that had led her astray.

Tomasso sensed her melancholy. "Wondering if things could have worked out differently?" he asked.

"Such speculation is illogical."

"But that's what you feel? Am I right?"

"Now I can see the mistakes I made two years ago. But at the time..."

Tomasso nodded. "I always thought you were foolish to blame yourself for the deaths of those priests. But the chain of events we're all caught up in, the cause and effect, it's complicated. I see that now."

Cristina knew what was haunting him. "Paolo's death isn't your fault."

"But I could have prevented it."

"Only if you'd known what was going to happen. Which is impossible."

"Isn't that what makes a good leader? Foresight?"

"I had to learn to forgive myself, Tomasso. And so must you."

"Will his mother ever forgive me? Or his brother? Someone has to take the blame." Tomasso reached for his flask, pulled out the stopper and took a swig.

"Drinking won't help."

"It's just water."

"Please. You've been drinking since before we set off this morning."

"That's not true."

"I can smell it on you!"

Tomasso slid the flask back into his saddle pouch. "Have I ever let you down, Cristina?"

"That's not the point."

"Have I?"

"No."

"I still do my duty. That's what matters."

"I'm not blaming you. But there are no answers in wine."

"Sometimes there's too much reality to deal with. This —" he gestured to the flask — "takes the edge off."

"I disagree. You can never have too much reality — too much truth," Cristina said. "You just have to understand how to process it."

"And yet you retreated to the convent." Tomasso patted the saddle pouch. "This is *my* retreat."

"There's a difference. I wasn't trying to block the world out. I was trying to understand it, so that I can reengage."

"Each to their own." Tomasso spurred his horse and continued along the road.

The main quarries were to the south, so they branched off before reaching Tivoli itself. What would once have been a sleepy country lane had been widened to accommodate the heavy carts transporting massive stone slabs down to the river jetties, but no-one had invested in the actual surface of the road, so deep grooves had been carved in the mud, forcing the horses to step carefully.

They heard the stone quarry before they saw it: an eerie chorus of a thousand hammers striking rock, driving away the starlings who could not compete with their raucous song. Closer still and the air began to fill with stone dust, irritating Cristina's lungs and powdering her hair. And then the wooden signs started to appear by the roadside:

Private Property!
No Trespassing!
Warning! Only those on official business allowed past this point.

Finally, they came to a large hoarding that bore the crest of the Orsini family, along with the word *PRIVATO* painted in large red letters. Underneath, some wit had graffitied, *Asini di Orsini.* The donkeys of Orsini.

"I assume whoever wrote this did it after he'd been fired," Tomasso said, running his fingers over the carved letters.

"Doesn't bode well for working conditions in the quarry."

"But that's how the oligarchs treat all of us, isn't it? As human donkeys."

Cristina glanced over her shoulder. "Where are the guards? Shouldn't someone be stopping us?"

"It's only a matter of time," Tomasso replied, dismounting. "We should get off this road before they discover us."

They led their horses into a dense copse of trees and secured the reins to some low branches, then scrambled up the wooded hill on foot. After a quarter of an hour, the path opened out and they found themselves standing on the lip of an enormous chasm that had been scarred across the landscape — the Orsini quarry.

It was as if they had slipped into a mythological underworld. Thousands of men —who looked like nothing more than ants from this distance — crawled across brilliant white faces of rock as they dragged newly quarried slabs behind them. Smoke rose from dozens of bonfires that had been lit inside fissures to fracture the cliffs from within. Ropes criss-crossed the manmade valleys as gangs of workers tried to dislodge vast travertine teeth from the mouth of the mountain. It was as terrifying as it was impressive.

"When St Peter's Basilica is completed, and people gaze on its beauty, how many will think of quarries like this?" Cristina wondered aloud. "The architect's drawings look so clean and effortless."

"And so quiet," Tomasso agreed. "You never imagine this cacophony." He pointed to the floor of the chasm. "You can see how it's organised: all the rock is dragged to the central ravine, then winched onto the mule trains. They transport it down the road we just came along to the river. Then the barges can sail all the way to the centre of Rome."

"It makes you wonder how much of the mountain will be left by the time they've finished."

"And how many men will have died."

Even from this distance they could hear the shouts of the foremen and the cracking of their whips. Cristina shook her head. "Who could take more than a few months of that?"

"This quarry — I bet it chews people up and spits out their remains," Tomasso said grimly. "It's a monster."

Cristina stood up. "And I'm afraid we need to crawl into its belly."

20: GRIEF

Paolo's coffin had been placed in the nave of Santa Bibiana to receive prayers prior to burial. The small church lay in the shadow of the ancient Aurelian walls, next to the Porta Tiburtina which dominated the Roman neighbourhood where the twins had lived with their parents.

The gloomy space was poorly lit by scattered banks of candles, but as Domenico's eyes adjusted to the darkness, he saw Marco and his parents kneeling in the side chapel. Their hands were clasped together; their lips whispered fervent prayers. On the wall above them was a fresco showing the *Descent from the Cross*: Joseph of Arimathea tenderly lowering Christ's body into the waiting arms of the grief-stricken Mary Magdalene.

Domenico stood in silence for a few minutes, not wanting to interrupt the family's prayers, until Marco sensed his presence and turned around.

"Capitano Falchoni, sir."

"Forgive the intrusion."

"No, no. Please." Marco stood up and introduced Domenico to his parents.

"I cannot imagine the pain you are suffering," Domenico said. "But I wanted you to know how highly Paolo was regarded. He was a fine soldier, dedicated to justice, and his sacrifice was made in the line of duty."

The mother and father said nothing.

"Everyone loved him," Marco said, trying to ease the awkwardness. "I'm sure Capitano Falchoni speaks on behalf of the whole regiment."

"I do."

Still the parents said nothing. It was as if accepting empathy would somehow betray their son's memory.

"I just came to give you this." Domenico offered them a leather satchel. "Paolo had some things in his locker at the barracks. I wanted to hand them to you personally."

Marco's mother took the satchel and sat on a pew, gazing at the bag as if it was a holy relic. Finally, she undid the buckle, opened the flap and reached inside. She pulled out a small tin which contained a set of ivory dice, and smiled to herself as she remembered her son playing endless games of hazard. She reached into the satchel again and took out a pewter drinking beaker etched with Paolo's initials. Tenderly she traced her fingers over the letters. Next came two clean handkerchiefs and a string of rosary beads. "My sister gave him those," she said. She reached in again and took out a neatly folded shirt. "He always wanted to be prepared," she whispered. "I made sure he had a spare shirt at work. Always."

Finally, she pulled out a pair of Paolo's leather gloves. She closed her eyes and held them against either side of her face, as if her dead son's hands were cradling her.

As fresh tears rolled down his wife's face, Marco's father turned accusingly to Domenico. "How could this happen? We're not at war. My son should never have died."

"Battles are fought on many fronts," Domenico said, trying to be tactful. "Apostolic Guards are now fighting a wave of corruption and fraud —"

"It's the foreigners, isn't it?" the father interrupted. "Swarming into our city."

"Your sons were conducting a difficult surveillance operation. That's all I can say at the moment."

"Of course it's the foreigners," the mother said through her tears. "You said as much." She turned to her son for support, but Marco looked suddenly tense.

"It's official business, Mama. We're not to discuss it," he whispered.

"There's nothing secret about it!" She wiped her eyes with her sleeve. "Rome doesn't feel like Rome anymore. This is *our* home. It should be for *us*." She looked at Domenico, desperate for him to agree

"This new St Peter's. It's brought unwelcome hordes of workers to our country," the father pronounced.

"What was wrong with the old basilica?" the mother demanded. "Why did they tear it down? Why does everything have to change?"

"It's just change for the sake of change," the father said.

"If only they'd left things alone, Paolo would still be with us…" Just saying his name was too painful, and Marco's mother gave in to fresh tears.

Domenico looked at this broken family. What could he say to comfort them? There were no words to heal their loss, but he sensed real danger in their grief. This was how riots were born. For every time these parents spoke of Paolo, they would apportion blame. And since they couldn't blame their pope or their Church, they would turn their anger on someone else. The foreigner. The other.

"All I can do is express my deep gratitude for Paolo's service to this city," Domenico said. "And I speak on behalf of Pope Julius himself when I pray for you to find peace in your suffering."

But far from offering comfort, Domenico's words plunged the mother deeper into despair. He caught Marco's eye, and there was a moment of understanding between the two men, a moment of shared helplessness in the face of such overwhelming emotion.

Domenico gave a small bow, crossed himself, then left the side chapel.

It was a relief to get out of the suffocating gloom and into the sunlight and noise of the street. Domenico glanced at the faces pushing past him on their way to the markets — people were chatting and laughing, seemingly without a care in the world. Yet in an instant, any one of them could be plunged into the abyss of grief. And trapped in that darkness, they too would lash out and lay the blame at someone's feet.

Did the oligarchs think about this when they created their illegal networks to traffic cheap labour into the Papal States? Did they even care? It would not be the families of the wealthy who would suffer in the rioting. No, they would be out of harm's reach in their country villas or locked behind the solid gates of their palazzos. Because that was what wealth bought you: the protective bubble of peace.

21: IDLE

To understand what was really going on, Cristina and Tomasso needed to put their ears to the ground, so they rode directly to the tavern closest to the travertine quarry. At this time of day, they assumed there would be a few old men drinking and gossiping, as everyone of working age would be busy cutting stone from the quarry.

The Fig Tree was a simple country inn; once through the honeysuckle-covered arch, they found themselves in a courtyard that contained two long tables with benches on either side. Men were huddled in groups — some playing cards without any great enthusiasm, some staring silently into their mugs of wine, others devouring bowls of steaming brown stew that had emerged from the kitchen hatch on the far wall. This was a long way from the bucolic jollity of folk paintings, and strangely, all the customers were young men. *Idle* young men, who nursed their drinks to make them last longer.

In the centre of the courtyard was a huge, dead fig tree, scratching in vain at the air with a thousand woody fingers.

"Ever thought about renaming the tavern?" Tomasso quipped.

The drinkers stared at him coldly.

Cristina leaned towards Tomasso and whispered, "Perhaps it's best we sit inside."

"It was just a joke."

"I think they have heard it before."

She led the way into the tavern building. Even though it was empty, the bar managed to exude an oppressive gloom. They took a seat by the small bay window, and a few moments later a wiry man in his fifties approached. "Drinking or eating?"

"Did somebody die?" Tomasso replied.

"Why? Are you volunteering?" the man said without a glimmer of humour.

"No. It's just…" Tomasso glanced in the direction of the courtyard.

"Just?"

"Nothing. We're drinking."

The innkeeper plonked two beakers on the table and filled them with wine from a pottery jug.

"We meant no offence," Cristina explained. "We've only just arrived."

"You don't say."

"Do people here hate all strangers?" Cristina asked. "Or is it just us?"

The innkeeper shrugged. "There's a saying in Tivoli: nothing good ever comes from Rome. Which would include you."

"And yet without Rome, this place would be nothing," Tomasso objected. "The travertine quarry puts food on the table of every house in the area."

The innkeeper sighed, picked up the two beakers and poured the wine back into the jug. "You should leave."

"Why?" Cristina asked, starting to get irritated. "We've only just arrived."

"When you both get stabbed, I don't want the blood on my floorboards. It never comes out, no matter how much you scrub."

Cristina locked eyes with the man. "Seriously? Those villagers would stab someone sent by Pope Julius?"

The innkeeper blinked. "The Pope?"

"The Holy Father himself."

"Prove it."

Tomasso rummaged in his jacket and pulled out his Warrant of Authority that bore the Pope's seal.

The innkeeper inspected it. "So … you're not working for Orsini?"

"Quite the opposite," Cristina replied. "I think we're working against him."

"Well. In that case…" The innkeeper refilled the two beakers with wine. "These are on the house."

But just as he turned to go, Cristina said, "You must be Antonio."

The innkeeper scrutinised her. "What makes you think that?"

"The licensing plate above the bar is for Antonio Morodi. And who else could give us free wine but the owner? Please —" Cristina drew up a stool — "won't you join us?"

"I'll get another cup."

"No need." Cristina slid Tomasso's beaker across the table and offered it to Antonio instead.

"But —" Tomasso objected.

Cristina ignored him. "It's all right. Deputy Tomasso's on duty."

"Oh." Antonio sat down and clinked beakers with Cristina; Tomasso could only watch as they slugged back the wine.

"So," Cristina smiled. "Now we're all friends, Antonio, perhaps you could tell us what's really going on here?"

Antonio painted a worrying picture. When the new St Peter's had first been announced, everyone in Tivoli Province had been excited about the good times that were coming. There would be work lasting for decades, giving families a chance to clear their debts, renovate their homes, and build up their savings. But within months, the Orsini family had started laying off local men and bringing in cheap labour to replace them.

"Every week another convoy of carts arrives, usually under cover of darkness. They take the foreigners into the quarries and that's where they stay."

"They don't come in here to drink?" Cristina asked. "Or get provisions from the market?"

Antonio shook his head. "Never. Maybe they're scared of what people will do to them."

"But it's not their fault. They're just trying to survive."

"You don't understand how people have been betrayed. All those big-money contracts and still the people here live in poverty."

"Well, we want to do something about that," Cristina said.

"It's too late," Antonio scoffed. "The damage has been done. People round here have been let down too many times. They've given up on trusting anyone."

"You've seen our warrants," Tomasso interjected. "We are here with the moral authority of the Vatican."

"These men have been stabbed in the back by one of their own. What chance does an outsider stand?"

Cristina leaned forward. "Who wielded the knife, Antonio? What happened here?"

"Caposquadra Spiro happened."

Without warning, the sound of smashing pottery echoed around the courtyard. Antonio leapt to his feet and rushed towards the door, where he slammed into a large, drunk man looming over the bar.

"Throw them out, Antonio!" the drunk man shouted, pointing at Cristina and Tomasso.

"Outside!" Antonio tried to wrestle the man into the courtyard, but it was like pushing a mountain.

"Send them back to Rome!"

In a well-practised move, Antonio slipped his foot behind the drunkard's heels and nudged him backwards, sending the man-mountain crashing into the flagstones.

"*Oof!*" He lay there, clutching his ribs.

"I warned you." Antonio shook his head. "You never listen."

The drunkard rolled onto his side and groaned.

"And no-one tells me who to throw out of my own tavern. It's one of the joys of being a landlord." Antonio slammed the door shut, crossed the room and sat back down at the table. "You see what I mean?"

Cristina poured Antonio another beaker of wine. "You were telling us about Caposquadra Spiro."

"He wasn't always a capo. He used to be one of us. But he was determined to crawl up the greasy pole, and to do it, he crawled up to Orsini."

Cristina's eyes narrowed. "And how exactly does one do that?"

"By proving where your loyalties lie. Spiro told Orsini there was a rich seam of travertine running right underneath his own village, and if they destroyed the village, they could double the size of the quarry. So Orsini did just that." Antonio spat on the floor, trying to clear the bad taste left by the memory. "Spiro betrayed his people to become a capo. Now even his own mother hates him. But what does he care? Giulio Orsini loves him."

"For now. But once Spiro stops making Orsini money…"

Antonio shook his head. "You've seen the size of the quarry. That buys a lot of love."

"I can't believe a man would betray his own mother," Tomasso said.

"Oh, he felt guilty about it. Tried to buy back her love by building her a grand villa in the hills."

"Did it work?"

Antonio smirked. "Go see for yourself."

22: GUILDS

"Are you hiding a killer in the Scalpellini Guild?" Domenico's question was uncompromising.

Master Linciare looked shocked. "What did you say?"

"We have surveillance operations running across Rome —"

"Are you spying on us?"

"That information is classified. But one of my own men was murdered by a stonemason," Domenico placed the blood-stained chisel on the desk. "Which would make the killer a member of the Scalpellini."

The Master of the Guild was caught between fear and indignation. His mouth twitched as he tried to find the right words to respond. It was rare to see Linciare speechless, as his rise to power had been largely due to his glib eloquence, but Domenico let him flounder; this was when witnesses were most vulnerable. Caught off guard, they were more likely to reveal a secret.

Even allowing for their grief, the extreme views expressed by Paolo's parents had disturbed Domenico. It underlined the importance of catching the killer, so he'd started interrogating the leaders of Rome's craft guilds. At this stage in the construction of St Peter's, Master Stonemason Linciare, head of the Scalpellini, was one of the key players in the city.

"How dare you come into my guildhall and make libellous accusations?" Linciare found his voice at last.

"Perhaps you'd rather meet at the cemetery where my soldier is buried?" Domenico suggested. "You can talk to the man's distraught parents at the same time."

"We are not a protection racket and we do not shelter criminals!" Linciare boomed. "We are a guild of master craftsmen representing the interests of working men. Each member has gone through an exacting apprenticeship and spent years mastering his craft. Why would anyone throw all that away by turning to murder?"

"Sometimes the most highly educated are the most violent," Domenico replied. "Look at the Borgias."

"I'd rather look here." Linciare walked to the doors on the far side of his office and slid them back to reveal a small balcony overlooking the guild's meeting hall. He ushered Domenico onto the viewing platform. "This is what we do, Capitano Falchoni. This is how we further the interests of working people. By supporting each other and training the young."

A dozen men in their late teens were working at separate tables dotted across the hall; on each table was a large artichoke and a block of stone, and the men were hard at work carving the stone into the shape of the thistle.

"This is how we ensure that the standard of masonry in Rome is the highest in the world," Linciare boasted.

Domenico was impressed by how diligently the men worked, wielding their chisels with incredible speed and accuracy, then patiently brushing away the stone debris and checking their progress from different angles.

"These *giovani* are halfway through their apprenticeships. They have already mastered the point chisel, the bullnose and the roughing claw, but if they fail this exam they will be expelled from the guild and will no longer be able to call themselves scalpellini."

"Sounds harsh."

"It's what we do to preserve the integrity of our craft. So do you seriously think we would destroy our hard-won reputation by harbouring a killer?"

"I appreciate your sincerity," Domenico replied, relenting, "and I meant no offence. But I need you to understand the gravity of the crimes we're investigating."

"Apology accepted." Linciare led them back into his office and slid the doors shut to block out the tap-and-chink of the apprentices.

"We know the oligarchs are building their fortunes on the back of St Peter's. One way or another, they control all the contracts. Your guild has rules and regulations, but the oligarchs are a law unto themselves. And that is causing a lot of suffering."

Linciare looked cagey. "Constructing great buildings is a complicated business."

"But it doesn't have to be a criminal one."

"Maybe. Maybe not." The mason moved behind his desk and sat down in his voluminous chair. "Either way, do not ask me to speak against the oligarchs."

"Even if they're breaking the law?"

"Only a fool bites the hand that feeds him."

"What happened to the 'integrity' of stonemasons?"

"Capitano Falchoni, do you know how much building work the oligarchs generate every year in this city?"

"That's not the point."

"It very much is the point. And I will not say anything that might harm my members' interests or damage their chances of getting work."

Domenico could feel his anger rising. This was supposed to be a city of God, but everywhere you turned, people preferred to worship gold. He paced towards Linciare's desk. "Paolo was just twenty-four. He was loved by his parents, loved by his twin brother. He was hard-working, good at his job and popular. Do you know how he died?"

"I am sorry for your loss, truly. But —"

Domenico picked up the chisel and tapped it on top of the master mason's bald head. "This chisel was driven through his skull. From top to bottom."

The blood drained from Linciare's face. He reached into his desk for a bottle of brandy, poured a small glass with trembling hands and slugged the spirit down. "Would you like some?"

"All I want is information. Paolo was on surveillance. He saw a group of builders moonlighting at Palazzo Volpe. Next thing, he's killed. A stonemason working in Rome is going to be a member of the Scalpellini. Which brings us full circle: are you hiding a killer?"

Linciare stroked his scalp thoughtfully. "If the killer was moonlighting, then maybe he wasn't even in the guild."

"Is that really the best you can give me?"

"It's a possibility."

"There is another way of doing this, Linciare. I get a warrant to raid the guild offices, then we go through every piece of paper and check every ledger entry. I wonder what that might turn up?"

Linciare raised his hands. "There's no need to be so hostile, Capitano Falchoni."

"You want friendly? Then start cooperating."

Master Linciare poured himself some more brandy to buy himself a few moments. "Look, there are some things you should know. But you must understand, you never heard any of this from me."

"This had better be worth it."

"There are many corrupt practices. The oligarchs are funnelling money into their own pockets. For every ducat spent by the Vatican, only half actually ends up in St Peter's. There are bribes at every stage, even to get onto the tender lists."

"Tell me something I don't know," Domenico growled. "Tell me about the *Speranza*."

"A tragedy." Linciare crossed himself piously. "But when it comes to unskilled labour, those men are not under the protection of the guilds. That makes them vulnerable, because competitive tendering pushes the price *below* the point of viability. It means that whoever wins the contract cannot afford to employ Italian labourers. So they have to bring in cheap workers. Foreign workers."

"And the guilds accept this?" Domenico looked at the mason in disbelief.

"Of course we're not happy. But what choice do we have?" Linciare glared impatiently at Domenico. "The oligarchs control ninety per cent of the building work in Rome. Go to war with them, and you may as well be dead."

"You don't know the meaning of the word."

"And you don't know the power of a blacklist!"

"Those two hundred and ninety-three souls on the *Speranza* — who is fighting for them?"

Linciare sighed. "Look, all I know is the situation is going to get a lot worse. Every month, ships leave the North African coast loaded with migrant workers. As the construction ramps up, there will be more and more boatloads."

"I need names," Domenico said. "Who is organising all this? Where are they based? Which oligarch is behind it?"

Linciare shook his head. "They keep the operations secret. They change their routes. They're always one step ahead.

Anyone who asks awkward questions … well, you saw what happened to your own man."

"You do know that withholding evidence is a crime?"

"I've told you what I know, Capitano. But I've been in Rome long enough to know what I shouldn't ask. And I'll tell you this for nothing: do not cross the people-traffickers. The only thing those men care about is money. The *only* thing."

23: REFUGE

Caposquadra Spiro hadn't just bought his mother a grand villa in Monti Tiburtini, he'd bought her half the hillside as well. From the wooded ridge, down a gentle slope to the twisting stream must have been at least seven acres. A swathe of trees curved through the meadow like a brushstroke, and at the bottom of the hill, surrounded by a neat phalanx of poplar trees, was the gleaming white villa itself.

"It must have been beautiful when Spiro bought it," Cristina said as she gazed at the estate.

"I bet he never thought it would end up like this," Tomasso replied.

Because there was a problem: the rural idyll had been turned into a refugee camp. Tents and makeshift huts had been constructed across the hillside, awnings had been slung between the trees to give shelter from the sun, and smoke from countless campfires rose into the sharp blue sky. Bits of furniture had been arranged into alfresco rooms, and trunks of possessions had been stacked up to partition areas for dozens of different families. Needless to say, the goats ignored the boundaries and roamed wherever they wanted, much like the children who shrieked with joy as they played hide and seek in the ramshackle settlement.

Cristina and Tomasso tied their horses to a wooden fence that surrounded the encampment and approached the villa on foot.

"You must be lost!" a voice called out.

Cristina looked up and saw a robust woman in her late forties standing on the balcony; her long hair was bunched up tightly and her arms were filled with a huge bundle of wet laundry.

"We're looking for Sofia, the mother of Caposquadra Spiro?" Immediately Cristina regretted being so honest, as everyone within earshot stopped what they were doing and glared at her.

"Has he sent you?" the laundrywoman asked warily.

"No. We've never met him."

"Then why are you here?"

"Can we talk inside?"

"Do you have any weapons?"

Tomasso opened his jacket to show that he was unarmed.

"We just want to talk," Cristina said. "Are you Sofia?"

"You'd better come up."

By the time they arrived on the balcony, Sofia was busy hanging up the laundry on a web of ropes that ran between the balustrades.

"You can sit there." She nodded towards a wooden bench. "But you'll understand if I don't join you. Need to get this dry before the rain comes." She glanced at the horizon, where a bank of dark clouds was lurking.

"We're not going to sit while you work." Cristina turned to Tomasso. "Come on, roll up your sleeves."

"Me? But what am I supposed to do?"

"You've never done laundry before?"

"Have you?"

"I've watched Isra." Cristina pointed to a large metal tub in the kitchen. "All the clothes in there need to be wrung out for a start."

Tomasso rolled his eyes but did as he was told, while Cristina picked up some wet clothes and pegs, and stood next to Sofia to hang them out. "One day, someone will invent something to do all this work."

"They have. It's called children."

Cristina laughed. "But it sounds as if your son doesn't visit much."

"He wouldn't dare. Not now."

"Still, he bought this villa for you, am I right? It's quite something."

Sofia looked sceptical. "I'm hoping he'll learn, but maybe it's too late."

"If you don't mind me saying, you don't sound very grateful."

"Are you a mother?"

"No."

"You do everything you can to raise them right, but sometimes they just choose their own path, and there's nothing you can do."

"He must have grown into a very generous man."

"Or a very guilty one." Sofia picked up a pair of wet breeches and shook them out. "I can't believe he thought I could live here in peace, while all the people I've grown up with were thrown out of their homes."

Cristina looked at the garden-turned-encampment; it had all the life and energy of a village, just without the buildings. "So, you offered everyone a home here?"

"It doesn't make up for what they've lost, but it's something."

Tomasso emerged from the kitchen and plonked a fresh pile of wet laundry on the table. "Must be confusing for the villagers. The son makes them homeless, then the mother gives them refuge."

"It's confusing for me," Sofia admitted. "And I raised him." She pegged up the last shirt she was holding, but rather than start on the fresh pile, she sat down on a stool. "He wasn't an easy child."

Cristina pulled up a stool and sat next to her. "Are any children easy?"

"I always forgave him, and I tried to understand. Maybe I forgave too much. Indulged him. But the other children..." Sofia's face tensed as she remembered. "They were merciless."

"He was bullied?"

"Spiro was different to the other children. He liked everything to be ordered. He wasn't scruffy or untidy. Everything had to be in its place."

"There's nothing wrong with having an orderly mind," Cristina said, thinking of her own obsessions.

But that was not what Sofia meant. "Most children, when they get undressed to go to bed, they just throw their clothes on the floor. Not Spiro. Every piece of clothing had to be folded over the back of a chair and placed in a particular order. Every night, the same ritual."

"Oh, I see."

"From an early age he read books about courtiers and started copying their ways. He found a tinker's stall at the flea market selling old fabrics — bits of velvet and brocade, trims of fur, that sort of thing. Spiro begged me to buy them and got me to sew all the bits together to make this extravagant cloak. He would strut around the village, cloak on his shoulders, pretending to be a wealthy landowner."

"Don't all children play dressing-up games?"

"It wasn't a game to Spiro. And when the other children mocked him, it soured him. He withdrew. Never went out to play, never had friends back. All he would do was read books about the lives of princes. He'd been born a peasant, but in his mind, he was an aristocrat."

Sofia stood up and grabbed another armful of laundry. "I suppose it was inevitable that as soon as he could, he went to Rome and got a position in the Orsini household. A footman. It suited him — he idolised the family. Of course, they saw him as nothing more than an amusing dog. But when they won the contract to supply the travertine for St Peter's, Spiro knew his moment had come. Now he could be a *useful* dog."

"Yet for all his sins, he still felt guilty," Cristina observed.

"Only for me. Not for the villagers. He despises them. His heart still hurts from the wounds they inflicted. When he watched the bailiffs throw people out of their houses, I saw a dreadful look in his eyes ... as if he was enjoying every moment. To Spiro it wasn't revenge, it was justice. He couldn't understand how cruel he was. So when he found out I'd let everyone make a home here, he was furious. We had a terrible argument. Since then, I've barely seen him."

"Is Spiro still working for the Orsini family?"

Sofia nodded. "The rich always have a place for poodles. As long as he does their bidding, they'll reward him and protect him. But in the end ... when he's no longer useful to them..."

"By that time, he'll be rich enough not to care," Tomasso said.

"It's not about the money." A sadness came over Sofia. "Spiro thinks they love him. When he finally realises they despise him, and always have, it will destroy him. And no mother wants to see her son destroyed, no matter what he's done."

24: QUARRY

Sofia offered to make them lunch, but Cristina didn't want to outstay their welcome, and Tomasso was keen not to get roped into doing any more laundry.

As they rode away, they gazed at the displaced families who were hard at work, trying to create an illusion of home in the open meadows. As always, the burden seemed to fall most heavily on the women, who remained houseproud despite having no houses.

"If Spiro is as ruthless as his mother says, he may well have been involved in the *Speranza* tragedy," Tomasso said. "People-trafficking sounds right up his street."

"And the best way to get proof is to get inside that quarry," Cristina replied. "We'll see if there's an army of migrant workers being held there."

"They'll never let us in."

"How can they stop us if they don't know we're there?"

"We'll never get past their security. And even if we did, we'd stick out a mile."

"First, it's not 'we', it's 'I'."

"No, no. Wait a minute —"

"And second, there'll be no need to hide."

"We can't just demand entry, Cristina! It's too dangerous to reveal our identities."

"Agreed."

Tomasso frowned, trying to work out what she was proposing. "Aren't we supposed to make these plans together?"

"That's precisely what we're doing now."

"Huh. Strange. Because it feels like you've made up your mind and I'm just listening."

"Maybe that's because you're still in shock from doing so much laundry."

"Have you forgotten how dangerous these people are? You saw what they did to Paolo. If they catch us spying —"

"God is on our side, Tomasso. We are acting with the moral authority of the Pope."

"I'm not sure God's protection is enough anymore."

For once, greed became their ally. Rather than bear the expense of having to feed the quarry workers, the Orsini family had set up a system they called 'flexible food', whereby local women were allowed into the quarry every four hours to sell food and wine. The capos who ran the quarry tried to present this as a perk, but really it was just a way of cutting costs and boosting profits.

Cristina bought a basket filled with bread from the market, covered her head with a long shawl that hung down over her shoulders, then joined the crowd of enterprising women milling in front of the locked gates of the quarry. She had agreed with Tomasso that they would meet in The Fig Tree tavern at dusk, and although she was reluctant to leave him alone within such easy reach of wine, it was the best place to wait without arousing suspicion. In any case, if all went well, Cristina would be there long before sunset.

As she waited to be let into the quarry, Cristina looked at the other women gathered in the unforgiving afternoon sun; she was struck by the resilience and dignity in their faces. The food they were offering was simple but appetising: olives, cheese wrapped in cloth, dates, slices of prosciutto, great chunks of bread still warm from the oven.

The women said little but listened intently to the grim wall of sound rising from behind the huge wooden gates. The cacophony of hammers blended with the angry shouts of foremen and the slicing crack of their leather whips; the harsh scraping of rock on rock and the deep rumble of cartwheels labouring under immense weight completed the grim chorale.

Finally, the wicket gates in the huge doors opened, and three guards emerged. With all the swagger of feudal lords, they wandered down the line of women, inspecting their food baskets and sampling whatever took their fancy. Sometimes they would pass comment on the quality of the food; sometimes they would combine different ingredients and sandwich them between two chunks of bread. The women said nothing, even though each piece of food taken by the guards cut into their profits. They knew from bitter experience that protest would result in them being barred from the quarry, and that would plunge their own children into hunger. So the women accepted what they could not change.

When they had eaten their fill, the guards ushered the women through the gates and into the quarry.

In an instant, all Cristina's senses were assaulted. Heat was trapped in the great bowl of the quarry as if it was a witch's cauldron, sending rivulets of sweat tumbling down her back. The powdery dust hanging in the air turned her tongue dry and caught in her throat. Worst of all was the blinding light that bounced off the walls of white rock. It was so bright it hurt, forcing Cristina to screw her eyes shut. She waited for a few moments, then tentatively opened her eyelids a crack. As her vision adjusted, she realised that the other women were old hands at this, for they had scattered in all directions and were now clambering up rickety wooden walkways as they headed for their regular customers. Where should Cristina start?

Different capisquadra roamed through the quarry on horseback, barking orders and reprimands, eagerly punishing the slightest infraction; Cristina knew she had to avoid attracting their attention at all costs.

All along the hillside, teams of men were dragging wooden sleds loaded with massive rectangular slabs of freshly cut travertine down to the quarry floor. Once there, the rocks were inspected, graded and sorted into different shipments; while they were loaded onto transports, the sleds were dragged back up to the cutting line. It seemed the most arduous and dangerous work was higher up, which meant it was the most likely place to find trafficked men. Cristina headed towards the steepest walkway and started to climb.

It was punishing. After scrambling up the narrow planks for just a few minutes, she was exhausted. There was no breeze, no shade, no plants to break up the scorched monotony, not even a few weeds. The light made her eyes water, but she didn't dare close them for fear of stumbling on the narrow planks and tumbling down the rockface. The higher Cristina clambered, the steeper the walkway became, forcing her to crouch on all fours, but then the sharp rocks cut her fingers and seared her palms. She had only been in this hell for a few minutes and already she was struggling; how did these men manage to survive the long shifts from dawn until dusk?

Suddenly the capisquadra blew on their whistles — it was the signal for a break. All the men stopped working and put down their tools. The hammers and grinding saws fell silent. Now all Cristina could hear was the sound of thousands of men panting for breath in the heat. She saw them slump down onto their haunches, or collapse against the slabs of rock they were dragging, their bodies glistening with sweat. She studied the men. They weren't local. They probably weren't even Italian, but it was impossible to talk to them without one of the capos seeing. A few hundred yards further along, the walkway disappeared into an enormous crack in the rockface; the workers up there were most likely hidden from the capos, so that was where she needed to reach.

But just as she was about to set off, Cristina heard a man scream out in agony. She peered over the edge of the walkway — further down the slope, one of the capos was flogging a labourer with a chain whip, tearing stripes of skin from his back.

"Behave like an animal, I'll treat you like an animal!" the capo yelled, lashing the man across his legs.

"Please! I beg you!"

"Disgusting, slovenly behaviour! Get out of my sight!"

The man stumbled down the slope.

Cristina caught the eye of a teenage boy who was slumped on the walkway above her; a heavy bag of chisels was slung over his shoulders. "What did he do?" she whispered.

"Looks like he took a piss," the boy replied softly.

"What's wrong with that?"

The boy shrugged. "It's not allowed."

Cristina looked at the capo who had inflicted the punishment. He had thick hair that had gone prematurely white, for his face was still quite young. He didn't look like a thug — put him in different clothes and he could easily pass for a priest or a professor. Yet his behaviour told a different story. Cristina watched as he took a cloth from his pocket and carefully wiped the blood off the chain whip.

"Who is he?" she asked the boy.

"The devil."

"But what's his name?"

"Spiro. Caposquadra Spiro."

25: TRAFFICKED

After precious few minutes, the capisquadra blew their whistles again to signal the end of the meagre break; across the quarry, thousands of men picked up their tools and resumed the arduous work.

Cristina pressed on up the hillside, keen to put distance between herself and Caposquadra Spiro. She followed the zigzagging walkway for a while, then came across a huge loom of sled ropes — the lower end trailed down the hillside, but the upper end disappeared into a gully in the rocks. Cristina stepped off the wooden planks, followed the ropes through the gap, and found herself confronted by the cutting face of the quarry.

A team of thirty men sweated in the brutal heat: two men stood on top of a huge boulder using pickaxes to hack a line of holes into the rock; another two followed in their wake, using the chisel edge of a stone hammer to connect the holes with a scored line. Then came the rest of the men, placing metal wedges into each of the holes and driving them into the rock with sledgehammers until the boulder was perforated by a line of metal spikes.

As the men worked, Cristina studied them. The four tracing out the line of the cut had complexions that could be Mediterranean, but the vigorous work of driving in the wedges was being done by men with much darker, sub-Saharan skin. Many of the workers had geometric tattoos on their arms and bodies, just like those on Alnaaji and the souls who perished on the *Speranza*.

A hollow crack reverberated in the gulley. Deftly the men jumped back from the rock, sensing an imminent shift in weight. But nothing happened. The rock had changed its mind.

Finally, one man stepped forward, raised his sledgehammer high into the air and swung it with immense strength onto the central wedge. The rock groaned, then a painful cracking screamed into the gulley as a huge slab of travertine sheared away from the boulder. It toppled forward and slammed to the ground, sending up a cloud of dust. A ripple of satisfaction passed through the team; even though they'd done this countless times, the moment of triumph over the mountain never lost its fascination.

Cristina gazed at the smooth plane of newly exposed rock. How many millions of years had it been locked away in the darkness, only to be suddenly exposed to sunlight in order to serve the grand vision of St Peter's? For a brief moment, doubt fluttered in her heart. Was the new basilica really just a monumental act of vandalism? Did piety and devotion justify this gross violation of God's mountain?

"Stand back! Step away!" The leader of the sled team pushed the quarrymen aside as he directed his team to start running ropes around the fallen travertine slab.

In the hiatus, Cristina approached the stonecutters and started handing out bread from her basket. The first two men she approached shook their heads, but the third started rummaging in his ragged trousers for coins.

"No. No money," Cristina said. "It's free. Here — take the bread. It's free."

This changed everything. The famished stonecutters quickly surrounded Cristina, holding out their hands for bread, thanking her in words she couldn't understand.

"I'm here to help you," she said quietly. "Does anyone speak Italian?"

But the men were too busy stuffing bread into their mouths to talk.

"The people who run the quarry, they're holding you prisoner, am I right?"

The men could sense from her tone that this was something conspiratorial and started to look anxious.

"You should not be working like this," Cristina continued. "You're not slaves. You need to be paid and fed properly."

Suddenly the leader of the sled team whistled a signal to his men, and they dropped their ropes and hurried away down the gulley towards the open hillside. Cristina looked at the slab of travertine — the ropes had not been secured, so why had the men left? What was going on?

Before she had time to understand, a hand touched her shoulder. She spun round and saw a tall black man with geometric tattoos across his chest; he clutched a hammer in his right hand.

"I speak a little."

He had a thick accent, and Cristina had to concentrate to unravel his words. "I'm here to help you. All of you," she said. "But I need to know where you've come from. How did you get here?"

The man shook his head. "You escape from here, lady. Get away." He pointed to the gulley. "Get away. This is hell."

"I'm not running away. I'm here to help you. This is wrong." She gestured towards the quarry. "You're being worked to death. It cannot continue."

The man turned to the other workers and said something in an incomprehensible language.

"Where do you come from?" Cristina asked.

"Ifriqiya," the man replied. "Over the water."

"And how long have you been here?"

He didn't understand.

"Here." Cristina pointed to the ground. "How long here? Months? Years?"

"Ah. Long time. Too long. They told us one year." He held up a blistered finger. "They promise gold. But..." The man searched for the words to express himself, then in frustration broke into Arabic.

"Yes!" Cristina pounced on the moment. "You speak Arabic?"

"Some."

Using a mixture of broken Italian and Arabic, Cristina and the man started talking more fluently. Slowly, a grim picture emerged.

Foremen from Italy had travelled to remote desert villages in the Hafsid Kingdom of Ifriqiya with offers of work. They handed out gold coins, but promised that most would be paid when the villagers had completed a year's contract.

"They gave our families money," the man said. "We trusted them. One year of work to free our families from poverty."

But when they were halfway across the Mediterranean Sea, everything changed. The men were chained up and transported in guarded carts straight to the quarry, where they were locked away in huts. They were not allowed to write to their families or leave the quarry at any time; they worked from sunrise to dusk, and the few coins they were paid were barely enough to keep themselves alive.

"How many of you are here?" Cristina asked.

The man shook his head mournfully. "Many, many have come."

"Can you escape? Run away? Through the mountains?" Cristina gestured towards the ragged top of the quarry, which was unguarded.

"Some tried. They were hunted like dogs. Their bodies dragged back to rot in the sun. There is no escape, lady." The man's words caught in his throat and he lowered his head. "We will never see our families again. We are lost. We are lost." He started to weep.

Cristina reached out and put her hand on the man's shoulder. "Do not give up hope. This is why I'm here."

He looked up at her. "It is too late for us. But please, get word to our families, I beg you. Tell them what has happened here. Tell them we love them." He gripped Cristina's hand. "Tell our sons and daughters to never trust men who come from Europe. Never."

His words were like a punch. All her life Cristina had felt privileged to be part of the European tradition. Europe was where civilisation was defended and learning flourished. Europe was where Eastern scholarship had found refuge after the sack of Constantinople. To hear it condemned as a continent of untrustworthy criminals was difficult.

"You have not been abandoned. I will return with the force of the law, I swear." Cristina started to back away. "Do not give up."

She turned and hurried down the gulley, anxious to get away from those accusing eyes. Her dream of a magnificent basilica had met the real world and created all this suffering. Could it be that St Peter's was defiled before it had even risen? Was the entire project now fatally compromised?

The clattering of hooves on rock jolted Cristina from her thoughts. She looked up and saw Caposquadra Spiro riding into the gulley, with the men from the sled team scrambling behind him.

"Is this the woman?" Spiro demanded.

The leader of the sled team nodded. "Yes, sir."

Spiro turned his gaze on Cristina. "Who are you?" His left hand reached for the chain whip which hung from his saddle. "Why are you stirring up trouble in my quarry?"

26: FLIGHT

Cristina adopted her most innocent expression and held up the empty basket. "These men were hungry, sir. But they work so high up the quarry, they get forgotten."

"Is that so?" Caposquadra Spiro was not impressed.

"It's the truth."

Spiro's arm flashed across his body as he unleashed the whip. The chain cut through the air, snatched the basket from Cristina's hands and sent it bouncing down the side of the quarry. "You may want to rephrase your answer."

Cristina drew a breath to try and talk her way out of trouble, but before she could utter a word, Spiro held up a finger to silence her.

"Consider: there is nothing I abhor more than a liar." Spiro glanced at the men from the sled team who cowered behind him. "These peasants have already told me that you are agitating. And I have asked what you are really doing up here. So now that it is your turn to speak, do so wisely."

Cristina knew that he was goading her. There was nothing he would relish more than a fight, and no matter what she said, he would use it to attack her. Unless perhaps the truth could protect her? If Spiro knew she was acting with the authority of the Vatican, that she had the backing of the Holy Father himself, maybe he would think twice. Or would the admission make her even more vulnerable? Would it force Spiro to ensure that she never returned to Rome to report her findings? She looked at the metal links of the chain whip dangling from his hand — just one lash across her throat could kill her.

"*Look out!*" The warning cry came from further up the gully. Everyone turned to see a boulder hurtling towards them, bouncing off the sides of the gully, dislodging more rocks as it gathered momentum.

Men scattered to avoid getting caught in the rockfall. Spiro's horse panicked and reared up on its hind legs, snorting in fear. Spiro hauled on the reins to try and wrestle back control, but that just added to the sense of alarm. As its hooves landed on the smooth rocks, the horse slipped.

"Run!" In the chaos, two hands grabbed Cristina and hauled her backwards up the gully. "You must run!"

Cristina struggled to break free, but the hands were too strong. She craned her neck and saw that she'd been grabbed by the man she had spoken to.

"Go! Now!"

"No! I have to confront him!"

"Lady, listen! He will kill you!" The man lifted her high into the air, then the workers on top of the rocks grabbed Cristina's arms and hoisted her onto the cliff edge.

"Run!" The man shouted at her again.

Cristina peered down and saw fear in his eyes. Further along the gully, Spiro was still struggling to control his horse.

"*Go!*"

Cristina spun round, taking in the horizon. It was a forbidding sight — untamed hilltops strewn with rocks as far as the eye could see, swathed in patches of wild vegetation. "Go where?" she cried.

"Anywhere! Just go!"

Cristina heard the chain whip crack violently on the rocks. She glanced down the gully and saw that Spiro had regained control of his horse and was now staring up at her. "Do not move!" he bellowed.

"Get word to our families!" the man begged. "Tell them what has happened. Please, go!"

Cristina saw the desperation in his face — she was now their only link to the outside world, and if she didn't escape, these men would vanish forever. So she turned and bolted into the wilderness.

It was hard going.

There wasn't even the smallest track to follow, which meant that with every step she had to take her chances with rough ground and loose stones. When she passed through stretches of dense bushes, she couldn't even see where her feet were, so she had to run on blind faith and pray that she didn't land badly. This was why there were no fences or guards up here — the terrain was treacherous, and the only destination was more wilderness.

She glanced over her shoulder, but no-one was chasing her. Surely it was impossible to get a horse up here; Caposquadra Spiro would just have to accept that she had escaped.

Cristina ran on until she reached the far edge of the plateau and paused to catch her breath. The slope down was steep and covered in unstable scree, but at the very bottom of the gorge there was a vast, ramshackle encampment made from salvaged wood and bits of canvas. It sprawled untidily across the canyon floor with no discernible structure or pattern; a couple of the shelters had spirals of smoke rising from campfires, and some tattered clothes had been laid across the tent roofs to dry. This must be where all the trafficked workmen were kept. The man had said it was impossible to leave, so it was more than likely that the encampment was guarded. Best to stay well away.

Instead, Cristina headed in the opposite direction until she came to a series of gulches that scarred the hillside; it looked as if an angry giant had clawed the side of the mountain. If she could scramble down one of these, at least she would be on the valley floor, and if she kept walking, eventually she would come to a river. There had to be a river; that was how this landscape was formed.

She looked at each of the gulches in turn, trying to decide which one was safest, but just as she made her choice, Cristina heard the sound of dogs barking in the distance.

She looked back in the direction of the encampment and saw a small cloud of dust rising from the canyon floor. Instinctively she crouched down, her gaze locked on the dust, her ears focussed on the chorus of barking. The noise wasn't receding, it was heading her way. As she studied the moving shapes, she could make out a posse — dogs leading the hunt, followed by their handlers. Then came a couple of trackers with heads bowed down, and at the rear was a man on horseback who seemed to be in charge — Cristina was sure it was Spiro. There must be a path from the quarry to the encampment which the posse had used to outflank her.

The dogs surged forward, eager to pick up a scent, then rushed back to their handlers to sniff the basket Cristina had been holding. More worrying were the trackers who studied the ground with chilling patience, searching for fresh footprints. When they didn't find any, they stopped and looked up at the ridge — they must have realised that Cristina was trapped up here on the high plateau. She watched as the posse veered to the right and started to scramble up the nearest gulch.

She sprang to her feet and bolted once again. She didn't have a plan; all she could do was run to the far edge of the plateau. But what then? Would there be another way down?

Cristina glanced over her shoulder — the barking was getting louder, but there was no sign of the dogs yet. How long had she got?

Suddenly her left foot landed on a loose rock and she tumbled headfirst to the ground.

"*Figlio di puttana!*" She stretched out her arms to break her fall and felt the rocks slash her palms. She rolled to a stop and lay gasping for breath, pain shooting through her body. She could only pray that she hadn't broken any bones. Cristina looked at her hands — blood was oozing from three deep cuts that scarred her flesh. More scent for the dogs to follow.

She rolled onto her front and knelt on all fours, then tested her ankles by putting her weight onto each of them in turn. The right one was good, but the left was agony. It wouldn't be long before it swelled up and reduced her pace to a hobble.

Cristina tentatively raised her head above the scrub and looked back towards the gulch: the dog handlers were just arriving on top of the plateau and being greeted by their excited hounds, who were eager to pick up the pursuit.

She couldn't risk standing. She would have to try and crawl away. Every time she put her hand down, she would leave fresh traces of blood for the dogs to find, but she had no choice.

Cristina braced herself to start crawling, then turned towards the far edge of the plateau ... and found herself staring into the pale yellow eyes of an Apennine wolf.

27: WOLF

Cristina didn't dare breathe.

Had she strayed into a wolf pack's territory? Was she now surrounded and about to be torn to pieces? Or was this a lone scout?

Its grey fur was already turning red with the season, and its mouth was open, showing a line of savage teeth. But even though she was bleeding, the wolf wasn't snarling at her.

"Easy boy. Easy," she whispered.

The wolf didn't respond. Cristina held its gaze. She knew there was no reasoning with a wild animal; the important thing was to show no fear, no hint of weakness. She must not look away.

Suddenly the wolf's ears pricked up as it heard the sound of dogs in the distance.

"They're after me," Cristina whispered.

Did the wolf sense her fear, one hunted animal to another?

It glanced at her bloodied hands, then turned and trotted a few yards into the undergrowth. It stopped and looked back. Was it waiting for her?

Cristina heard the dogs barking behind her, getting closer with every heartbeat. She had no choice; wherever the wolf was taking her, she would just have to trust it. So she followed, limping, crouching low, desperately trying to stay hidden, while the wolf led the way, running ahead, then stopping to wait for her to catch up. Stop, start, slowly moving across the plateau while all the time the barking of the pursuing dogs got louder.

What would Spiro do if he caught her? Up in these wild mountains she could be murdered without consequence, for they were beyond the reach of the law. How easy it would be for Spiro to have her thrown off the edge of a cliff, so that when her body was found, everyone would assume it had just been a terrible accident.

The wolf paused, but this time when Cristina caught up, she tried to shoo it away.

"Go! Run! Don't let them catch you as well."

The wolf stared at Cristina with its mysterious gaze, then bounded towards a rocky outcrop that jutted above the plateau. Cristina hobbled after the animal until she found herself staring at a fissure in the rocks that was barely big enough to squeeze through.

"Oh no. I'm not going in there," Cristina said. The wolf darted into the fissure, then a few moments later reemerged, as if to show her that it was safe.

"No! There could be snakes in there, or a bees' nest. Or anything."

The wolf brushed past her and dived into some bushes of wild garlic that were growing close by. Cristina watched, bewildered, as the wolf rolled around in the foliage. This was no time to play — the hunting dogs were almost upon them.

Suddenly the wolf leapt out of the bush and rubbed its fur against Cristina's legs. And now she understood. Garlic. Dogs hated the scent of garlic, and the wolf knew it. She grabbed some blossoms and leaves, then crushed them between her fingers. The wolf watched as she ran her hands over her face and arms, covering herself in the pungent scent, then they both slipped into the darkness of the fissure.

After a few yards, the crack became too narrow to move any further, but it was enough to keep them out of sight. Cristina squeezed herself round so that she could look out; the wolf lay on the floor in front of her.

They waited, listening to the sounds of the posse — dogs barking and snuffling the ground, men shouting instructions, the horse's hooves clattering on the loose ground.

Closer and closer the hunters got, until they were just yards from the fissure. Cristina held her breath; the wolf remained absolutely still.

Suddenly the hunting dogs leapt back from the garlic bushes, whining their disapproval. The handlers tried to urge them on, but the dogs were having none of it and veered away from the fissure. Spiro stopped his horse and looked around but could see nowhere that a person could hide.

"Get those damn dogs under control!" he shouted.

The handlers scolded their hounds and drove them on, heading towards the far edge of the plateau.

Cristina and the wolf waited as the sound of the posse grew fainter, until all was silent again.

She looked at the wolf, reached out and gently stroked his head. "Thank you."

The wolf stood up, glanced at Cristina one last time, then bolted from the fissure out into the undergrowth. In a moment, he was gone.

Cristina slithered out of the fissure and looked up at the sky. The sun was getting low; as soon as it set, the posse would be forced to give up. But she wanted to be off this plateau before it got dark. She would have to make her way back to the gulch and slide down that way. It would be painful, but it was her only chance of surviving.

She set off, one agonising step at a time, senses bristling, alert for humans or other wild animals that might not be as compassionate as the wolf.

28: HALF-DEAD

All Tomasso could do was wait. He had been staring at the same table in The Fig Tree for hours and now knew every curl and notch in the grain, every wine stain that had soaked into the wood over the years.

He'd deliberately chosen a table by one of the windows overlooking the courtyard so that he could see Cristina the moment she arrived.

But she hadn't.

Instead, he had watched the sun set, dusk fade into night, and the moon rise over the jagged hills. It was a bad idea for a woman to be out anywhere after dark, let alone in an unfamiliar place, and least of all in the depths of the countryside which was well known to be favoured by thieves and bandits.

Tomasso glanced around the tavern. Many of the men were the same ones who had been here when they had first arrived in Tivoli, and most of them were sitting on the same benches. This must be how they whiled away their long hours of unemployment; but their loss was the innkeeper's gain, and he seemed to be the only man here without a cloud of gloom floating above his head. "It's time to alert the authorities," Antonio said, putting another jug of wine on the table.

"I *am* the authority," Tomasso replied.

"Not around here. You're just a stranger."

"No-one gossips quite like a constable." Tomasso refilled his beaker. "If we tell the magistrates in Tivoli, within hours everyone in the province will know. We're supposed to be on covert surveillance."

Antonio glanced at the other customers. "You think they don't already know you've been sent to spy on us?"

"Not on you. We're trying to help you."

"That's what everyone says. Then they betray us all the same."

Tomasso took a swig of wine. "If Cristina hasn't returned by the morning, I'll get the magistrate to organise a search party."

Antonio gazed out of the window at the dark of the night. "The difference between now and the morning might be life and death. This is wild country. You have no idea what's out there."

There was a loud clatter as the main doors swung open. The murmur of conversation in the tavern suddenly stopped, and Tomasso turned to see a woman standing in the doorway. She looked half-dead. Her body and arms were covered in grimy sweat. She had torn strips off her clothing to bandage her hands, but these rags were now caked in dried blood. Her face was blistered and sunburnt, and she was using a salvaged branch as an improvised crutch because she could barely walk.

"Cristina?" Tomasso gazed at her in disbelief.

The innkeeper gave a stoical shrug. "Like I said: wild country."

"What happened to you?" Tomasso exclaimed.

Cristina started to hobble across the room. "A drink," she whispered. "Drink ... and food." She swayed gently, trying to hold her balance; but being here, safe in familiar surroundings with someone she trusted, made her body finally accept the truth about its own exhaustion. The stick fell from her grip, and she slumped forward.

Tomasso caught her just in time and held her tightly; for once Cristina didn't recoil. She closed her eyes and pressed her face into his shoulder, feeling the scratchy linen on her cheek, breathing in the different scents lingering on his jacket: smoke from the tavern fire, beeswax from his leather cross belts, the sweet aroma of sweat mingling with wine. She was surprised at how safe it made her feel to be enveloped by Tomasso's arms.

Then she heard a strange sound, like staccato breathing. She look up at Tomasso — his eyes were screwed shut.

"I thought you were dead," he whispered.

"So did I." Cristina wiped away his tears with her bandaged hands. "So did I."

They looked at each other as smiles of relief drove away the tears. Tomasso went to hug her again, but now that Cristina was feeling safer, the embrace felt awkward, and she pulled back.

Tomasso laughed. "That's more like it."

"I didn't mean…"

"No, no. I understand."

"Thank you."

"And the garlic is a bit strong," he smiled.

They lapsed into silence, then mercifully, the innkeeper returned with wine and food to bundle the moment back to normality.

"I reckon you've got a touch of heatstroke," Antonio said as he poured Cristina a beaker of wine. "So don't drink it all at once. And eat slowly. Small mouthfuls. Don't want you keeling over in my tavern."

Grateful for the distraction, Cristina and Tomasso sat down at the table and busied themselves with the food. As she ate, Cristina recounted what she had witnessed in the quarry and how she had managed to escape. Tomasso listened intently, without interruption. He did wonder if her encounter with the Apennine wolf had really happened, or whether it was a hallucination triggered by the onset of heatstroke; either way, the important thing was that she had made it down from the plateau.

"Spiro's mother was not exaggerating," Cristina concluded as she mopped up the last of the pepper sauce with a chunk of bread. "He is ruthless, cruel, and determined. You'd think he owned the quarry himself, the way he behaves. That every rock was money in his own pocket."

"Which is probably why the Orsini family loves him," Tomasso observed. "The rich always love people who make them richer."

Cristina sat back and wiped her mouth with a napkin. "Spiro is just a caposquadra, but in his head … he's an aristocrat."

"They really hate him," Tomasso nodded to a group of men huddled round a table playing cards. "It's bad enough being exploited by the rich, but when one of your own switches sides, that is unforgiveable. To betray your own people for a few ducats…"

"The man has no moral compass. That's what makes him dangerous."

"What about evidence, Cristina? We need hard evidence to present to Pope Julius that links Spiro to the *Speranza*."

"The proof is up there in the quarry — hundreds and hundreds of men, sweating themselves to death every single day."

"How do we know they didn't come willingly from Ifriqiya?"

"They did at first. They were even paid money. But as soon as they were at sea, everything changed."

"So, they were kidnapped?"

"Effectively. They will never see home again. They're not even allowed to get a message out. They will die up in that quarry."

"But the proof?"

"It's all up there. The moment you set foot in the quarry, it's undeniable."

Tomasso nodded. "Then we must head to Rome at first light."

29: GHOSTED

Pope Julius never looked happy. Deep-set eyes emphasised a prominent brow, giving him a permanently worried look, and the long grey beard added a touch of hangdog to his expression. But hearing Cristina's account made him look particularly glum.

"This has long been my fear for the new St Peter's: loss of control," the Holy Father admitted. "The energy needed to create a basilica on such a magnificent scale is like an explosion of gunpower. Its effects are radical and momentous, but debris flies in all directions and sometimes the innocent get hurt."

It was rare for Julius to admit to any kind of weakness, but as the only other people in the room were Cardinal Riario, Domenico and Cristina, the Holy Father knew he could be candid. "We must instruct the Building Committee to review all quarrying contracts, then organise an official inspection of the Orsini works at Tivoli."

"Forgive me, Your Holiness, but that would be a very bad idea." Cristina immediately bowed her head to add a veneer of respect to her rebellious words.

"The Pope does not have 'bad' ideas," Riario corrected. "He speaks with God's authority. Yet sometimes his words do inspire others to have ideas that are more apposite."

"Indeed." Pope Julius looked expectantly at Cristina.

"The reason I was able to gain access to the quarry is because I was incognito. An official inspector would only be shown the official quarrying operation, rather than the truth."

"And I'm afraid the Building Committee of St Peter's cannot be trusted either," Domenico added. "My investigations into the murder of Apostolic Guard Paolo have cast doubt on the committee's honesty and integrity."

Cardinal Riario scowled. "That's quite an accusation."

"But not unreasonable," Cristina replied. "Given their power and connections, it may well be that the Building Committee is complicit in the trafficking of workers."

"Rumour, rumour, rumour!" Pope Julius exclaimed. "I have asked for evidence, yet all you give me is rumour, supposition and accusation!"

"Holy Father, you need to see the quarry with your own eyes," Cristina suggested. "If you arrive unannounced, no-one will dare deny you entry. Then you can see what I saw."

"Impossible!" Riario exclaimed.

"Why? He is the Pope. Anything is possible."

"Except anonymity. When the Holy Father leaves Rome, dozens of people have to be informed." Cardinal Riario started counting them off on his fingers. "Bodyguards, confessors, advisors, cooks, servants of the wardrobe, the Holy Father's physician, messengers, the Keeper of the Warrants. He cannot simply jump on a horse and ride off."

"More's the pity," Julius muttered.

"But the same does not apply to you, Your Eminence," Domenico said to Riario. "With the greatest respect to your office, *you* can simply jump on a horse."

"That is not my job," the cardinal replied.

"It is now," Julius pronounced. "On this occasion, you must be my eyes and ears."

"But Your Holiness —"

"You will leave for Tivoli immediately." He turned to Domenico. "Capitano Falchoni, organise your fastest carriage and best drivers. With sufficient changes of horse, Cardinal Riario can be at the quarry before sunset."

"Is there no-one else?" Riario pleaded.

"Take it as a compliment. It shows how much I trust you." Pope Julius turned to Cristina. "You and anyone else who knows about what you witnessed in the quarry, are to remain inside the walls of the Vatican until the cardinal returns."

"You do not trust us?" Cristina asked.

"It is not a question of trust, merely one of maximising the chances of success."

It was the longest afternoon.

Cristina found it impossible to settle to anything while she waited for Riario's return. She wrote an account of what she had seen in the quarry and filed it as an official report. Then she went through Domenico's case notes on Paolo's murder investigation to see if there was anything that had been missed, after which she went to the Vatican kitchens to organise a meal for the guards in the barracks on late shift. After visiting the Holy Father's physician to have ointment applied to her sunburnt face, Cristina finally accepted there was nothing left to do but try to catch up on her sleep.

She lay down on the makeshift bed in her brother's office without expecting to actually sleep ... and was surprised to be jolted awake by Domenico's hand some hours later.

"He's back!"

"What?" Cristina sat up, disorientated.

"Listen."

Cristina turned towards the windows and heard horses panting as their hooves clopped on the flagstones.

"What time is it?"

"Three hours after midnight. Whatever the cardinal saw, he must have turned round and come straight back to Rome."

The servants of the bedchamber knew how much the Pope hated having his sleep interrupted, but Julius had left strict instructions that he was to be briefed the moment the cardinal returned, and who were they to defy the Holy Father?

When Cristina and Domenico arrived in the Pope's private office, they found Cardinal Riario already there. He looked pale and tired but refused the offer of a seat. Cristina studied him, trying to work out what he'd discovered by analysing his posture and expression, but the cardinal was a master of the inscrutable.

When Pope Julius was ushered into the room by one of his servants, he was wearing a silk gown and still had a sleeping cap on his head.

Cardinal Riario bowed. "Forgive me for interrupting your sleep, Holy Father."

"Forgive me for depriving you of yours altogether," Julius replied. "I hope it was worth the sacrifice."

Riario hesitated, and immediately Cristina sensed this was unwelcome news.

"When we arrived at the quarry, Caposquadra Spiro was already waiting to greet us."

"Did he try and forbid your entrance?"

"Quite the opposite. He was the epitome of cooperation. We were given escorts to guide us around the quarry and told we could venture wherever we wished."

"What did you see?"

Cardinal Riario shrugged. "A travertine quarry working as it should, Holy Father. The men we spoke to were all Italian and under no duress. Many live in the area; some had moved from other parts of the peninsula, but none have been forced to work against their will."

"How many men did you speak to?" Cristina asked.

"A fair number."

"But how many?"

"Twenty. Thirty."

"That still leaves a lot of men who could be migrant workers."

"We saw no-one with the tattoos you described. No-one was being whipped or punished or maltreated."

"This is wrong." Cristina's frustration was turning to anger. "Someone must have leaked news of your inspection. They're lying to you."

"I can only report what I saw," Riario said tersely.

"What about the encampment? Did you go up on the plateau? At the very top of the quarry?"

"I did. But I could see nothing remotely akin to what you described."

"They must have dismantled it overnight." Cristina was struggling to make sense of the contradictory account.

"Rather unlikely," the cardinal said, casting a sceptical glance at Pope Julius.

"Unlikely, but true. It has to be. What other explanation is there?" Cristina countered.

"That perhaps … you were mistaken?"

"I am not in the habit of imagining hundreds of makeshift tents!" Cristina snapped. "I know what I saw!"

"As do I," the cardinal replied.

Cristina turned to Pope Julius. "Spiro must have guessed that I was working on your authority, Holy Father. When he failed to catch me, he must have taken immediate action to destroy all evidence of migrant workers and people trafficking." She turned back to Riario. "How many excavation sites were actually operating?"

The cardinal cast his mind back. "Maybe eight, actually at the rockface."

"And there is the answer!" Cristina exclaimed. "When I was at the quarry, I counted over thirty-five separate gorges that were being excavated. Spiro has temporarily shrunk the operation. All those men, all the migrant workers, they have been hidden away somewhere."

"Hidden where, precisely?" the cardinal said sourly. "You make me out to be a fool who cannot see what is in front of his eyes."

"Those mountains are huge. There are many places to hide people. Caves, ravines…" Cristina knew that Riario didn't believe her, so she focussed solely on the Pope. "They have carts, Holy Father. Maybe the men were taken to the forest and hidden there."

"You assume a lot," Julius said darkly. "So much industry to conceal men … it seems improbable."

"With all due respect, you have not met this man Spiro. He is an evil man, and there is nothing quite so industrious as evil in pursuit of profit."

Pope Julius turned to Riario. "How did Spiro strike you?"

"I cannot lie, Holy Father. To me, he was the epitome of charm. And he certainly knows his job. Is he a difficult man to work for?" Riario shrugged. "This is hard manual labour. It is not work for the fainthearted."

"But he was cooperative?"

"Nothing was out of bounds, and he answered all my questions."

"Then I fear we are back where we started. With no evidence. No proof of wrongdoing."

Cristina sank to her knees in front of the pontiff. "Holy Father, I would never lie to you. I swear what I saw was true."

"I didn't say I doubted you."

"Then can you not act with the authority vested in your office? God is more powerful than all the oligarchs combined. Can you not strip the Orsini family of their contracts to put an end to this cruel trade in human souls? It will act as a warning to the world."

Pope Julius drew a deep breath, weighing up his options. As he exhaled, a rogue hair in his beard fluttered in the downdraught from his nose. "The simple truth is that I cannot build St Peter's without the oligarchs. If I go to war with them on nothing more than a rumour, they will make my life impossible. I need proof in order to act. Incontrovertible proof."

"But you are God's voice on Earth," Cristina pleaded.

"I am." Pope Julius nodded. "But even I cannot defy the golden rule of money: those with gold, rule. As long as the oligarchs enjoy enormous wealth, even a pope must tread carefully around them."

30: RETREAT

Cristina couldn't get back to sleep after that, and she didn't particularly want to walk home in the middle of the night, even though it was just a short distance across the Tiber to Piazza Navona. Instead, she decided to calm herself by watching the sunrise from the roof of the Sistine Chapel.

Everyone thought of *la Sistina* as a place of sacred worship and fine art, but when Pope Sixtus IV commissioned the building, he had something quite different in mind. Twice as long as it was high, and three times as long as it was wide, the chapel was constructed with massive brick walls supported by large buttresses to resemble a medieval castle — because that was exactly what it was: a place of refuge within the Vatican, where popes and cardinals could shelter from the violent and volatile politics of the peninsula. Which was why it had a protected rooftop walkway running around the entire building, commanding imposing views of both the city and the rolling hills beyond.

Cristina clambered up a narrow spiral staircase until she reached the access door, then pushed it open and immediately felt the cool night-breeze on her face. She strode along the walkway, startling some sleeping pigeons, until she found a spot on the southern face that was sheltered from the wind. She perched on the low brick wall and gazed up at the starscape.

Cristina felt crushed. How could she ever hope to bring the oligarchs to justice when they controlled so much? To make an army of migrant workers vanish in the space of a single day ... that was formidable power. The Apostolic Guards were investigating with the authority of Pope Julius, yet at every turn they were either blocked or outmanoeuvred. The truth no longer seemed to have any leverage over the dynastic families; they were a law unto themselves, and a world where truth had no traction was not a world Cristina wanted to inhabit.

Her mind drifted back to the House of Eternal Grace, where a peaceful room was still waiting for her. Right now, that cloistered space seemed more inviting than ever.

Cristina watched the sky gradually lighten in the east, until a red glow bloomed on the horizon; moments later, the first rays of the day's sun touched her face. She felt their warmth and made up her mind: she would return to the convent and continue writing her diaries; she would retreat to a place where God was paramount and where truth did not have to compromise — a world of purity, outside the fray.

Walking home in the damp morning air, Cristina felt as if an enormous weight had been lifted from her shoulders. No longer did she have to win this battle; her enemies had triumphed, they'd driven her from the field, and accepting that brought a kind of peace.

But almost immediately, another feeling started to gnaw at her … the grey flatness of boredom.

No. Not boredom. She scolded herself for using that word. She was never bored; there was too much to see and do in the world. To be bored was to have failed at life. Tranquillity — that was a better word. And wasn't that what mystics had been pursuing since the dawn of civilization? The peace of enlightenment? Yes, that was still a worthwhile cause; she would content herself with serenity.

Assuming that everyone would still be asleep, Cristina let herself quietly into the house, but when she entered the kitchen, she was surprised to see Isra and Alnaaji busy preparing food.

"You're back!" Isra exclaimed. "And still in one piece." She hurried over and took Cristina's face in her hands. "You look like you need some home comforts. And a hot bath."

Not wanting to be left out of the reunion, Alnaaji hurried over, threw his arms around Cristina's waist and squeezed her tightly. She ran her fingers through his hair and looked down to see a beaming smile on his face.

"I missed you both," she said.

"Well, you timed your return perfectly." Isra gestured towards the table, which was covered with bowls and dishes containing all sorts of delicious-looking food. "Breakfast Ifriqiya-style is being served."

"What?"

"A Berber breakfast. Alnaaji has been teaching me how to cook his family's food."

"It certainly smells good."

Alnaaji took Cristina's hand and led her to the scrubbed kitchen table. He pointed to the first dish, which contained a thick brown paste. "*Amlou*. It is almonds and honey."

"Your Italian is getting good."

The boy chuckled with pride. "Isra teach me. Every day. Many, many hours!"

"And he's an excellent student," Isra smiled.

Alnaaji pointed to the next dish. "Semolina bread. And here, roast chickpeas, here mint tea ... and here the best." He stopped by a skillet that contained a rich sauce in which two poached eggs nestled. "Shakshouka. Very good. Tomato, chilli, onions. You want try?"

Cristina drew up a stool. "I think we should all have breakfast together."

And they did. Alnaaji took control, offering the different dishes to Isra and Cristina, and studying their reactions with intense interest. "You like? Is good? Special from my village." His enthusiasm was infectious, and Cristina loved watching the pride in the boy's eyes. His desire to please was in such sharp contrast to the harsh cynicism of the circles she'd been moving in since leaving the convent. The three of them made an unusual little family, but they had found comfort in each other.

Cristina studied Alnaaji's face, amazed at the resilience he had shown as he recovered from his ordeal on the *Speranza*. This food could so easily have plunged him back into grief by reminding him of the world he had lost, but instead he seemed to draw strength from the connection it gave to his home.

When they had finished eating, Isra topped up their cups of mint tea and started clearing the table.

Alnaaji looked expectantly at Cristina. "So, you like? You really like?"

Cristina patted her stomach in appreciation. "A magnificent feast. Thank you."

"How is search, Miss Cristina?"

The question caught her off guard. "My search? For what?"

"For justice. For the *Speranza*."

The boy was looking at her with such hope, she couldn't bring herself to tell him the truth. "It's ... complicated."

"You find men who do this? Men who kill the *Speranza*?"

Her mind jolted back to the quarry. She remembered Spiro's thin lips tightening as he reached for the chain whip. She remembered the grief in the eyes of the men who knew they would die on the mountain without ever seeing their families again. If she retreated to the convent in search of tranquillity, it would mean abandoning those people. No matter what her heart craved, Cristina had to accept that leaving the battle did not end the conflict; it just meant someone else had to do the fighting.

She reached out and held Alnaaji's hand. "I think I know what needs to be done."

"To catch men?"

Cristina nodded. "To catch the men, I need to go to your country, to Ifriqiya."

The boy's eyes went wide.

Isra almost dropped the plates she was holding. "You didn't really say that?"

"Rome is under the boot of the oligarchs. The whole peninsula is. The only way I can find evidence to expose their corruption is by travelling to the source. Across the Mediterranean Sea … to the Hafsid Kingdom of Ifriqiya."

"That's absurd. You won't last a day."

"On my own, I won't. Which is why you're coming with me."

31: RISK

Nothing more was said over breakfast, but Cristina could sense Isra's disapproval by the way she clattered the dishes and tossed cutlery back into the drawer. She knew Isra would pick her moment for an argument, so there was no point forcing the issue.

Instead, Cristina decided to spend the morning tending to her own wellbeing. As she undressed, she examined each item of clothing to assess whether or not it had been damaged beyond repair by her flight through the mountains. Then she made a neat pile of laundry and slid into a tub of hot water. Finally, she could let her body relax.

This was the only house on Piazza Navona to have a plumbed bath, and installing it had been costly as well as time-consuming. Cristina had spent months lobbying Rome's surveyors to give her permission to build a dedicated pipe from the city's western aqueduct to her own house. She had then faced a barrage of criticism when she had asked the builders to design a grid of pipes around a large furnace in the cellar to heat the water.

"Immersing yourself in a hot liquid will open the pores of your skin and let disease enter your flesh!" one physician harangued her. "You will destroy the body's natural balance!" declared another.

Cristina dismissed these men as unenlightened and looked back fifteen hundred years for inspiration, when Rome was famous for its elaborate complexes of thermae and balneae. Now, having finally recreated a small piece of the classical world in her own home, Cristina decided that she would bathe at least once a week. She closed her eyes and luxuriated in the sensation of being enveloped by hot, perfumed water.

She must have dozed off, because the next thing she knew, she was coughing out a mouthful of water. She sat upright, then set about scrubbing herself clean, going gently around the areas where her skin had been burnt. She had to wash her hair twice to remove all the powdery dust from the quarry and was amused by the fine scum of travertine powder it left on the surface of the bath. After she had dried herself, Cristina applied the lily root and camphor ointment that the Pope's physician had given her to soothe her sunburn, then she got dressed.

Isra had already laid out a linen chemise dress in the bedroom, but Cristina ignored this, as she had no intention of lounging around the house today. Instead, she pulled on some grey breeches, a black doublet and leather riding boots — clothes she wore when she meant business. She went downstairs to her library to consult maps of the North African coast, and it was here that Isra was waiting to pounce.

"We have responsibilities now, Cristina. It's not like before. We can't just take off."

"We've always had responsibilities."

"But now we have to think about Alnaaji."

"It's him we're doing it for. And anyway, life doesn't stop just because we have a child to care for."

Isra slammed the atlas on the desk and opened the pages showing the Mediterranean Sea. "This is dangerous! It's swarming with Ottoman pirates." She pointed to the North African coast. "And that is even worse."

Cristina laughed. "Merchants have been trading around the Mediterranean for two and a half thousand years, ever since the Phoenicians."

"That boy has already lost so much. He relies on us. We can't risk him being abandoned again."

"We're not abandoning anyone."

"What if something goes wrong?"

"You've become so domesticated, Isra. What happened to the fearless woman who was by my side when we outwitted bandits in Otranto?"

"She grew up."

The two women stared at each other stubbornly for a few moments; finally Cristina looked down and started turning the pages of the atlas. "Isra, if everyone thought like that, these blank spaces on the map would remain blank forever."

"But why does it have to be us?"

"Because domestic life is closing your horizons down, and that is not the Isra I know. When your horizons shrink, the mind dies."

"Two women travelling alone in Ifriqiya? It doesn't get more vulnerable than that."

"A very sweeping generalisation."

"European women, Christians in a Muslim country?"

"We will be prosperous traders with money to spend. And everyone respects merchants, regardless of culture or creed."

Isra rolled her eyes. "So now we're going to dress up. That won't help us one bit."

"We will be textile merchants who have travelled to Ifriqiya to find new dyes for our fabrics. Better still, we have decided to start importing Bedouin rugs and fabrics to Europe. It's a big opportunity for them and we'll be welcomed with open arms. I'm sure of it."

"And I'm sure that we will be unmasked the moment we open our mouths," Isra scoffed. "What do we know about textiles and dyes? Nothing!"

"Actually, it's in my blood."

"What are you talking about?"

"Textiles. It's the family business."

Isra blinked. "But your father is a merchant."

"In textiles. Well, velvet actually. That's his speciality."

"You've never said anything about this before."

"It was never relevant."

Isra was struggling to absorb the new information. "So, the Falchoni family wealth is based on velvet?"

"My grandfather won the ecclesiastical contract to supply the Vatican. And once you dress cardinals, all the best families want your services."

Isra sat down and shook her head. "So that's where the money comes from. You certainly kept that quiet."

"There was never any intention to deceive you." Cristina sat down next to Isra. "I'm sorry."

"So why do you never talk about it?"

Cristina hesitated. "The truth is, my father is disappointed that neither Domenico nor I are interested in taking on the family business."

"More fool you. All this time you've been driving yourself mad investigating crimes, when you could have been a wealthy merchant."

"It's not that simple. My father spends every waking minute obsessing about contracts and silkworms and shipping deadlines and budgets. He has no time for anything else. That's why he's in such poor health; he never really has time to enjoy the money he makes. If I'd chosen that life, there would have been no time for learning or books. I'd have hated it. And what is the point of living a life you hate?"

"So, your father does all the work, and you get to enjoy the money?"

Cristina couldn't tell if this was criticism or praise. "My father chose to have children. He just didn't choose to have such wilful ones. We love him, but we can't be him."

"Well, we chose to look after Alnaaji. And we must honour that, just as your father honours your choices."

"Tolerates is probably a more accurate description."

"Nonetheless, if we travel to Ifriqiya, even if we can pass ourselves off as Falchoni velvet merchants, who will look after Alnaaji?"

Cristina gave a mischievous smile. "Someone who really needs to feel the pull of such responsibility."

32: MINDER

"No! No, no, no." Deputy Tomasso folded his arms defiantly.

Domenico drew up a chair so that Tomasso could sit at the desk. "Please, just calm down."

Reluctantly, Tomasso took a seat. "Paolo was brutally murdered on my watch. I should be out there getting justice for him, not looking after some child I don't even know."

"Being an Apostolic Guard makes strange demands on us," Domenico explained. "But that's what makes the work interesting."

"And if Cristina and Isra are going to Ifriqiya, shouldn't I be going too? They need someone to protect them."

Domenico winced. "Don't ever let them hear you say that."

"Come on. You know it's true."

"They want to go by themselves. They're convinced it's the best way to keep their cover."

"And you agree?"

Domenico sighed. "You know how stubborn my sister is."

"Look, even if you let them go alone, that doesn't mean I have to be a childminder." Tomasso pointed to the courtyard just outside the office window. "There are dozens of men in the barracks who are better suited. Men who have wives and children; they'll know what to do."

"But Cristina has specifically asked for you."

"Why? What did I do wrong?"

"Deputy Tomasso, this is not a punishment."

"It isn't?"

"Cristina chose you because she trusts you." Domenico opened his desk drawer and pulled out a sheaf of papers that had been bound with a loop of string. "She's even written a set of instructions to help you out."

Tomasso scoffed. "I really don't think looking after a child is that complicated."

"Please. Just read it."

Reluctantly Tomasso took the booklet and flicked through the pages, which contained detailed instructions on how to look after a twelve-year-old boy. There were sections on food, sleep, exercise, hygiene and education. There were appendices containing the names of market stalls selling special ingredients for North African food, and lists of useful vocabulary in Italian and Arabic. There were checklists to be filled in every day, and there were even diagrams illustrating the correct technique for brushing the boy's teeth. Tomasso's eyes glazed over.

"Look, between you and me, you don't have to read all that. Just keep the boy alive for a few weeks and wash him every now and then. And make sure he doesn't lose any weight — Cristina is sure to have weighed him, and it's the first thing she'll check when she gets back."

The handover took place at Tomasso's apartment on Via della Fontanella, but when Cristina and Isra entered, they left the boy outside on the landing. The two women wandered from room to room, casting their eyes over everything yet saying nothing, and Tomasso got the distinct impression that he was being judged.

"What's the matter?" he asked.

"Nothing," Cristina replied innocently.

"Why are you looking at my home like that?"

Cristina turned to Isra. "Do you know what he's talking about?"

"Not a clue," Isra replied.

The women moved into the kitchen, and Tomasso suddenly became acutely aware that the sink was full of unwashed plates. But Cristina was focussed on six bottles of red wine lined up on the shelf. Without a word, Isra hurried over and put the wine out of sight in the cupboard next to the window.

"You won't be needing those," Cristina explained.

"Won't I?" Tomasso was starting to feel bullied.

"Have you read the instruction pages?"

"I was only given them this morning."

"But you will read them, and study them?"

"I suppose."

Cristina frowned. "You don't sound sure."

"Yes. I will read the instruction pages."

"Good. Because all the answers are in there."

"Understood."

"Any problems, talk to Domenico."

Tomasso was struggling to contain his irritation. "And he understands children better than me?"

"No need to be so defensive," Cristina soothed. "I'm just trying to help."

"People have been raising children since the dawn of time. It can't be that hard."

"Women," Isra corrected. "*Women* have been raising children since the dawn of time."

Cristina noticed Tomasso roll his eyes, and suddenly felt sorry for him. Perhaps they were being too hard on the man. "I suppose it's not really your fault. Men are ignorant about childcare because they have been excluded from it. So why not think of this next month as a chance to expand your horizons?"

"Very well," Tomasso replied, having reached the point where he would say anything just to get this over with.

Inspection complete, Isra went onto the landing and led Alnaaji in by the hand. The boy kept his eyes glued to the floor — it was clear he didn't want to be doing this any more than Tomasso.

Cristina bent down and lifted his chin. "As you know, we're going away. We'll be gone a few weeks, but we are coming back."

Alnaaji screwed his eyes shut and threw his arms around Cristina's waist. "Stay. Please."

Cristina was desperate to stop him from crying and ruffled his hair playfully. "We want to reunite you with your real family. But first we have to make sure it's safe. That you won't be kidnapped again."

"I come with you."

"As soon as we know it's safe, we'll take you home. I promise. In the meantime —" Cristina gestured towards the deputy — "this man is going to be looking after you."

The boy looked up and studied Tomasso's face.

"One more thing." Cristina rummaged in her bag, pulled out a winding key engraved with symbols of the zodiac, and pressed it into Alnaaji's hand. "While we're away, your job is to keep the clock in my library running smoothly. Can you do that for me? It's very important."

The boy nodded.

"Once a week, Deputy Tomasso will take you to the house so that you can keep it wound."

Alnaaji gripped the key tightly and stood a bit straighter, inspired by the responsibility. Then Cristina and Isra hugged him tightly, kissed him, and left.

The man and the boy stood silently in the room, not sure what to do next. They looked at each other awkwardly, then Alnaaji walked over and clasped Tomasso's hand. "Do not worry. I will look after you."

33: CROSSING

Cristina and Isra chose one of the new class of merchant galleys to cross the Mediterranean Sea. Equipped with lateen sails as well as oars, it was designed for speed rather than cargo, as its principal business was the ferrying of diplomats and military dispatches across the region. From Civitavecchia sailing almost due south, it would take two days to reach Tunis. The weather couldn't have been better. The vast blue sky was dotted with occasional fluffy clouds that looked like lost sheep, the swell was gentle, and the wind held steady from the west, perfectly angled for optimum speed.

The two women spent most of the first morning standing on the raised deck by the foremast, mesmerised by the rhythmic, churning splash as the bow cut through the water and sent out a rippling V of white foam.

"It's a beautiful sight," Cristina said, breathing in the salt air. "And so peaceful."

Isra looked askance. "I can tell you're a city person."

"What's that supposed to mean? That I'm provincial?"

"If you'd had to cross this sea in a storm, or survive the bloodshed of battle, you'd have very different memories."

"You're not normally so negative, Isra."

"I'm just being honest. The Mediterranean is a deceiver. Its beauty hides its horrors. Think of all the lives these waters have claimed ... the armies they have swallowed ... the slaves that have been dragged to the depths, still chained to their oars."

"Well, mercifully, conditions for us are perfect. So let's focus on the positives."

Isra took the hint and fell silent. But having listened to her conjuring up so many ghosts, it was impossible for Cristina to enjoy the view anymore, and her mind drifted back to the *Speranza*. What were the men on that ship thinking as they sailed this route in the opposite direction? At what point did they realise they had been fatally deceived?

"You know, Isra, there's one thing that still baffles me. If cheap immigrant labour is how the oligarchs boost their profits, why did they let all those workers on the *Speranza* perish?"

"Perhaps they did try to rescue them."

"If they had, surely some of the men would have survived. Even just a handful. But the crew seemed more interested in covering up their own tracks and vanishing. They abandoned their valuable cargo as well as the ship — how does any of that help the rich get richer?"

Isra pondered the problem, but couldn't see a way through. "Well, let's hope we find the answer in Ifriqiya, or it'll have been a wasted journey."

"And we mustn't give Tomasso the pleasure of thinking we've failed," Cristina said with a sly smile.

"I wonder how he's getting on."

"With a bit of luck, caring for another will break his drinking habit."

"Has it really got that bad?" Isra seemed anxious at the thought. "Is he still reliable?"

"Tomasso was the first one to board the *Speranza*. He saw the full horror and it badly affected him. Then to have Paolo murdered a few days later … I think he's struggling to cope."

"But he's a soldier. They're trained for this."

"Can anyone be trained for horror? My brother just bottles everything up, refuses to talk about it, and slowly it eats into his soul. His salvation is being in command, taking responsibility for his men. But Tomasso … I think he's lost. He needs direction. Perhaps taking care of Alnaaji will help."

A bell tolled on the poop deck; Isra turned and saw one of the cooks waving a ladle above his head. "I assume that means lunch."

"Do you want to risk it?"

"We've got to have something. We won't last until tomorrow evening."

"All right. But if the soup is grey, I'm sticking to the hardtack."

They started making their way back along the walkway, allowing their bodies to roll in harmony with the movement of the galley. "I'm sure being a parent for a few weeks won't change Tomasso as much as it's changed you," Isra called over her shoulder.

Cristina looked confused. "I haven't changed."

"Please. The only reason Alnaaji isn't travelling with us now is that you don't really want to let him go home at all."

"That's not true."

"Nothing to be ashamed of in wanting to take care of him."

"Don't be absurd. I would never keep him from his real family."

"Then why aren't we taking him back to them?"

"There's no point taking him to Ifriqiya if he's just going to get trafficked to Rome again. We need to make sure his home is safe."

"Why do I get the feeling that's just an excuse?"

Cristina didn't reply. She was imagining what it would be like when that day finally came, when they would have to say goodbye to Alnaaji forever … and it filled her with dread.

34: GUARDIAN

Tomasso was surprised at how anxious he felt. He'd read the instruction booklet from start to finish the previous evening, but the numerous directives had all blurred into one, leaving him thoroughly confused. He'd gone to bed early but had woken in the middle of the night drenched in sweat, after dreaming that Alnaaji had disappeared into a crowd and been lost.

After that, Tomasso struggled to get back to sleep. He lay tossing and turning until the first bell of the watch sounded from the Porta del Popolo, then decided he might as well get up and get ahead of the day.

Tomasso wrapped himself in a gown and tied the knot at the front, then padded along the hallway and pushed open the door to Alnaaji's bedroom to check all was well. The boy was fast asleep, oblivious to everything.

How long did children sleep for?

Was this normal, or was something wrong?

And why was he sleeping at such a strange angle, with one leg resting on top of the headboard?

Better check the instruction booklet again.

Tomasso made his way through to the kitchen and lit the kindling inside the stove. He positioned some logs around the flames, and watched as the fire took hold. Once he was satisfied that it wouldn't sputter out, he closed the stove door and went to the larder cabinet.

Under normal circumstances this would be empty apart from some prosciutto crudo and a chunk of bread, but he and Alnaaji had spent the previous afternoon scouring the markets for all the foods that Cristina had listed, and the shelves were now groaning with supplies. Tomasso picked up an orange, sat down at the table and started peeling it. As he ate, he decided to read through the instruction booklet one more time — you never knew what problems the day might present, and he wanted to be prepared. With a well-rested mind, it all made more sense, and Tomasso was now able to see what a useful resource this was. Cristina really had thought of everything.

The floorboards creaked. Tomasso looked up and saw Alnaaji standing in the doorway, his hair sticking out in all directions.

"Morning," Tomasso said.

The boy rubbed his eyes and nodded, then shuffled across the kitchen, put his arms around Tomasso and hugged him.

The deputy froze. Was something wrong? Or was this what the child always did? He waited for the moment to pass, but it didn't. Gingerly, Tomasso patted Alnaaji on the back, and only then did the boy let go.

Happy that the morning greeting was done, Alnaaji sat down at the table opposite Tomasso. They looked at each other expectantly, each waiting for the other to make the first move. Hurriedly Tomasso flicked through the instruction pages to find out what was next.

"Ah. Breakfast. Yes. I wasn't sure if you got washed before food, or the other way around."

Alnaaji nodded. "Breakfast is good."

Fortunately, Tomasso had prepared for this moment by already deciding the night before what he was going to serve: eggs, olives, flatbread and hummus. He put the one skillet pan he owned on top of the stove and dashed in some olive oil, which sat there in a lifeless puddle. The pan clearly wasn't hot enough, so he started taking the ingredients he needed out of the larder.

Alnaaji watched in silence, intrigued by how this task that Isra made look easy, had suddenly become complicated.

There was a clatter of jars as a chain reaction tore through the packed cupboard. "*Testa di cazzo!*" Tomasso tried to regain control by grabbing a bottle of vinegar, but he was not quick enough to save a sack of chestnut flour, which rocked forward, tumbled from the shelf and burst on the floor, sending up a large cloud of powder.

They both stared at the pile of flour on the wooden floor, then Alnaaji burst into a fit of giggles.

"What's so funny?" Tomasso said. "We had to traipse round three markets to find that."

But the more serious Tomasso became, the more the boy laughed.

"What?"

Alnaaji pointed at Tomasso's face.

The deputy glanced in the mirror hanging next to the larder and saw that his face was covered in a fine dusting of flour from the explosion. "You think that's funny?" Tomasso said with a mischievous smile, then he bent down, grabbed a handful of flour and hurled it across the room at Alnaaji.

The boy ducked, but he wasn't quick enough.

Whoosh! The flour exploded on top of his head, instantly turning his hair grey.

Alnaaji roared with laughter, dodged around the table and grabbed a handful of flour himself.

"No, no! Don't you dare!"

Too late. The boy hurled the flour at Tomasso, catching him square on the chin.

Within moments, the kitchen had turned into a powdery battlefield, with Tomasso and Alnaaji laughing and yelping as they threw flour at each other then tried to take cover.

Suddenly there was a furious banging on the front door. They both froze.

"What are you doing in there?" a woman's voice screeched.

Alnaaji looked anxious.

"It's just the landlady," Tomasso whispered. Then, to pay his respects, he lifted his leg and farted.

Alnaaji roared with laughter again.

"Shh!" Tomasso hissed, and the boy buried his face in a cushion to try and smother his giggles.

"No noise that can be heard by other residents! Those are the terms. As if my life isn't hard enough without this nonsense," the voice in the corridor moaned. "You've been nothing but trouble since the day you moved in. This is the last straw. If there are any breakages, you'll be out on the street, you hear? *Out on the street!*"

As the landlady droned on, Tomasso moved his mouth in time to her words, mimicking the complaints he'd heard a thousand times in a grotesque impersonation of the padrona … which made Alnaaji laugh all the more.

35: SOUQ

Tunis wasn't one port, but two. Heavy cargo ships unloaded at Halq-al-Wadi, built on a sandbank overlooking the Mediterranean Sea; but if you sailed through the gap in the sandbar, you entered Lake Tunis, a vast natural lagoon on the far side of which lay the ancient Medina.

Cristina and Isra were stunned by the energy that radiated from the city. It was surrounded by a high wall studded with square watchtowers, but the scale and opulence of the mosques and palaces jostling for space beyond the city gates made it clear that this was one of the wealthiest cities in the Islamic world. The harbour was thronged with dockworkers and porters touting for work, whistling and shouting at each other in a multitude of dialects, and wheeling carts between vast mounds of goods which were being imported and exported.

As their galley tied up, Cristina braced herself to be overwhelmed by the commercial frenzy, but the dockers knew that this type of ship was light on cargo, which meant the scrummage was muted. She and Isra had managed to pack everything for the journey into two wooden trunks, and now needed a porter to ferry them to a lodging house, so they picked their way along the gangplank and addressed a huddle of thawb-clad men.

"I'm looking for lodgings in the Medina," Cristina said in Arabic. "Somewhere that's clean and reliable. Can you help?"

Her question triggered a cacophony of responses in Arabic, Italian, Spanish and English, accompanied by vigorous hand-waving and beckoning.

"Yes, yes!"

"I take you. Please, lady."

"Follow! You follow me!"

"I know very good place."

"Come, come. I take you best lodgings. Very best."

"These are liars! I take you to my brother's house."

"No! This house is brothel. Not safe."

"Very safe. Very nice. Very clean."

The men seemed to have picked up words from every ship that had ever docked here and were trying different dialects until Cristina responded. "I only need one porter!" she said, trying to fend them off.

"This my speciality, lady!"

"No! He will steal your money. I speak truth."

Eventually, Cristina selected a skinny man with an endearing smile which revealed that he was down to his last tooth, and all the other men moved on to the next ship that was tying up.

With strength that seemed out of proportion to his wiry body, the porter loaded both wooden trunks onto a cart and invited Cristina and Isra to sit on top of them.

"Where's the horse?" Isra wondered as she made herself comfortable.

"Perhaps it's having some water?"

As it turned out, the man was the horse. The porter checked everything was secure, then hurried to the front of the cart, slung a leather strap around his shoulder, picked up two long handles and started to pull the whole load towards the Bab el Bhar gate.

"That is impressive," Cristina said.

But it wasn't just about strength — the porter was incredibly agile, manoeuvring his cart through crowds of shoppers dawdling in the markets, and navigating alarmingly narrow alleys.

"Do you really think we can trust him?" Isra whispered. "Or is he going to take us to a den of thieves and demand money?"

"I trust him," Cristina replied.

"Because he's an old man?"

"Because if he was dishonest, he wouldn't be down to his last tooth."

From the moving cart they enjoyed an unofficial whistlestop tour of the city. Madrasas and mausoleums punctuated every street corner, labyrinthine souqs spilled from one square to the next, winding their way around elaborate fountains, and dozens of minarets stood ready to summon the faithful.

The porter was vaguely following the main axis that ran from the Bab el Bhar gate in the east to the Kasbah in the west, but just opposite the vast Al-Zaytuna Mosque, he veered north into Bab Souika, squeezed down an alley where some children were playing with a skipping rope, and emerged into a long square, where he finally stopped.

"Here, lady." He beckoned with his arm. "Please. You choose."

Cristina and Isra gazed at the signs hanging from the walls and realised that every building in this square was a lodging house. They hopped down from the cart, chose the best maintained building and went inside to haggle. Using classical Arabic, sign language and a smattering of words she'd picked up from Alnaaji, Cristina managed to secure a room for a whole month at a reasonable rate, which would enable them to keep a base in the city while pressing deeper into the desert in search of the boy's village. The porter made light work of lifting the trunks up the narrow staircase by hoisting them onto his back, then Cristina gave him a generous tip, and the two women set about unpacking.

One of the trunks contained samples of velvet and other fabrics to support their cover story, but these had been cleverly bundled to hide daggers, swords, a compass and two water flasks. The other trunk contained clothes, shoes, toiletries and other personal items for the trip. Cristina had brought a map of Ifriqiya with them, but it was quite threadbare; as far as Europeans were concerned, this was still a largely uncharted land, and Alnaaji had been unable to fill in any of the blanks as he had never left his home valley until the people-traffickers arrived. If they were going to gather hard evidence to present to Pope Julius, they needed to find the boy's village and record as many testimonies as possible, so Cristina had the idea of using Alnaaji's tattoos to trace his roots. Her suspicion was that each province had its own style of tattoo, and Isra had made a careful sketch of all the markings on Alnaaji's body. Armed with these, they set off for the nearest souq.

Rugs, leather slippers, copperware, perfumes, spices, fruit and fabrics, jewellery, bags, belts and biscuits … it might have been easier to list what *wasn't* sold in the souq. Each stall was supposed to stay within its allocated arch in the thirteenth-century colonnades, but invariably they spilled out onto the walkways, unable to contain their own exuberance. Makeshift awnings had been slung across the buildings to provide shade from the intense heat, enabling shoppers to browse at a leisurely pace and spend more money.

"*Shufti! Shufti!*" men would call out as the women strolled past.

"Good quality, very thick!"

Groups of men huddled round small tables, sipping tea.

"Look! Good quality. Best price."

Yet nothing on display actually had a price, as that should only be mentioned at the very end of any negotiation.

Cristina and Isra finally stopped at a tattoo stall which had bottles of ink neatly stacked on wooden shelves, and hundreds of design samples bound together in leather folios. Isra showed the tattoo artist the sketches of Alnaaji's markings, then pointed to the map. "Where do they make tattoos like this?" she asked. "Which region has these?"

The man put down his needles, studied the markings and frowned — nothing was familiar. This was a cue for all the men in the adjacent stalls to gather round and voice their opinions on the matter. In a few minutes, there was a spirited discussion in progress, with each man seemingly in heated disagreement with all the others. Yet by the end of it, all agreed on the origin of Alnaaji's tattoos, and with a delicate touch the tattoo artist traced a new web of lines on the blank spaces of Cristina's map.

"Here. You go here."

36: CARAVAN

Cristina had instructed Isra to only pack what they could easily carry if they were forced to run for safety. Isra had therefore bought a pair of leather knapsacks from the souq and was now trying to distil their belongings for an expedition inland that might last a number of weeks. Obviously, the weapons and navigation aids had to go with them; beyond that, Isra had chosen clothes that were loose-fitting and offered plenty of protection from the sun, yet were light enough to be washed and dried overnight. She tightened the buckles on one of the knapsacks and slipped it over her shoulders. The weight was good, but she was worried the straps might start to chafe. Just as she was about to make some adjustments, Cristina bowled into the room.

"I've found one! They're loading at the docks." Cristina glanced at the knapsacks. "Are we ready?"

"How far have they agreed to take us?"

"The caravan is heading south, right across the Sahara and down to the Oyo Empire. But we can peel off just before Gafsa and pick up the trail to Alnaaji's home province."

"And you trust them?"

"They're merchants. All they want is to live in peace and turn a profit."

"So how much are we paying them?"

"I showed them some of our most exquisite velvet samples and they were impressed." Cristina opened one of the wooden trunks and pulled out a roll of richly coloured velvet. "This will get us where we need to go."

"And what about the return journey? How do we get back to Tunis?"

"One step at a time, Isra."

"In other words, you don't know."

"All I know is that this is the safest way to travel into the desert. In a caravan we won't get lost or attacked by bandits or die of thirst." Cristina peered out of the window and looked up at the position of the sun. "They're setting off after the Zuhr prayer. We'd better get moving."

As they arrived at the docks, the porter from the previous day greeted Cristina and Isra like an old friend.

"Hello, hello! You happy, lady?"

"Yes, thank you." Cristina smiled and tried to dodge past him, but the porter was quicker.

"You want tour? I show you Medina. Very beautiful."

"No, thank you."

"You want perfumes?"

"No."

"Special offer. Very sweet."

It was clear that polite resistance was futile, so Cristina dipped into her purse and gave the porter a couple of coins.

"*Baarak Allahu fik!*" He smiled as he bestowed the blessing on Cristina, then hurried off to find another customer.

Suddenly Isra stopped and stared towards the end of the dock. "That is quite a camel train."

"Three hundred animals," Cristina replied. "And apparently, this caravan is a small one. Some of them have over two thousand."

The entire far end of the dock was congested with camels and men who were unloading goods from merchant galleys directly onto the animals. At first glance it all seemed chaotic, but each handler was responsible for his own file of ten camels and knew exactly what goods they were carrying and how to secure them for the long journey. The whole operation was being supervised by the caravan's khabir, a man in his sixties with a large, rectangular forehead, black eyebrows and a bushy silver moustache. He was not a man of many words, but he didn't need to be, for it was obvious the handlers had enormous respect for him; they knew the khabir would guide them safely across the most hostile terrain in the world without flinching. And just as they respected the khabir, he respected the Sahara; that was the secret of his survival.

Every now and then, the khabir would give a sharp whistle and point to some loading detail that he wasn't satisfied with, for he knew that the minutiae of weight distribution on the camels here could mean the difference between a profitable expedition and being burnt alive in the cauldron of the Sahara.

"What do you think they're trading?" Isra asked.

"From what I can make out, skins, cloth and leather are the bulk of what's coming from Italy. They'll sell all that as they head south, then return in six months with ivory, spices and hashab gum to sell to European merchants."

"Well, I have no idea why anyone living in the Sahara wants to wear velvet, but I'm glad they do." Isra took the muslin cover off the roll of crimson velvet, then she and Cristina approached the khabir and offered it up for his inspection. He reached out a hand and gently stroked the pile of the material, then pressed it between his fingers.

"It's the finest in Italy," Cristina said.

The khabir shrugged. In his many years of trading, he had heard every sales pitch in the book and had learnt to trust nothing but his own senses. He lifted the cloth to his nose, drew a deep breath, then nodded. "Welcome." He pointed to two camels that had been saddled for riders. "Please."

And that was it: Cristina and Isra were now under the protection of the caravan.

They approached their camels, but rather than try and clamber up on their own, the women decided to wait until their handler was ready to teach them the correct technique. As they were waiting, they saw a commotion break out further along the dock. A galley had just arrived and was tying up, but guards from Medina were bundling all the porters and hawkers away from the ship. Anyone who resisted found themselves on the wrong end of a guard's whip. When the space had been cleared, some more soldiers appeared, unfurled a red carpet at the bottom of the gangplank, then formed themselves into a welcome guard for whichever important dignitary was on board.

Expectation rippled across the curious crowd — who had just arrived? Some great warrior or powerful noble? A king, perhaps?

"*Yah! Yah!*" The sound of cracking whips cleared a path in the crowd. An official carriage emerged from the Bab el Bhar gate, sped towards the dockside and pulled to a stop at the end of the red carpet. The liveried driver leapt down from his perch and with great reverence clicked open the door.

The carriage rocked on its springs as a tall man unfurled himself from the darkness and stepped onto the carpet. He had a shiny bald head and his eyes were accentuated with kohl. The crowd seemed to visibly shrink under his gaze.

"Who on earth is that?" Isra whispered.

"One of the Hafsid rulers, I assume." Even though they were out of earshot, Cristina kept her voice down. "Perhaps the Vizier of Tunis?"

A drum on the galley deck started beating a solemn rhythm, and the crew lined up. Slowly, two men emerged from the officers' cabin and strode along the deck.

"I certainly know who *that* is," Cristina whispered, stunned. She watched in disbelief as Giulio Orsini walked down the gangplank, closely followed by Caposquadra Spiro.

"What are they doing here?" Isra exclaimed.

Cristina grabbed her arm and bundled them both out of sight behind the camels. "He mustn't know we're in Tunis."

"Did they follow us?"

"No-one knew we were coming except my brother and Tomasso. But if Spiro realises we're here, it's unlikely we'll ever make it back to Rome."

Cristina and Isra watched as the vizier greeted Orsini and Spiro like old friends. Jokes were exchanged, followed by small gifts, then the vizier invited his guests into the carriage, and they were all driven away.

The porters on the docks breathed easy again and everyone got back to work ... except Cristina and Isra.

"Why are they here, Cristina?"

"It must be to do with the people trafficking. They know we're investigating them. Maybe they're setting up a different smuggling route."

"Do you think the Hafsid rulers know what's really going on?"

"Orsini's probably paying him a fat bribe to turn a blind eye."

"Then it's just as well we're getting out of the city today," Isra said grimly. "Because if we get caught between the Hafsids and their bribes, it will end very badly indeed."

37: VASTNESS

It was difficult to comprehend the vastness of the Sahara.

Medina did not gradually merge into the desert; the change was abrupt and absolute. As soon as you passed through the walls of the city, you entered a world of scorched sand and searing light. Humans flinched, but the camels walked with steady, fearless determination; this was their world. After an hour, Cristina glanced back over her shoulder and saw that the city had vanished altogether. They had been embraced by the wilderness.

Daunting as this landscape was, Cristina knew they were only scratching the surface of the great emptiness. She and Isra would ride with the caravan for just under a week, travelling some three hundred miles to the trading post at Ferkane; but the khabir would lead his expedition another thousand miles south, directly across the blistering Sahara until they reached the fertile rainforests of the Oyo Empire. It was a thousand miles that would break most men, but for the khabir, it was just a way of life.

Immersed in this ancient landscape, time itself seemed to evaporate, and as the spirit of emptiness seeped into Cristina's soul, she started to appreciate the richness and variety of the desert.

This wasn't just a place of monstrous, drifting sand dunes; there were also large plains covered with sharp stones and wind-worn pebbles which clattered under the hooves of the camels. Sometimes they would follow a dried-up valley and emerge onto a low plateau that had been carved into strange shapes by water that had long since vanished. At other times they would pick their way across gulleys covered with clumps of spikey brown grasses which somehow managed to suck enough moisture from the furnace to survive.

And there were animals out here too. Lizards, hares and snakes darted from one patch of shade to the next; once, they even saw a herd of oryx roaming through a patch of scrub vegetation.

Occasionally, the caravan would pass remnants of human endeavour — some stones gathered into a small shelter, or a rocky shrine erected to memorialise some intrepid traveller who had underestimated the savagery of the desert. The sight of these failed human endeavours made the ache of loneliness more acute, and Cristina started to understand why the camel trains were so large — the only community out here was the one you brought with you.

Momentary respite came from a handful of tiny oases that were dotted along the caravan routes. They seemed almost magical, pockets of green flourishing in the middle of an infinite heat, but in fact they owed their life to the diligence of generations of khabirs. Where one traveller had found a watering hole, the next had planted some date palms, which the next had tended, eventually creating an umbrella of shade in which dwarf orange trees could flourish. Everyone who passed through the desert nurtured these precious islands of life, and in return were given succour.

When they finally arrived at the Oasis of Dew, it was as much as Cristina and Isra could do to clamber off their camels, scramble to the pool of fresh water and plunge their heads into it. But for the men of the caravan, this was the busiest time of day, and it was quite something to watch them set up camp, tend and groom the camels, light fires, refill water skins, check on the health of the oasis plants and prepare dinner.

As the heat vanished into the cloudless sky, Cristina and Isra felt the first pangs of hunger, and eagerly sat around a flickering fire to eat dinner with the men. A soup flavoured with plenty of salt, accompanied by bread and dates, was followed by a vegetable stew with onions and turnips. With her stomach full, Cristina could barely keep her eyes open, and was glad to crawl into the little tent she shared with Isra.

It was just as well she went to sleep early, as the next day began shortly after sunrise. One of the drivers boiled large kettles of water so that the others could perform their ritual washing before the first prayers of the day. Breakfast itself was simple: hot tea, served with oats mixed into a mush.

"Did you see?" Isra whispered. "We're eating the same food as the camels."

Cristina glanced from the feed sacks in front of the camels to the tin dish in her own hands — the food looked worryingly similar. "Are we eating their food, or are they eating ours?"

Isra laughed. "Best not to ask."

The tents were packed quickly after breakfast, and the drivers loaded all the precious merchandise back onto their camels, taking great care to ensure everything was well balanced. As soon as everyone was ready, the camel train moved off, leaving no trace that they had ever been at the oasis.

The second day was quite different to the first. Rather than taking in the details of the landscape, Cristina's mind slipped into a different gear. Now she was not so much thinking as meditating. It was like spending hours caught in that strange state between sleep and waking, and the entire day passed in this almost hallucinogenic trance. The sense of disorientation became more intense as Cristina sipped verbena tea after dinner while listening to one of the older drivers, Khalif, play haunting music on a rababa.

The instrument itself was quite crude — a small, rounded body covered in stretched skin; attached to this was a long, thin neck, and running between the pegboard and the base was a single string which Khalif played with a small bow. The music he produced was sublime, like a lone voice calling out to the enigma of the desert.

Cristina lay back and studied the million pinpricks of light in the black sky as the music washed over her. How many stars were there on the celestial sphere that surrounded the earth, she wondered? And what lay beyond them? Was that where you might finally glimpse the face of God?

The music held the whole caravan in thrall, for no-one spoke a word, and when Khalif stopped playing, most of the camel drivers retreated to their tents. But Cristina was keen to learn more about the rababa.

"That was beautiful," she said, crouching down next to the old man. "Would you teach me?"

Khalif said nothing, but carefully wrapped the instrument in woollen cloth and slid it into one of his saddlebags.

"Is it difficult to play?" Cristina persisted.

The old man poured himself another cup of tea and sipped it silently.

"I don't think he understands," Isra whispered. "Try a different dialect."

"Oh, I understand," Khalif said in Italian. "I just don't want to talk to you."

Cristina hadn't expected such a blunt snub. "Because we're women?"

"No. Because you are European."

Cristina remembered hearing this same hostility in the quarry. "You've obviously been to Italy, judging by your command of the language," she replied. "Was it really so terrible?"

For the first time, Khalif turned his gaze on her. "I have seen into the European heart. I know what devils lurk there."

"In some men, yes. But not all."

"In all the men who come to Ifriqiya, there are devils. I have seen them with my own eyes. I have felt their whip on my back."

"Were you enslaved?" Cristina asked.

Khalif said nothing, but Cristina could see the pain in the old man's eyes.

"We are here precisely to stop that evil trade," Cristina explained.

Khalif scoffed.

"If you know something that could help us, you owe it to your countrymen to tell us," Cristina persisted.

"Do not tell me to whom I owe what!" Khalif snapped.

"I'm sorry. I only meant —"

"Do not presume! That is the European way, to lecture the world. But I will not have it. For I have seen you in action and I know how devious your minds are."

"You cannot judge all of us by the actions of a few."

"Yet you all share one thing." Khalif tapped a finger on the side of his head. "You admire cleverness and learning. But the cleverness of the European is the very thing that enables his evil."

"They are two separate things."

"No. They are hand in hand. The Europeans who come here, they learn every weakness of this land so that they can use it against us. The Berbers are a proud people, but we are scattered across a thousand valleys, with a thousand different tongues. The European knows this and it is why he steals our people. How can we warn each other if we do not know each other, or even speak the same language? The European comes with just enough gold to turn us against each other. He divides us to weaken us. And then he crushes us." Khalif gazed at her with contempt. "That is why I do not want to talk to you."

"I hear your anger," Cristina pleaded, "and you are right. But this evil trade in people can be stopped."

"By you?" He gave a scornful laugh.

"By Pope Julius II. One of the most powerful men in Europe."

"Which means he has the most to lose by change."

"Come to Rome with me, Khalif. Let the Pope hear your testimony. In your own words, from your own mouth."

Khalif roared with mocking laughter. "If you knew what I had to do to escape from Rome, to see my own country and family again, you would not ask such a thing."

"I will guarantee your safety."

"I never want to set foot on that continent again!" Khalif bellowed. "Never."

His anger was quickly absorbed by the immensity of the desert, but the conflict had made everyone in the caravan feel uncomfortable. Harsh words spoken out here could fester in the long days ahead.

"Forgive me, Khalif." Cristina lowered her gaze. "Forgive my ignorance. I am only trying to help."

Khalif shook his head. "The only thing the European wants is to have the world under his boot. You come to Ifriqiya, and all you see is something to be plundered."

"But Europe is changing. New ways of thinking are spreading. There is new learning, and a new understanding."

Khalif wrapped a blanket around his shoulders. "New learning only means the European will find new ways to exercise his cruelty. His heart will never change."

Then Khalif turned his back on Cristina and closed his eyes.

38: PROVISIONS

For the next three days, Cristina and Isra kept themselves to themselves. They didn't try to make conversation with any of the drivers or volunteer for extra duties; they just did as they were told and stayed quiet. It was a relief to finally arrive at the desert trading post where they would split from the caravan.

Ferkane was a ramshackle affair. Several dozen semi-permanent black tents were clustered alongside a dense grove of date palms which had flourished around a bubbling waterhole. The settlement was surrounded by a low rim of barren hills, which sheltered it from the worst of the scorching desert winds.

Everything here was geared up to service the caravans which passed through, for Ferkane was where five different routes converged from all parts of the Hafsid kingdom. Some tents served freshly cooked meals; others were stocked with piles of dried fruits and salted meats. There were tents specialising in repairing camel saddles and leather water pouches, while others offered tattoos and shaves. Here you could hire a desert guide, a camel doctor or a fortune teller; there was even one tent with no sign outside, just an old woman who collected money from men who would enter furtively on their own and emerge half an hour later looking calm and satisfied. Trinkets and jewellery, headscarves and blankets, pottery and pieces of parchment inscribed with verses from the Quran — the traders of Ferkane had thought of everything. The only dwelling here that wasn't a tent, was a tiny mosque constructed from crude mud bricks that looked as if they were about to crumble back to dust.

While the camel drivers restocked their provisions, Cristina and Isra studied the map and planned the next leg of their journey. The trail which they thought led to Alnaaji's village was the one leading east from Ferkane, but quite how many miles they would have to travel along it remained a mystery. It was too dangerous to attempt the journey on their own, so they decided to talk to a local guide, who told them that the village was a full day's camel ride away.

"Would you take us there?" Cristina asked.

The guide shrugged.

"We'll pay a good rate and hire camels from you as well."

The guide shrugged again.

"So … is that a yes?"

"Not today."

"Tomorrow?"

The guide shook his head.

"Well, when can you take us?"

The guide waved his hand to indicate some indeterminate day in the future.

"He's just negotiating," Isra whispered. "Let's try somewhere else."

But they encountered the same surly attitude in every tent they entered. It was as if their money was no good in Ferkane, and the traders only sold them basic provisions with great reluctance. The drivers from the camel train, however, encountered no such problems. They loaded up with armfuls of provisions, and when they could carry no more, the traders offered to carry it for them.

As they approached a tent selling dried olives, Cristina saw Khalif walking in the opposite direction.

"Enjoying yourselves?" he asked with a dry smile.

Cristina didn't find it amusing. "What are we doing wrong? Why won't they serve us?"

"It's just their way."

"Don't they want our money?"

"Getting angry won't help."

"If they won't trade, we'll be stuck here forever!"

"They are just reminding you that out here in the desert, you are not the masters."

"This again." Cristina sighed with frustration.

But Isra was furious. She held up her purse and loudly chinked the coins. "We don't need reminding of anything. We just need provisions and a guide. And our money is as good as yours!"

Khalif looked the two women up and down. "If I were you, I'd try again in the morning."

"What good will that do?"

"Today they're busy selling to us. But tomorrow will be quiet, and then your money will look more attractive."

As the drivers finished getting provisions and returned to their camels, the traders lowered their awnings and closed up for the day. An hour later, the caravan had left, and Cristina and Isra found themselves standing in the middle of a ghost town. They could see trickles of smoke rising from the tent chimneys as the air filled with the delicious smell of cooked meat, but they were not welcome at any of the family tables.

"This is absurd!" Cristina protested.

"It is," Isra replied. "But what can we do? Let's just make camp and try again in the morning."

Fortunately, they had purchased a small tent from the khabir, and it didn't take them long to find a secluded spot on the edge of the oasis. While Cristina pitched the tent, Isra gathered some sticks to make a fire.

"Do you think we'll be safe here?" Cristina asked. "Maybe we should move closer to the mosque."

Isra glanced up at the ramshackle dome on the far side of the trading post. "I'm not sure the Imam would take kindly to European women camping in the shadow of his walls. You can imagine what kind of an imam gets stuck out here."

They lit a fire and prepared a simple meal, but just as the sun was starting to set, there was a sudden bustle of activity around the trading post. Cristina and Isra peered through the trees and saw all the traders opening up their tents for business again. They lit torches and called out greetings, and one of them even started playing music.

"Has the caravan returned?" Isra asked.

"I'm not sure." Cristina tiptoed through the palm grove until she could see onto the main square of tents. Six heavily armed men had ridden into the trading post on camels; their leader was Caposquadra Spiro.

"He must be following us," Isra hissed.

But Cristina was more worried by the reception Spiro was getting — it was clear the traders knew him and loved him. They beckoned him into their tents, offered him and his men tea, gave them samples of fruit and bread to taste; they laughed at Spiro's jokes and embraced him warmly.

"So much for not liking Europeans," Cristina muttered.

"He must have passed through this trading post many times."

Cristina's gaze darted around the tents. "There's no sign of Orsini. He's probably still in Medina."

"Do you think Spiro's already recruited more labourers? Or is he on his way to do that?"

Cristina watched Spiro strut around the trading post; how he loved being a man of importance. Shoulders back, head held high like a haughty god, he plucked anything he fancied from the baskets of food to see if it amused his palette; whatever displeased him, he dismissed with a flick of his fingers. For the first time, Cristina saw Spiro as Khalif saw all Europeans.

Piecing together fragments of overheard conversation, Cristina realised that Spiro had made camp on the other side of the low ridge. "We need to go and take a look."

"Now?" Isra glanced up at the last flickers of daylight draining from the sky.

"They won't be able to see us in the dark."

"And we won't be able to see where we're going! I don't want to break my neck."

Cristina looked at the ridge. "That's nothing compared to the quarry."

"Where you almost died!"

"You worry too much, Isra. Stay close to me and you'll be fine."

They set off immediately and found a well-worn path leading up through the rocks.

"The traders must use this ridge as a lookout point, to see when camel trains are approaching."

"I bet they don't do it in the dark, though," Isra grumbled.

Although the path was steep, there were no boulders to scramble over or ravines to cross. By the time the moon had risen, Cristina and Isra were standing on top of the ridge looking down at Spiro's encampment.

Dozens of young Berber men were sitting around small fires, laughing and eating. One man was singing whilst another accompanied him on a rababa, and many of the others were playing dice games. Several men were gathered round a chessboard offering advice to the players, who were trying their best to ignore them so that they could concentrate.

"And there's the fresh meat," Isra whispered.

"Spiro must be taking them back to Medina for shipment."

"Look at them all, so full of hope. Probably thinking about how they will return with pockets full of gold."

"They have no idea what horrors await them," Cristina whispered. "No idea…"

39: IMAM

Huddled together in their tent, Cristina and Isra spent all night locked in discussion. Somehow, they needed to raise the alarm, but they were outnumbered, in another country, and with no recourse to the law.

Cristina was all for confronting Spiro in public when he came into Ferkane for more supplies later that morning. "Once the traders know what's really going on, they'll boycott him. How far can he get without supplies?"

"It won't work." Isra was adamant. "You've seen how much money he brings to the trading post. Spiro will deny everything, and the traders will take his side."

"We can't unsee what we witnessed last night, Isra. We have to do something."

"Our mission was to find Alnaaji's village and gather evidence —"

"But this overrides everything. A crime is unfolding in front of us. If we act now, maybe we can eradicate this evil trade."

"We're foreigners and we're women. Worse, you're a white woman. Our voices count for nothing out here."

Cristina growled her frustration and slumped back on the roll of blanket that served as a pillow. "I hate being silenced."

The women lay quietly, trying to think of a way out of the impasse.

Cristina gazed through a crack in the tent awning, watching a sliver of sky slowly turn from deep indigo to milky grey … until a clear voice reached across the desert silence as the first call to prayer began. Cristina listened to its plaintive tones for a few moments, then suddenly sat up.

"They may not listen to us, but they *will* listen to their imam."

"You can't hustle a holy man."

But that was exactly what Cristina intended. She scrambled out of the tent and strode in the direction of the tiny mosque.

"Wait!" Isra crawled from the tent and chased after her, dodging through the palm trees. By the time she caught up with Cristina, they were already at the mosque gates. Considering how rickety the building seemed, the gates were surprisingly solid and carved with intricate geometric patterns.

They listened as the Salah cast its eerie spell across the remote settlement.

"I seek refuge with Allah from Satan, the accursed... You alone do we worship, and You alone do we ask for help... God's peace and blessing be upon you."

The recitation stopped. Cristina waited for the echo of the last syllable to fade to nothing, then she hammered on the doors with her fist. A few moments later, they heard sandals slapping on the floor inside.

"Who is it?" a man's voice called out.

"We need to speak to the imam," Cristina replied in Arabic. "Is he awake?"

"I am the imam," the voice confessed from behind the doors.

"We are travellers passing through Ferkane. We need your help."

"At this hour?"

"Every hour that passes puts innocent lives at risk."

They heard some muttering, then the sound of bolts being slid back; the doors opened to reveal a tall, black man with tufts of hair sticking out in all directions as if he had just crawled out of bed.

Cristina gave a little bow. "I am sorry to disturb you, Imam. We thought maybe your servant would answer."

"Servant?" The man's face lit up with amusement. "Very good. Very funny. In this mosque, I am servant, cleaner, cook and imam."

"Well, I am Cristina Falchoni, and this is Isra."

"Sufian. Imam Sufian." He extended his hand, and they shook with a firm grip.

"May we come in?" Cristina asked.

Sufian stuck his head out of the doorway and looked around with sharp, restless eyes. "Is that a good idea?"

"We have come from Rome, in Italy."

"I know where Rome is."

"Then you'll understand how far we've travelled."

"The length of a journey is unrelated to its importance." Sufian's eyes darted from one woman to the other, trying to fathom their intentions. "Why are you here?"

"To right a terrible wrong," Cristina replied. "To reunite families that have been torn apart. And to stamp out an evil trade."

"All before breakfast?" The imam's eyes twinkled, and he swung open the doors. "I had better make some cardamom tea."

While Imam Sufian busied himself in a side room, Cristina and Isra studied the little mosque. Although it was a humble space, it was well looked after. The rough walls were freshly whitewashed, an array of multicoloured rugs covered the floor, three crudely hewn pillars held up the roof beams, and in the far wall was the mihrab niche facing the Kaaba in Mecca.

Finally, Sufian emerged carrying a tray with three small beakers of tea. "I have put honey in. We all need sugar at this hour."

"Where's the dome?" Isra asked, looking up at the flat ceiling. "From the outside there's a small dome."

"Ah," Sufian chuckled. "The dome is where my heart is kept. Please." He beckoned them to follow him through a door that was hidden behind a curtain, to reveal a small private library that Sufian had built underneath the dome.

Isra saw the joy in Cristina's face as she gazed at the shelves stacked with scrolls and books.

"Who would have imagined?" Cristina whispered. "All this, in the middle of the desert."

"It is my special place."

"I know exactly what you mean. I have one at home."

Sufian looked surprised. "Women are allowed books?"

"That depends on who you ask," Cristina replied, craning her head to read the spines.

"Some of these texts are also disputed," the imam confessed. "But who is looking all the way out here? It is between me and the Prophet, Peace Be Upon Him."

Cristina turned to the imam and studied his face. "How did a man like you end up in the middle of the desert? Someone with your learning should be in a madrasa in Tunis."

"The madrasas..." Sufian shrugged. "They are a nest of scorpions. To be an imam in Tunis, you must face a choice: agree with your superiors and get promoted, or be true to the words of Muhammad, Peace Be Upon Him."

"And you chose the latter?"

"The authorities believed sending me here was a punishment, but I have turned it to my advantage." He held his arms out to embrace his private library.

"Then you are exactly the man we need," Cristina smiled.

Sufian arranged three large cushions on the floor. "Please. Sit. Talk."

They made themselves comfortable and the imam topped up their beakers with fresh tea.

"An Italian passed through the trading post last night — Caposquadra Spiro. Did you see him?" Cristina asked.

"He has been many times. He is a friend of yours?"

"Quite the opposite."

"This I am glad to hear."

"Then you know about him?"

Sufian hesitated, trying to be diplomatic. "I know that he never goes anywhere without armed guards. I know that there is malice in his eyes. And I know that in the many months I have seen him pass through Ferkane, I have never seen him perform a single act of kindness. The Prophet, Peace Be Upon Him, said 'God is kind and likes kindness in all things.' This Italian has much to learn."

"Do you know what he is trading?" Cristina asked.

"He hires men to travel far and work for him. But why should another country benefit from the sweat of our men? It is not right."

"Did you not wonder why these men never come back?"

The imam looked confused. "But they do return."

"You've seen them come home?"

Sufian cast his mind back. "They do not come as a procession. But on their own … I think so."

"And you've seen this with your own eyes? Men who went away with Spiro coming home?"

"I have heard that is what happens. But many settle near the coast. With the money they earned, they can build a house overlooking the sea."

"You know this for certain?" Cristina pressed.

Sufian shook his head. "Why? Is it not so?"

"I fear you have been deceived, Imam. A few men may have returned, but the vast majority … once they leave Ifriqiya, they are put in chains. In Italy they are treated like slaves and worked like donkeys. Many die broken men, in a foreign land, far from home."

Sufian looked stunned. "But I would have heard this. Someone would have spoken the truth."

"They take men from isolated villages. They lie to cover their tracks. They will do anything and say anything to steal your men and enslave them. And Caposquadra Spiro, he is the architect of their misery."

40: RESIST

It was important no-one in the trading post knew Cristina and Isra were involved in the agitation, so they retreated to the shadows of the palm trees while Imam Sufian made his way from tent to tent, talking to each of the traders in turn, explaining what Spiro was really doing. It was like watching a ripple of enlightenment spread through the settlement.

As the men listened to the imam, their faces would crease with confusion; instinctively they would back away, refusing to let his words contaminate them. But Sufian was as persistent as he was persuasive, and the more he spoke, the more his ideas managed to penetrate the traders' defences and take root. As the truth grew in their minds, the men started to see how it made sense of things they had witnessed over these past months, and how it connected disparate rumours they had heard whispered.

Once they had embraced the truth, anger became inevitable.

Caposquadra Spiro rode at the head of the procession as he always did. Behind him came six waggons loaded with newly recruited men; two strong camels pulled each waggon, and on either side of the caravan rode Spiro's armed guards. It should have been a routine stop at the trading post to load up with provisions that would carry them north to the Mediterranean Sea, but this time the traders had abandoned their tents and were standing in the middle of the clearing, blocking the road.

The men in the waggons were confused; Spiro looked uneasy but straightened himself in his saddle to deal with the nuisance.

"What a touching tableau," he quipped. "I know it breaks your hearts to see me leave, but fear not! I will return."

Spiro's banter fell on deaf ears. No-one smiled.

"Let me pass," Spiro ordered with more gravity. "I have no quarrel with you. We are heading to the coast."

Imam Sufian stepped forward and stood directly in front of Spiro's camel. "Set these men free. They are no longer your prisoners."

"Prisoners?" the capo exclaimed. "You have misunderstood the situation. These workers are free men. See for yourself."

He beckoned magnanimously to the waggons, but the imam didn't move. "We have seen through your lies, Spiro. Chains are waiting for these men. Chains, enslavement and a premature death."

Spiro looked perplexed. "These are outrageous accusations. Either offer proof for your paranoia or clear this road and let us pass."

"*I* am the proof," Cristina said as she stepped out from the crowd and stood next to Sufian. "I have witnessed what happens to men like these."

Spiro flinched in his saddle as he recognised Cristina. "I'd hoped you were dead. What a disappointment. But it makes little difference. You have no authority here."

"I work directly for His Holiness Pope Julius II, Supreme Pontiff, Bishop of Rome and leader of the Papal States," she replied. "Wherever God is present, so is the authority of the Pope. And on that basis, I demand that you release the men you are trying to kidnap."

"You're quite the wordgrubber," Spiro scoffed. "But you have completely misunderstood what is going on here."

"Let them go!"

"These men are not mine to release. They are self-employed craftsmen, recruited for their skills. They will return from Rome next year with pockets full of gold. Isn't that right?" Spiro turned to look at the men, who stared at him blankly; they hadn't understood a word he'd said.

"Be happy!" he commanded. "We're going to make you rich!"

"Smile! Smile!" the guards commanded, prodding the waggons with their swords, adding to the sense of confusion.

Imam Sufian stepped closer to the waggons and started shouting to the men in Arabic, trying to explain what was happening. Cristina saw bewilderment on the men's faces — they had come from such remote villages they didn't understand Arabic. All except one man, who suddenly looked anxious.

"Over there!" Cristina pointed. "I think he understands."

Sufian hurried towards the man, but immediately Spiro spurred his camel forward and knocked the imam to the ground.

The traders gasped to see Sufian treated with such disrespect. Isra rushed forward to help him get back on his feet.

"No harm, no harm," Sufian said as he dusted himself down. "I'm all right."

But Cristina could feel anger bristling among the traders. She turned to Spiro. "It's over. You're not taking these men anywhere. You can run back to Medina and tell Orsini his plans are in ruins."

"Orsini?" the caposquadra mocked. "You think Orsini had the wit to create a scheme like this? You clearly haven't spent enough time with aristocrats. They have all the charm and polish of wealth, but most of them are really quite stupid."

"Then you admit you are the architect of this criminal abuse."

"Very emotive language."

"How else should I describe the kidnap and enslavement of innocent people?"

Spiro considered for a moment. "This is merely supply and demand in action. It is the hidden hand of the free market ensuring the best use of men and materials. It is the way of the future."

"If it's so wonderful, why do you attack our imam?" Cristina replied. "Why do you travel with armed guards? Why do you have to put men in chains?"

"I see no chains." Spiro looked innocently at the waggons.

Cristina strode past him and addressed the one man who seemed to understand Arabic. "If you value your freedom and your life, get off this cart and make your way home again." She pointed to Spiro. "The only thing this man offers is death."

The man looked from Cristina to the imam, then grabbed his small travelling sack, leapt over the side of the waggon and hurried towards the crowd of traders. They applauded his courage, and one of them immediately offered him a beaker of fresh tea.

Emboldened by the warmth of the reception, another two men clambered out of the waggons, followed by a few more who didn't know what was happening, but sensed the tide was turning. The trickle quickly became a flood as men realised this was a choice between life and death.

A few minutes later, Caposquadra Spiro and his armed guards were left in charge of nothing but empty waggons. It was humiliating, but Spiro's face remained impassive.

"Well, well, it looks as if the free market has spoken after all," Cristina said.

Spiro ignored her and turned to the workmen. "If that is your choice, you must repay the money we gave you! That money was an advance. You have broken your contracts."

"We do not follow European law here," the imam replied. "These men owe you nothing."

Spiro glared at Sufian. "Heathen!"

Cristina stepped protectively in front of the imam. "For your own safety, Spiro, leave now. And be grateful you're leaving with your life."

"Do not think you have heard the last of this." Spiro whipped the side of his camel and led his bodyguards back out into the desert.

41: FLIES

They celebrated victory with fresh pastries and copious amounts of mint tea.

Ovens were fired up, wives, children and bakers set to work, and it wasn't long before trays of delicious sweetmeats were being passed around the trading post. Deep-fried chebakia coated in honey were the most popular, followed by qurabiya almond biscuits, m'hencha pastries rolled into miniature swirling snakes, and soft sfenj doughnuts served warm.

When everyone was buzzing with sugar, the rababa players tuned their instruments and the dancing started. There was much laughter amidst the relief, and a genuine sense that truth had triumphed over evil. The rescued migrant workers had long journeys to make back to their home villages, and since it was now too late in the day to set out, the traders opened up the domestic quarters of their tents and offered the men shelter for the night.

Cristina and Imam Sufian chatted to the workers, hoping to discover more details about the organisation of the people-trafficking operation. They knew it would take more than one victory to dismantle the terrible trade, but perhaps today would be a turning point. Amongst the workers themselves, feelings were more mixed. Some knew they had just had a lucky escape and were grateful, but others lamented the lost opportunity. The money Spiro had promised would have transformed their lives, and now those dreams had been shattered.

"He would never have paid you," Cristina reassured them, using Sufian as an interpreter. "It was all a lie. And worse, you would never have seen your homes again."

The men nodded, yet still there was a part of them that mourned what could have been.

As the sun set, Imam Sufian was hoisted onto one of the tables and urged to give a speech. After thanking the traders for showing generous hospitality, Sufian turned to more serious business. "If today is to have meaning, it must be the start of real change. And that can only happen if you carry word of what you have witnessed." The imam extended his arms as if to embrace the crowd. "Whoever you meet, tell them what happened here. Whenever you trade or go to the market, warn people about the false promises of the men from Europe. It is down to each of you to spread the word from tribe to tribe, and village to village, until the whole of Ifriqiya knows the truth. Only then will we defeat evil, for men like Spiro use our isolation against us. But when we talk to each other, when we overcome tribal differences to help our brothers, then we take back control of our destinies."

The crowd burst into enthusiastic applause, the music struck up again, and Sufian was hoisted onto the shoulders of the migrant workers and paraded around the trading post like a conquering hero.

By the time everyone finally gave in to sleep, people felt as if they had done a good day's work.

Until the flies came.

At first, Cristina thought she was dreaming.

She was back in her library in Rome, trying to help a lost bluebottle escape, but it had become trapped between two panes of glass. The more she tried to guide it out, the more panicked it became, and the angrier the buzzing grew. Round and round her head, buzzing louder and louder without making progress, until suddenly the fly darted towards her and landed on her face.

Cristina snapped open her eyes and brushed her hand across her nose, trying to sweep the insect away. But there was something wrong. In the pre-dawn gloom, the air seemed to be rippling. She sat up. Her eyes focussed. Then she recoiled in horror.

The tent was swarming with flies.

"Figlio di puttana!" Cristina shook Isra awake and scrambled outside, but there was no respite — thousands of flies were swarming around the palm trees.

Isra emerged from the tent, covering her mouth with her arm. "What happened? Where did they come from?"

"God knows!" Cristina looked over to the trading post. "Maybe someone's left cakes out."

Isra shook her head clear of the insects. "That wouldn't cause all this."

Cristina grabbed Isra's hand and led her away from the palm trees and into the main trading post. No food had been left out, yet still the swarms of flies swirled frantically in search of something.

"Over there!" a voice cried.

They spun round and saw Imam Sufian emerge from the mosque with a robe draped over his face. "They're coming from over there!" He pointed to the track which led west from the trading post. Cristina looked across and saw a writhing black ribbon of flies twisting into the distance, then disappearing behind a towering sand dune.

"Why are they swarming?" Cristina shouted.

"Something's out there." There was a tremble of fear in Sufian's voice. "They're in a feeding frenzy."

Cristina studied the sand dune, wondering what horrors it was hiding.

"We should wait until the sun's up," Isra said. "We can put together a search party to go and…"

But Cristina was already walking away, heading in the direction of the dune.

"It might be dangerous!" Isra warned.

Cristina shook her head and kept walking. "Whatever's there is dead already. And rotting."

Isra and the imam hurried along the track until they caught up with Cristina, then the three of them trudged anxiously towards the sand dune.

With every step they took, the febrile buzzing became more intense, and the flies more agitated. At first, Cristina tried to swat the insects from her face, but she soon realised it was hopeless. You couldn't beat them, you just had to let them land on your skin and remember to keep your mouth shut.

They walked in silence until eventually they reached the bottom of the sand dune. With rising dread, they started to scramble up the soft slopes. Instinctively, they paused just before the crest to brace themselves for whatever lay beyond, then hauled themselves the final few feet.

What they looked down on was a scene of horror.

A tribe of nomadic Berbers had been massacred. Men, women, children, camels — every living thing had been butchered, and their body parts strewn across the encampment. The ropes on the tents had been cut so that the awnings fluttered wildly in the wind. Pots had been smashed and pans scattered in all directions. All the food sacks had been slashed, letting precious grain and rice ooze into the desert.

And everything was covered in a blanket of hungry flies, determined to suck as much life as they could from all this death.

Daubed in blood across the sand were the words *Coloro Che Resistono.* 'Those Who Resist.'

Imam Sufian cradled his head in his hands and started to weep. Isra closed her eyes, but Cristina forced herself to stare at the atrocity. She owed it to the dead to witness their suffering.

Desert nomads had such incredible knowledge. They understood how to survive in a hostile world, they were the most skilled camel-herders, they could read weather patterns, memorise changing water sources, and they carried the traditions of generations in their songs. Yet all their skill and wisdom counted for nothing against the ruthless swords of the caposquadra and his thugs. Spiro had vented his rage on the first living things he had come across after being humiliated at the trading post. He had killed without mercy and turned the atrocity into a trophy that celebrated his own cruel power.

There were no words that could match the horror of this moment, so Cristina, Isra and Sufian just clung to each other and prayed. They prayed in different languages to different gods because those differences counted for nothing when set against the horror of the slaughter.

Suddenly Cristina broke away. "Why did God allow this?"

"We cannot know the mind of God," Sufian replied.

"He is supposed to be the most powerful force in the universe. Yet He lets this happen?" Cristina pointed to the butchered bodies that lay at the foot of the sand dune.

"That is not God, it is Man," the imam said with unwavering faith.

"What use is philosophy to those dead children?" Cristina exclaimed, fighting back tears. "God gave me reason and intelligence and learning, but if they are powerless to defeat evil, what is the point of them?"

Sufian lowered his gaze. He knew that now was a time for mourning, not argument. "Prayer is all we have."

"Well, it's not enough." Cristina started picking her way down the side of the dune. "We need action, not prayer."

42: GATE

"Even if the Pope doubts my word, he cannot doubt yours." Cristina pointed to a beautiful copy of the Quran perched on the lectern in the tiny mosque. "You are both men of God."

Imam Sufian hesitated. "You know how tense relations are between our religions."

"But you are both People of the Book."

"The Ottomans want to conquer Europe, as you are well aware. And the Pope wants to send the Muslim fleets to the bottom of the sea."

"Yet on this issue, you are both aligned. Pope Julius wants to eradicate this terrible trade in people, and so do you. To raise his hand against the oligarchs, the Pope needs hard evidence, and what could be more powerful than the sworn testimony of an imam?"

Sufian started pacing round the small, circular library, trying to ease his agitation. "You are asking me to leave this place of solitude and learning, to go and confront ruthless men who will sacrifice anyone to satisfy their greed?"

"It is only what I'm asking of myself."

"Then probably we will both die."

Cristina clasped Sufian's hand to stop him pacing. "Imam, I will guarantee your safe passage in Rome."

"Assuming we get there. And what about the people here in the trading post? These men and women need me more than ever. They have just buried those slaughtered families with their own hands. They are frightened; they need good counsel and wise prayer."

"Sufian, the greater victory would be to stop anything like this from ever happening again. If you come with me to Rome, we stand a chance of achieving that."

The imam gazed at all the volumes he had lovingly collected over the years as if he would never see them again. Then his eyes landed on a set of scrolls. "You say the Pope needs hard evidence?"

"My word alone is not enough. I've already tried."

"There are many terrible things about the Hafsid Dynasty, but one of the worst is their obsession with money. This trade in people is illegal, but it is almost certain the Hafsids will be taking a share of the profits."

"How does that help us?"

"Thieves distrust the world. There will be a trail of paper. Records and ledgers to prove that no crooked man is being cheated by the other crooked men."

Cristina's mind started racing ahead. "Yes, yes. The bureaucracy of greed might give us the evidence we need."

"Most likely the Vizier of Tunis will be levying an excise duty on each man who is shipped to Rome."

"And the records will be in Medina?"

"Perhaps the names of ships, numbers of men in each cargo, duty paid, dates of sailing. Maybe more."

"So we find the ledger entries for the *Speranza*, and if Spiro is named, it proves he was responsible for that atrocity."

"Quite."

"But how do we get our hands on those records?"

The imam gave a knowing smile. "I may be in the wilderness now, but there is a brotherhood among imams that never dies. All knowledge in Medina flows through the madrasas. Including government records."

Early the following morning, Imam Sufian locked up his tiny mosque and said a small prayer to keep the building safe in his absence.

"Don't worry," Cristina reassured him. "You'll be back soon enough."

"Will I?"

"And the world will be a better place on your return."

Knowing what was at stake, the traders lent Cristina, Isra and Sufian a small team of camels, gave them generous provisions for the journey, and a guide to prevent them getting lost in the wilderness.

They made swift progress across the desert, largely because this was a much smaller caravan, which meant there was far less time needed to set up and break camp each day. Yet it was a sombre caravan, and they travelled mostly in silence, as the relentless hours of intense heat were still not enough to burn away memories of the appalling massacre.

One night, Cristina and Isra sat by their tent gazing up at the vast starscape.

"How can we bring Alnaaji back to a country where this happens?" Cristina said quietly.

Isra nodded. She had also been thinking about Alnaaji's fate. "That Bedouin tribe could just as easily have been his people."

"Nowhere is safe until we have destroyed this terrible trade. Nowhere."

Their approach to Medina was on the road leading to the Gate of the Lantern, but as they drew close, they saw that a big crowd had built up outside the city walls. Extra guards were positioned at the gates, and every traveller wanting to enter the city was being checked and searched.

"It seems they were expecting us," Sufian said.

"Are those Spiro's men on the gates?"

Isra narrowed her eyes to try and see more clearly. "Could be. They're not wearing uniforms."

"As soon as they stop us, we'll be arrested," Cristina replied. "We should try a different gate."

"They will all be the same," the imam replied. "And if we cannot get into the city, we cannot get our hands on the evidence we need."

"Do you think they have put extra guards on the port as well?" Isra asked.

"Possibly."

"So, we might not even be able to get on a ship back to Rome."

"Negative thinking doesn't help us," Cristina rebuked.

"I'm just being realistic."

"What solution do you propose?" Sufian asked, as he turned his searching gaze on Cristina.

Her eyes locked on the city skyline as she tried to think. "Let's change the dynamics of this fight."

"Meaning?"

"I will hand myself in to the guards."

Sufian looked alarmed.

"I am the one Spiro is after. Once they have arrested me, the gates should return to normal, and you'll be able to get into the city."

"They'll throw you in gaol!" Isra protested.

"I doubt that."

"Or they'll have you executed."

"They wouldn't dare."

"Either way, you'll never see Rome again. It's a stupid idea."

"Isra, nothing's going to happen to me. I'm travelling with the authority of the Pope."

"You think the vizier cares about the Supreme Pontiff?" Sufian interjected.

"The Hafsids won't risk antagonising the Pope. If they harm me, they might find themselves at war with the Vatican."

Isra and Sufian held back in the shadows of a small grove of olive trees, while Cristina strode towards the Gate of the Lantern. They watched as she pushed her way to the front of the queue and deliberately picked an argument with one of the guards. Moments later, alarm whistles rang out, and the guards grabbed Cristina and hauled her inside the city walls.

"Do you really think she'll be safe?" Isra asked anxiously.

"There is a prayer we say in the mosque: 'May God protect and keep the vizier, far away from us.'"

"That doesn't fill me with confidence."

"Yet I believe Cristina knows what she's doing. Look…"

Now that the main suspect was under arrest, all the extra guards were melting away and taking the roadblock with them. A few minutes later, people were once again moving freely in and out of Medina. Isra and Sufian joined the crowd and slipped through the gate undetected.

43: MADRASA

Isra and Sufian made their way through crowded streets and bustling souqs until they arrived at the Amber Mosque, where the imam was one of Sufian's old friends.

"That is a mosque and a half," Isra said, gazing at the huge and beautifully appointed building. The minaret stretched over fifty feet into the sky and was topped with a gilt cone; the huge dome was covered in glazed blue roof tiles which glinted in the sun, and the courtyard echoed with the splash of fountains.

"You could fit my little mosque into one corner of the prayer hall," Sufian said with amusement.

"Your friend must be much better at politics than you."

"Indeed. But success is not the question. Happiness is."

They heard sandals slapping across the courtyard. "Sufian? Is that you?" A burly man was hurrying towards them. He had a neatly trimmed beard, and a crocheted taqiyah perched on his shiny bald head.

"The prodigal son returns, but not for long," Sufian laughed.

"Welcome, welcome!" The two men embraced each other warmly. "It's so good to see you!"

"Imam Nafurat, this is Isra."

"Ah. Your wife?"

"No!" Isra exclaimed.

"No, no. Not at all," Sufian added.

Nafurat was taken aback by the vehemence of their denials. "There is nothing wrong with taking a wife. Our beloved Prophet, Peace Be Upon Him, had eleven wives."

"I'm not sure how much peace he would have got with eleven wives," Isra quipped.

Nafurat hesitated — was the woman blaspheming?

But Sufian roared with laughter until Nafurat joined in. "I like her!"

"Brother, I have come because I need your help."

"My door is always open to you."

"It is urgent, but it needs discretion."

"Come, come." Nafurat ushered them across the courtyard. "You are safe here. Under my protection, nothing can harm you."

Imam Nafurat led them both into his private study and prepared a large pot of jasmine tea, while Sufian gave a full account of Spiro, the massacre, and the hunt for records that would finally bring the man to justice. Nafurat listened with grave intensity, then took a sheet of paper from his desk, dipped a quill into the silver inkpot, and started writing a letter. "This situation cannot be allowed to continue."

Sufian smiled with relief. "I knew you would understand. You have much integrity."

"Not as much as you, brother. The difference between us is that I know when to keep my mouth shut." He folded the letter, then took a candle and started melting sealing wax over the fold. "These records that you seek, they are held in Madrasa al-Shamma'iya. The oldest madrasa in the city." He pressed his signet ring into the hot wax, then wrote a name on the front of the letter. "One of their scholars owes me a favour. He can be trusted." Nafurat handed the letter to Isra. "Take this to Madrasa al-Shamma'iya. Say you need to give it to the man named on the front. Do not hand it to anyone else, you understand? Only him."

Isra took the letter and looked at the Arabic script on the front.

"He will get you the documents you need," Nafurat promised.

"I will take the letter," Sufian said. "It's best if Isra stays here, under the protection of the mosque."

Nafurat looked askance. "Is that wise, brother?"

"Isra is a stranger in this city."

"Precisely. Unlike you. Which means she has no enemies here."

"Enemies?" Sufian sounded hurt. "Who are we talking about?"

"You left this city under a cloud, remember? Not everyone is as understanding as me."

"If I have enemies, then I need to make peace with them before I journey back to the desert."

"Very well, Sufian. But first she must deliver that." He pointed to the letter in Isra's hand. "Once she and her friend are safely out of Tunis, you can start your mission of reconciliation."

Isra knew exactly how to move through a city without attracting attention: head covered with a scarf, eyes down, route memorised. The trick was to walk briskly, as if you were a local who knew exactly where you were going.

She arrived at the madrasa without incident and gave the letter to the porter sitting behind a grand mahogany desk in the entrance hall. He gave Isra a strange look, shook his head and handed the letter back.

"I need to give this to him." Isra pointed to the name on the front of the letter. "It's important."

The porter didn't understand what she was saying and answered in a torrent of Arabic.

"Please! It's really important."

The porter gestured for her to calm down, then spoke to a young boy sitting in the corner, who immediately disappeared up a stone staircase. A few minutes later, a distinguished-looking man appeared and took the letter from her hands. He looked at the name written on the front and shook his head.

"What is the problem?" Isra was getting exasperated.

The man explained in Arabic, using hand gestures to try and clarify what he was saying, but it was no use.

Suddenly Isra had an idea. "*Latine loqueris?*"

The scholar's eyes lit up. "*Sane faciam.*"

Pleased that her Latin lessons had finally come in handy, Isra dug through her memory and explained what she was trying to do.

The scholar replied slowly, using simple sentences. At first Isra thought she had misunderstood, but the man repeated himself. "*Hic est mortuus.*"

"*Mortuus?*"

"*Et mortuus est annum.*"

Isra shook her head in disbelief. "*Quod est impossibile.*"

"*Hic est mortuus.*" Gently the scholar put the letter back in Isra's hands with an apology. "*Doleo.*"

Isra staggered out of the madrasa, utterly baffled. Did Nafurat not know that his friend had been dead for over a year? Surely that was impossible. Could there be two men with the same name?

A voice rang out from a minaret, startling Isra, but it was just the call to prayer. A few moments later, the city was filled with competing mosques, each summoning the faithful in their own way, but now the noise put Isra on edge. With a rising sense of dread, she ran through the streets, but just as she turned the final corner, she froze. At the far end of the street, she saw Imam Nafurat leading a troop of guards towards his mosque.

He swung open the gates and beckoned them inside. The guards hurried into the courtyard, swords drawn, while Nafurat hung back in the shadows.

A few moments later, the guards reappeared, dragging Sufian with them. His hands had been manacled and there was blood running down his face, yet despite everything, the imam remained calm.

Only when the guards had vanished with their prisoner did Nafurat emerge from his hiding place. Furtively, he looked up and down the street to see if anybody had been watching, brushed away the spots of fresh blood on the pavement with his foot, then entered his mosque and closed the gates behind him.

Imam Nafurat had betrayed them to the authorities — the same authorities who were holding Cristina prisoner.

44: AUTHORITY

Cristina crouched in the cell, head resting in her hands, waiting for the sound of the guards' footsteps.

But they didn't come.

Hours passed. Through the stone walls, she heard prisoners shuffling idly in adjacent cells. She heard the chirrup of a sparrow that had found its way into these basement dungeons and couldn't find its way out again. But she didn't hear the clink of keys or the brisk footsteps of authority. It was as if anyone incarcerated in these dungeons was immediately forgotten.

Cristina looked at the tiny window positioned high up in the wall that let in a trickle of light. She glanced at the jug of water in one corner of her cell, and the bowl for relieving herself in the opposite corner. At some point they would feed the prisoners, and she would have to seize that moment. She would remind the guards that she was in Tunis on the Pope's orders, and demand to be treated with the respect due to a visiting diplomat. The problem was, she had already said that when she was arrested, and no-one seemed to be listening.

Cristina watched the tiny puddle of sunlight creep across the far wall as the afternoon waned. Then, just as the remnants of her confidence were draining away, the gates at the far end of the corridor were unbolted and footsteps hurried closer. The door to her cell burst open and three guards stormed in. Cristina tried to get to her feet but she wasn't quick enough, and the guards hauled her from the cell, feet dragging on the rough stone floor.

"Wait! Wait!" she pleaded, but they weren't interested.

The guards dragged her stumbling down the long corridor. They paused at the bottom of some steps, but just as Cristina regained her balance, a muslin sack was pulled over her head.

"No! Please don't!"

The guards gripped her arms and hauled her up the steps, then veered right along another corridor. Blindfolded and outpaced, it was impossible for Cristina to keep up; all she could do was submit to what she couldn't control.

Eventually she felt the floor under her feet change to a polished surface; they must have reached the formal part of the palace. Moments later she was thrown down and the sack was pulled from her head.

Cristina blinked as her eyes struggled to adjust to the light in this gleaming audience chamber. She looked up and saw the Vizier of Tunis sitting on an ebony throne perched on a dais. His dress was simple: a blue tunic with matching shalwars, because this was a man who didn't need extravagant robes to remind everyone of his position. He exuded power.

"You asked for an audience; now you have it. When it is over, you may wish you had never asked." The vizier spoke fluent Italian, albeit with a thick accent. Cristina realised he must have spent many hours negotiating with merchants and diplomats from across the Mediterranean.

She glanced around the hall — it was laid out in a semi-circle, with marble pillars at regular intervals. In front of every pillar was a guard armed with two glinting swords. The only way Cristina was going to get out of this room was by talking.

So she began.

In a calm, clear voice, she told the vizier about the cruel trade in human souls that she had witnessed. She told him of the agonising deaths of the men and boys on the *Speranza*, and the tortured lives of the workers enslaved in the travertine quarry. She told him of how Berber men were tricked and trafficked, and how any resistance was met with violent revenge.

"Excellency, you have been deceived by the very men you have trusted. You welcomed Orsini and Spiro into your country as merchants, and I know you believe that trade will benefit your people and enrich your land. But these Italians are stealing your young men; they are robbing your country of its strength and its future. I believe you are a ruler who cares for his people; that is why I have surrendered myself to your mercy. If I can prove that Orsini and Spiro committed these crimes, Pope Julius will take action, and justice will be done."

The vizier considered everything he had heard, then stroked his chin with his right hand. "Interesting."

He beckoned one of his servants and whispered some instructions. The servant hurried to the edge of the chamber and opened a secret door that had been disguised to look like a decorated panel. Cristina was astonished to see Duke Giulio Orsini and Caposquadra Spiro step out from the gloom.

"These are the men you speak of?" the vizier asked.

"Yes," Cristina replied, recovering her composure. "They have been abusing your hospitality and your trust."

"Indeed?" The vizier turned his stern gaze on Orsini and Spiro. "You have heard the accusations against you. Do you have anything to say?"

Orsini bowed low. "As you know, Excellency, I was with you here in the medina the whole time. I have no knowledge of what happened in the desert." He took a half-step away from Spiro, as if trying to distance himself from any taint of guilt.

"Excellency, we were attacked in the desert," Spiro said quickly. "It was a violent and unprovoked attack by bandits disguised as Bedouin."

"That is a lie!" Cristina exclaimed.

"My men fought bravely, and only just escaped with their lives."

"I saw the bodies! You butchered women and children!"

Spiro ignored her and focussed solely on the vizier. "Excellency, I believe this woman travelled into the desert with the sole aim of stirring up insurrection. She is a danger to the peace and prosperity of your nation."

The vizier said nothing. He let the silence drag on, waiting to see who would crack under its pressure.

Finally, Orsini pointed an accusing finger at Cristina. "Excellency, how much gold has this woman put into your treasury?"

"The real treasure of any country is its people," Cristina interrupted. "And I am trying to protect them from the rapacious appetites of these men."

"By my calculations, we have gifted Your Excellency a thousand ducats this year alone."

"Really?" The vizier beckoned to one of his servants. Moments later, a clerk appeared with a ledger and offered it to the vizier, who ran his eyes down the columns of figures. "Slightly under, I believe. But close enough." He waved the ledger away and looked at Cristina. "Can you outbid Orsini?"

Cristina shook her head. "Excellency, this is not about money, it is about truth."

"No. It's about power."

"Truth is power."

"Wrong again. Money is power."

Cristina could feel everything slipping away from her. These men only seemed to understand gold. But she had one last card to play. "I have a witness. And he has given us hard evidence of the crimes committed by Orsini and Spiro. When this evidence is laid before the Pope, he will bring everyone responsible for this evil trade to justice. When that happens, Excellency, do you not wish to be on the right side of history?"

The vizier's brow creased into a frown. "When you say 'witness', do you mean the imam?"

Cristina felt her breath catch. "There are many imams in Ifriqiya. To which do you refer?"

"Bring him in!" the vizier commanded.

The same door through which Cristina had been brought just minutes earlier swung open, and two guards dragged a man into the chamber. His feet didn't make any attempt to keep up; they just trailed on the polished marble floor. And in his wake, he left a trail of blood.

The guards dumped the body in the centre of the room and turned it over with their feet so that everyone could see the bloodied face. It was Imam Sufian, beaten to a lifeless pulp.

"Please, no…" Cristina felt sick. She had promised Sufian that she would protect him; she had persuaded him to give up his life of contemplation and help her change the world. Now blood oozed from his body and pooled on the beautiful marble floor.

She looked at the vizier, Orsini and Spiro through her tears. If these men would kill an imam in their frenzy of greed, was there any authority in the world that could control them?

Orsini seemed chillingly untroubled by the corpse. "It appears you have no evidence after all, Signorina Falchoni, just wild accusations. The Holy Father must be getting tired of your hysteria."

Cristina looked accusingly at the vizier. "So, the very rulers who should be protecting their people are selling them out for gold."

"Do not lecture me!" Anger tensed the vizier's face. "I have seen the hypocrisy of Europeans. Do you really care for the people of this land, or are we only of interest when it suits your purpose? When Mahdia was destroyed by an earthquake, did you send soldiers to dig my people out from under the rubble? When our crops failed, did you send galleys laden with grain? You did not. So do not interfere now."

The vizier snapped his fingers. Two guards strode over to Cristina, grabbed her arms and hauled her to her feet. "Leave. Never return. And consider yourself lucky to still be alive."

The guards bundled Cristina towards a set of doors leading out of the chamber. As she went, she turned and glared at Orsini and Spiro. "You have not won! You have not."

"Oh, I think we have," Orsini replied.

"*Ciao bella!*" Spiro smiled and offered a little wave.

45: PATERNOSTERS

The moment the merchant galley docked in Civitavecchia, the two women got to work. While Isra made her way back to the centre of Rome to open up the house and restock the larders, Cristina went straight to the Vatican to lobby Pope Julius. But the urgency of her mission slammed into a stone wall of papal resistance.

"Where is the evidence?" the Holy Father demanded.

"Lying dead in Tunis!" Cristina replied. "Butchered in the vizier's palace. And hacked to death in the middle of the desert."

"Show some respect to the Holy Father!" Domenico whispered. "He is not the enemy."

"Forgive me," Cristina said with a bow to Julius. "But I fear Orsini and Spiro will stop at nothing to protect their abhorrent trade."

"I have already warned the dynasties," Julius said. "They have read the papal edicts forbidding the use of slave labour. They know the consequences if they disobey me."

"Holy Father, the oligarchs are making so much money from trafficking cheap labour, I fear they are willing to take that risk."

"They would gamble with God?" Pope Julius looked askance. "They would put their immortal souls at risk of damnation?"

"They will take a tiny fraction of their vast profits and build sombre chapels where pious monks can pray for their souls for a thousand years. The oligarchs think it's a small price to pay for a life lived with all the indulgences of extreme wealth."

Pope Julius slid the red velvet camauro from his head and scratched his scalp with long, bony fingers. "Why do you refuse to acknowledge the dilemma I face? A pope should never compromise with sin, but if I make accusations against the oligarchs without incontrovertible evidence, it will unite them against me, they will down tools, and St Peter's will never be finished. Moral absolutism will lead to the failure of the greatest Christian monument in the world."

"But how can St Peter's be a great monument if every stone is tarnished with the blood of slavery?"

"Does that stop us admiring the Great Pyramid of Giza? Or the Colosseum at the heart of our own city?"

"They are not Christian buildings, Holy Father. This time, the guilt will be yours."

"How dare you?"

"Forgive me —"

"I am not the one wielding the whip!"

"Holy Father, to be guilty is not just about committing evil acts. Averting our gaze to avoid confronting evil makes us just as guilty as the perpetrators. We can be guilty even though our hands are clean."

"I will not be judged by you!" Pope Julius thundered, his hands trembling. "You dare to come in here and lecture God's anointed voice on Earth? You are precisely the sort of arrogant woman who the Inquisition is tasked with humbling."

Cristina sank to her knees and bowed her head so low her fringe touched the marble floor. "Forgive me, I beg you, Holy Father. I am exhausted from the long journey. I meant no offence."

Julius drew a breath and looked at Cristina's folded body. He knew this show of humility was just theatre for his benefit, but the truth was, this woman had been a valuable servant of the

Vatican for many years, and it was her very passion that made her so effective. Julius slid the camauro back onto his head and adjusted it. "There is a simple, hard fact of the universe: we cannot build a great basilica with paternosters alone. Gold is needed. And that means compromise."

Domenico gripped Cristina's arm firmly as he hurried her down the corridor leading from the papal apartments. They had been lucky to get out of the room unscathed, and he didn't want his sister bursting back in with another idea.

"I must say, Cristina, I'm impressed by how you continually find new ways to insult the Pope."

She shrugged. "A philosophical argument is never insulting. Even if it gets heated."

"You called the Holy Father a sinner with blood on his hands."

"Only theoretically. But he also has the power to forgive himself, which lets him off the hook."

"Cristina, perhaps it's time to think about returning to the convent for a while?"

She glared at Domenico. "If you think I'm giving up on this case, you really don't know me at all."

"But those diaries won't write themselves, will they?"

"I need evidence to bring down Orsini and Spiro. And I will not find that in the House of Eternal Grace." Cristina shook her arm free of her brother's grip and continued striding towards the doors.

They emerged from the Vatican into the sound and fury of the construction site. Domenico wanted to pause and see how close the builders were to completing the first barrel vault linking the westerly piers, but knowing what she did about the human cost of this basilica, Cristina couldn't bear to look at it.

"What has got into the Pope since I went away? First he sends me to investigate, now he finds me embarrassing."

"I think the oligarchs are tightening their grip on him."

Cristina walked briskly through the tangle of alleys heading down towards the river. "He needs to flex his muscles. I mean, he holds the keys to Heaven, they're on his coat of arms. Why should he be wary of a few corrupt aristocrats?"

"Because they control this city. And right now, we live here, not in Heaven."

"Short-term thinking, Domenico."

"We've had the same struggle investigating Paolo's murder. Every lead has hit a dead end. Witnesses who could be useful mysteriously vanish. Suddenly no-one knows anything."

Cristina knew the entire investigation was teetering on the verge of collapse. "If an Apostolic Guard can be murdered with impunity, none of us are safe."

"I'm afraid the oligarchs know our investigations threaten their lucrative contracts. And God help the man — or woman — who gets between aristocrats and their wealth."

46: FAMILY

Tomasso opened the door of his lodgings and for a moment was too overwhelmed to speak. He gazed at Cristina and Isra, barely able to believe they looked so well. Their skin had turned nut-brown, while their eyebrows and hair were flecked with blonde highlights from the intense sunlight. They looked dusty from the voyage, but they had no wounds or scars, no bandages, and both of them were smiling.

"You're alive," he whispered.

"Of course," Cristina replied. "Why wouldn't we be?"

"Because…" Tomasso's mouth momentarily resembled that of a goldfish. "Ifriqiya … the Sahara…"

"Do you really have so little faith in us?"

Before he could answer there was a yelp of excitement from inside the apartment, followed by the sound of running feet as Alnaaji swerved past Tomasso and threw his arms around both women. Isra hugged the boy tightly. "We missed you so much!"

Cristina kissed the top of his head. "It's so good to see you again!"

Alnaaji tried to talk, but he was too overjoyed to say anything, so he just clung to the women. They crouched in a huddle for a while, holding each other tightly, immersed in the happiness and tears of reunion.

Finally, Cristina looked up at Tomasso and whispered, "Thank you for taking care of him."

"No, no. It was a pleasure."

"And he looks so well."

"Why wouldn't he?"

"Well … you know…"

"Do you really have so little faith in me?"

Cristina laughed. "*Touché*, Tomasso."

He ruffled the boy's hair. "We had a good time, didn't we?"

Alnaaji nodded, though his head was still buried in Isra's skirts.

Predictably, the landlady didn't share in their joy. "What is all that noise about?" she complained from somewhere on the floor above.

"Sorry, Padrona!" Tomasso called up.

"You know the rules about women in the house!"

"It's just my family," Tomasso lied, as he ushered everyone inside and shut the door behind them.

Alnaaji danced the women towards the chairs that were set in the middle of the room, where Isra produced a gift that had been carefully wrapped in a silk cloth. "This is for you. A present, from us."

The boy's eyes widened as he took the bundle. "A present?"

"Something from home."

Alnaaji unwrapped the cloth to reveal a conical wooden instrument about a foot long. "A mizmar!"

"We saw people charming cobras with them in the souq," Cristina said.

"What do you say?" Tomasso prompted.

"Thank you! Thank you!" Alnaaji hurried round the room, hugging each of the adults in turn.

"Do you know how to play it?" Cristina asked.

"I have seen old men play." Alnaaji studied the instrument carefully. The dark wood was inlaid with traditional patterns. It had a dozen fingerholes running down the shaft, and a feathery reed projecting from one end. "But before we play, we must put water on here. See?" He pointed to the reed.

"Come on then." Isra took the boy's hand and led him to the kitchen.

Left alone, Tomasso turned to Cristina. "What happened out there? Did you find the evidence we need?"

Cristina shook her head. "They outmanoeuvred us. Again. All we found was death and corruption."

"So, what now?"

"Now I'm going to go home and have a hot bath and a good night's sleep. Then tomorrow, we'll have to start again."

"Sounds like a plan," Tomasso said with a nod.

As Cristina's eyes wandered around the room, she started to smile.

"What?" Tomasso said defensively.

"Nothing."

"Tell me."

"There's been quite a change here."

"Has there?"

"Everything seems strangely tidy, Tomasso."

There were no bottles of wine waiting to be drunk or dirty dishes on the table. Cushions were on the seats, and there were even a few ornaments lined up on the shelf. Tomasso had turned his rooms into a home.

He shrugged. "I hadn't noticed."

Cristina studied him. "Are you blushing, Tomasso?"

"No!" He bent down to straighten one of his newly acquired rugs.

"I think parenthood suits you," Cristina mused.

Before he could reply, there was a loud honk from the kitchen that sounded like a duck being squashed, followed by howls of laughter.

Alnaaji hurried back into the room, honking on the mizmar. "I love it!" he declared.

"But does it actually play a tune?" Tomasso asked.

"Of course!" Alnaaji composed himself and held the instrument high, just like he'd seen the street musicians do back home. Then he squeezed his breath between the reeds and produced a long, haunting note that momentarily transported them back to North Africa.

As the note trailed off, there was a loud banging on the ceiling. "I SAID QUIET!"

"Yes, Padrona!"

"Maybe it's just as well he's leaving," Isra said as she picked up the boy's leather bag and started packing all his clothes.

"There's no rush, is there?" Tomasso asked. "We could make some supper."

"Honestly, I think I would fall asleep at the table," Cristina replied. "I'm that tired."

"Well, we kept your clock going, didn't we, Alnaaji?" said Tomasso.

But the boy was too busy squeezing notes out of the mizmar to reply.

The three of them made their way back to the house on Piazza Navona in a joyful procession. Alnaaji regaled Cristina and Isra with stories of his adventures with Tomasso, occasionally breaking off to startle passers-by with some raucous notes from the mizmar. Only when they had all eaten supper did the boy bring himself to ask what they had done in Ifriqiya. "Did you find my family? Are they safe?"

Cristina didn't lie, but she was economical with the truth, and concentrated on providing colourful details about the towns and desert that might prompt fond memories for the boy.

"But is it safe?" he repeated when she had finished.

Cristina clasped his hand. "Be patient. Just a little longer."

Alnaaji nodded. "Very well. I be patient."

But as Isra looked from Alnaaji to Cristina, she wondered whether the boy was starting to change his mind about where home really was.

The family reunion did not last long.

Domenico stormed into the house in the middle of the night with the ominous news that their father had suffered another stroke, and their mother had sent word urging them to return to the family estates in Frascati without delay. Her brother had brought two horses, saddled and provisioned for the journey; all Cristina had to do was throw on some riding clothes.

Instructions had been sent ahead to the guards on the Porta Tiburtina, and the gates were already open when the siblings arrived. As they galloped through the ancient walls and out into the dark countryside, Cristina clung to the thought that her father had suffered apoplexy attacks before, and although weakened, he had survived. There was no reason it should be different this time.

But there was something alarming about the urgency of Domenico's manner. He'd always had a good understanding of how to pace a horse, but now he urged it on relentlessly. All that seemed to matter was getting to Frascati as quickly as possible.

Did Domenico know more than he was saying?

Was her father dying?

The strangeness of the moonlit landscape added to Cristina's sense of unease. They passed no other people on the road — which was just as well, for travellers at this hour were invariably looking for trouble — but the fields they rode past were alive with strange shadows darting furtively between bushes. Owls and nighthawks circled above the olive groves, terrorising the mice, and the howl of wolves echoed around the valleys as rival packs assembled to slaughter unsuspecting sheep. In these night hours, Cristina felt as if she was a stranger in the very landscape she had grown up in.

Suddenly she had the feeling that God was mocking her. He had led her to the travertine quarries to show her cruelty, then denied her the means of stopping it. He had guided her to Ifriqiya and made her witness the bloody barbarism of men, then betrayed her when she came back to Rome to demand justice. Now He was driving her through the dark side of His Creation, where nocturnal beasts stalked the land. And what was waiting for her at the end of this desperate journey? Was God watching over her father, or had he turned his back on this family altogether?

They glimpsed the outline of the villa just as dawn was flickering in the sky. Two stablehands were already waiting in the courtyard, and as Cristina and Domenico galloped up the tree-lined approach, they ran forward to take the reins and lead the horses straight to water.

The siblings hurried through the corridors towards their parents' rooms; as they entered, they saw their mother on her knees beside the bed, rosary beads clasped in her hands as she prayed for divine intervention.

Cristina moved to the opposite side of the bed and held her father's hand. It felt clammy, and didn't respond to her touch.

"It's me, Father — Cristina," she whispered.

There was a slight flicker of movement on her father's forehead. Did he recognise her voice? Did he know she was here? His mouth was open, his cheeks hollowed out, and his breathing was heavy and uneven.

"When did it happen?" Domenico whispered to his mother.

"After lunch," she said, trying to swallow her tears. "He went down at the table, and that was it."

"Has he had the last rites?"

His mother nodded and buried her head in her hands.

Domenico held her tightly, but Cristina's gaze was locked on her father's face, willing him to open his eyes, to sit up and make one of his stupid jokes.

But the man had moved to a different place.

She leant forward and gently stroked his hair, hoping that touch might still convey how much she loved him.

And then his body tensed, and he drew one very deep breath, summoning all the energy he had left. He exhaled, long and steady and slow … and then there was nothing.

A strange peace descended on the room as the spirit of Cristina's beloved father slipped away. The lifelessness of the body left behind was absolute.

All the tension in Cristina's own body broke. She lowered her head onto her father's rapidly cooling hand, and she wept.

47: INHERITANCE

Cristina was numb. In the hours following her father's passing she felt disconnected from herself, like a bystander watching the rituals of death unfold.

Two priests arrived early in the morning, breathless from their journey up the hill, and lit candles around the corpse to mark the start of the vigil. The head housekeeper, who had been with the family for as long as anyone could remember, washed the body and dressed it in formal clothes ready for the funeral. In whispered discussions, the priests made arrangements for the mourning procession and interment in the family vault. Then all at once the rush of activity subsided, and Cristina and Domenico found themselves alone with their mother.

They sat in silence around the fireplace in their late father's study. No-one knew what to say. What could anyone say? Each of them needed time to adjust to this new reality. Surprisingly, it was Cristina's mother who broke the silence. "Your father always said that business abhors a vacuum. He would want us to honour that."

Cristina looked at her mother in disbelief. "Do you really want to talk about the family business today?"

"We all know that difficult decisions need to be made."

Cristina and Domenico glanced at each other. They understood precisely how difficult this was going to be, for they had spent many evenings in Rome discussing the problem. As the only son, Domenico was now expected to give up his career in the Vatican and return to Frascati to run the family business and estates. In truth, that was the very last thing he wanted, but how could he tell his mother without breaking her heart?

Cristina felt too fragile to have this argument now. "Perhaps we should rest for a couple of days," she said. "After the funeral, there will be plenty of time to discuss the future."

"But that is not what your father wanted." Her mother was resolute. "Nurturing the business was his life's work, and now it is ours."

She looked expectantly at Domenico, whose hands were fidgeting.

"The thing is…" he began. "I'm not really…" He trailed off, unable to say the words.

"Domenico, I am your mother. I have known you since you drew your first breath. Do you think I cannot read what's in your heart?"

Domenico looked up. He had expected to see anger in his mother's face, but mercifully there was none. "Then you know?"

"Of course. And so did your father."

"Was he angry with me?"

His mother shook her head. "He knew you had found your true vocation, and what more can a father want for his son? If your heart is in Rome with the Apostolic Guard, then you are not the right person to run the Falchoni estates."

Cristina saw the relief on her brother's face. He crossed the room and hugged his mother. "Thank you."

But his relief triggered anxiety for Cristina. Did this mean the burden was going to fall on her? Was she now expected to give up everything she had built in Rome and retreat to the provinces? What of her library, and her studies? What of the diaries she was writing? But her mother had read the panic in Cristina's eyes. "Don't worry, the last thing our velvet needs is a philosopher in charge. In business, decisions need to be made, not analysed."

"Then who *is* going to take over?" Cristina asked.

Her mother stood up and strode to the fireplace. For a few moments she studied the glowing embers, then turned to face her children. "I loved your father. He was everything to me. Yet it is also true that I have spent the last forty years living in his shadow."

Domenico frowned. "You mean, under his protection?"

"Yes. But also in his shadow. There have been many occasions, especially recently, since his health started to decline, when I believed different decisions should have been taken."

"About the family, or the business?" Cristina asked.

"Both." Domenico and Cristina exchanged a wary glance, wondering how different their lives might have been had their mother been in charge all along. "The best way to find solace in my grief is to put my ideas into action," she continued. "From now on, I will be running the Falchoni textile business and estates."

Domenico's relief at not being burdened was suddenly forgotten. "I cannot see how that is going to work. What does it say in father's will? And who is going to accept a woman being in charge of so much?"

"Ask Queen Isabella of Spain," Cristina quipped.

"We are not in Spain!"

"You're sounding very defensive, Domenico."

"The reality is that the world simply will not accept our mother being head of the family business."

"Then the world will have to change."

"With all due respect, Cristina, what do you know about the real world?"

She refused to take the bait. "I think the business, the estates and the family will thrive under mother's leadership."

"But it's not you she has to convince, Cristina. It's the ordinary workers. Will they accept a woman being in charge?"

"They won't have a choice. This is a family business, and it always will be. Now the matriarch is taking control." Cristina looked at her mother. "You have my full support. And my admiration."

Her mother nodded. "Thank you, Cristina. But do not think this lets you off the hook."

"What do you mean?"

"A family business cannot survive without a new generation to take on the challenge. Neither of you are interested in textiles, and I have accepted that and indulged it. But I need grandchildren." Her stern gaze darted between Domenico and Cristina. "As that task is beyond me, at least one of you must show their commitment to this family by providing for its continuation."

An awkward silence followed this pronouncement. At forty-one, there were plenty of options still open to Domenico; but at thirty-six, time was running out for Cristina. If she didn't have children soon, they would never come, and right now she didn't even have a husband. It meant the pressure from her mother would only increase. "I have an idea," Cristina said, steering the conversation back to safer ground. "Domenico, you questioned the loyalty of the workforce to our mother." She stood up and pulled on her jacket. "I am going to visit the foreman straight away and discuss the matter with him. Then we'll know for sure, and our minds can be at rest." Cristina strode out of the study before her mother could say another word.

48: VELVET

The Falchoni workshops were housed in a series of interlinked stone barns at the bottom of the valley, where a running brook supplied plenty of water for washing and dyeing. As Cristina hauled open the great wooden doors of the main building, the sound of clattering treadle looms transported her back to her childhood … only now the workshop was twice the size she remembered.

Twenty large-frame double looms were set at regular intervals in the barn, each machine tended by a team of women who worked the treadles with their feet, hauled on battens to push the weft into place, fed fresh thread into the platen, and made sure that the thousands of strands of silk never tangled under the shuttle. These weavers had a meticulous eye for detail, and the moment any one of them spotted a blemish, they would ring a handbell, and the peddling would stop until the error had been corrected.

Famously, Falchoni velvet was made from Syrian silk, transported across the Ottoman Empire and traded through Venice. Every week, fresh cartloads of thread arrived on enormous reels that were hauled into the warehouse at the far end of the complex. Teams of men would then put the thread through various stages of dyeing, winding and bundling before it arrived in the weaving room. After passing through the looms, more teams of women would supervise the finishing, cutting and rolling of the fabric. It was an incredible operation, a precision dance of people and machines that turned humble silk thread into the most opulent velvets that had ever adorned the backs of kings and cardinals.

But watching it now gave Cristina a pang of guilt — her father was so proud of his success in growing the business, and she realised how much it must have hurt him that neither of his children showed the slightest interest. The wealth that was produced in these workshops gave Cristina and Domenico freedom and opportunity, yet they had never wanted to roll up their sleeves and immerse themselves in the mechanics. And now it was too late to apologise.

"Signorina Falchoni, my deepest condolences."

Cristina turned and saw a slight man with a kind face walking towards her. He extended his hand. "Paglio. I'm the foreman here."

"You don't need to introduce yourself. I remember you, Signor Paglio." Cristina shook his hand warmly.

The man gave an apologetic smile. "It's been so long since I saw you. And you've been away."

"How could I forget? I used to play in these workshops with your daughter. You would tell us off, I remember!"

"Which is why you still have ten fingers."

"Thank you for looking after us."

"I'm so sorry about your father. We all are," he said, indicating the workshop. "We would have shut the factory down as a mark of respect, but this order must be completed, and you know what your father was like about deadlines."

Cristina picked up a sample of the material — it was a particularly luxurious type of double velvet with subtle patterns created using different heights of pile. "Who is it for?"

"The ruler of Siena," Paglio replied. "Not a man to cross, apparently."

"Absolutely. He's a tyrant called Pandolfo Petrucci."

"I'm sure we've clothed worse," the foreman said with a shrug. "And he has paid in advance."

Cristina handed the sample back. "Well, I won't delay you; I just wanted to ask you something."

"Of course." Paglio looked at her expectantly.

"How long were you with my father?"

"Oh." The foreman looked thoughtful, trying to remember. "Well, I was already here when you were born, if that helps."

Cristina looked at the teams of women, all focussed on tending their looms. "So, no-one knows these workers better than you?"

"I'd say not."

"Then, how do you think people would feel if my mother took over running the business? Would they accept her?"

"It'd be a relief, I'd say."

"A relief?"

"Truth be told, your father's powers had been fading for some time."

"And you didn't say anything?"

"It would have been disloyal. I'd never do such a thing."

"So, is my mother already running things?"

"No, no. The padrone wouldn't let her near the business, even when he couldn't cope."

Cristina was puzzled. "So … how did things keep going?"

Paglio shuffled uneasily.

"Don't worry, Signor Paglio, no-one's in trouble. You can tell me."

"Best you come into the office."

The foreman led Cristina up some wooden steps in the corner of the building and into a room that had been built on a platform that overlooked the workshop. He closed the door, then unbuttoned his shirt and took out a heavy key that hung around his neck on a leather cord. He pulled a blanket aside to reveal a strongbox, then methodically slid back the bolts and undid the locks. He opened the lid to reveal a heavy ledger book, along with racks of coin holders neatly stacked with a small fortune in gold and silver.

"About a year ago, your father started making mistakes," Paglio explained. "Orders were left unopened, he was giving loss-making quotes, deliveries were sent out before full payment had been received. I tried to correct him, but you know your father. So, I started tidying things up, quietly." He took out the ledger and opened it for Cristina to inspect. "The padrone thought he was in control, but in truth, the business was run from this office. It's all accounted for, down to the last ducat. I was waiting for your brother to take over, then I would have handed all this to him."

Cristina turned the pages of the ledger, studying the rows and columns that meticulously recorded every transaction. "A whole year of this?" she whispered.

"Your father was a proud man, but he had become lost to himself. I believe he would have approved of what I did."

"As do I." Cristina looked at the gold and silver coins in the strongbox. "Let me pay you for your labours." She reached out to pick up some gold, but Paglio backed away.

"No, no. I don't want anything. I'm paid a wage."

Cristina pointed to the ledger. "But this was above and beyond your work."

"I don't want anything, signorina. It was for the good of the business. And anyway, if you take money from there, the books won't balance."

Cristina didn't know what to say. She had spent so long chasing people who would do anything to acquire wealth, who would lie and cheat and murder, yet here was this man sitting on a small fortune who refused to take a single ducat. Why was the foreman so honest? Had he never been tempted to vanish in the middle of the night with the strongbox? After dedicating years of his life to building the Falchoni fortune, did he not think he deserved a slice of the wealth sitting under his desk?

"It's not my money. It's yours," Paglio said, as if reading Cristina's mind.

"But you created the wealth." Cristina gestured towards the workshop below. "All of you. With your hands and your labour."

"We are the workers. You are the owners."

Paglio spoke without any hint of resentment or irony; he was just stating the obvious. This was the way of the world, and he accepted it. But this made it even more puzzling for Cristina. Why did the foreman accept that his labour should make other people wealthy? Every day for the past year, Paglio had had the chance to make his own family rich, but he had remained loyal — what was holding him back?

The door to the office clattered open, and a woman of Cristina's age entered; she was carrying a wooden template with dozens of small holes cut in an elaborate constellation.

"Father, I need you to look at..." Her voice petered out when she saw Cristina. The two women gazed at each other across a chasm of time.

"Hello, Alba," Cristina said.

The woman nodded respectfully. "Condolences on the loss of your father, Signorina Falchoni."

Cristina was taken aback by her formality. When they had been girls, the two of them were always running amok in the workshops, playing hide and seek amongst the huge silk reels, and painting pictures on the floor using water from the dyeing vats. They had been inseparable ... until Cristina had gone to Rome, nearly twenty years ago.

"How are you?" Cristina stepped forward to give Alba a hug, but the woman backed away.

"Good, thank you, signorina. Married, four children. Busy. You can imagine."

"Yes, yes ... and it's been so long."

An awkward silence descended on the room.

"Could you check this against the thread?" Alba offered the wooden template to her father.

"Give me a minute," he said to Cristina, then accompanied his daughter down the stairs to the looms.

Cristina watched father and daughter through the office window as they bent over one of the weaving looms. It was clear that Alba was a skilled worker, yet still she wore faded clothes and down-at-heel boots. It didn't look as if there was much money left over after feeding four children. Cristina thought of the money she would spend on a single book for her library without even thinking. She and Alba had once been so close, yet now the space between them seemed unbridgeable.

49: VAULT

Nestled in a corner of the rustic cemetery wall, under the shade of a huge oak tree, sat the Falchoni family vault. From the outside it looked like a folly — a miniature church built in the High Gothic style of a north European cathedral. But inside, it housed the bones of the Falchoni dynasty stretching back almost two hundred years.

Cristina approached the building warily and saw that the vault doors had already been unlocked by the stonemasons who had spent the morning preparing for her father's entombment. In her hand she clutched a dozen lilies. She hadn't been here since that terrible day when they had buried her baby brother a quarter of a century earlier.

As she stepped inside, Cristina was embraced by the cool gloom of death. Her ancestors were entombed in neat rows, stacked six high along the left-hand wall, each grave sealed with a stone slab engraved with names and dates. The opposite wall had a similar arrangement, but most of the sealing slabs were blank because these tombs were still awaiting their occupants. Cristina's eyes ran over the wall as she wondered which niche would eventually be her own resting place. Finally, her gaze settled on the niche that had been prepared for her father. She knelt down and placed a single lily in the dark space, then turned her attention to the smallest tomb in the vault, which was set under the stone altar. She ran her fingers over the words carved on the slab:

Aldo Falchoni
1482–1484

Untimely death. Two words that captured the family's inability to accept the passing of their beloved baby.

Cristina arranged the rest of the lilies on the little tomb, then whispered, "Papa is coming to look after you now." She closed her eyes and was about to say a prayer when she heard a noise behind her.

Cristina turned and saw Domenico standing in the doorway to the vault.

"I wonder ... was father thinking about Aldo in those last hours?" he asked.

"Maybe. I know I think about him every day." Cristina stood up and brushed the dust from her knees. "Do you ever wonder what Aldo would have been like if he'd lived? What kind of man he would have grown into? I imagine him as a scholar."

"More like a soldier, I think," Domenico replied.

"Maybe he would have had a career in the Church. Cardinal Aldo has a certain ring to it."

"Or maybe, just maybe, he would have been the son who was actually interested in manufacturing velvet. That would have made Father happy."

Cristina smiled. "It would have made him Papa's favourite for sure."

Domenico bent down and inspected the niche that had been prepared for their father. "Did you speak to the foreman?"

Cristina nodded. "He thinks it's a good idea for Mother to take over. They all do."

Domenico could see worry etched on his sister's face. "But?"

"Time and again the Bible warns us about the folly of wealth, doesn't it? 'The love of money is the root of all evil.' 'It is easier for a camel to pass through the eye of a needle than for a rich person to enter the kingdom of God.' And yet, in the real world, Christ's words count for nothing against the power of money."

Domenico really wasn't in the mood to be lured into one of his sister's philosophical debates. "We should think ourselves lucky that we weren't born into a poor family, or we'd end up out there for all eternity." He gestured towards the uneven rows of pauper graves.

"But that's the point." Cristina sat down on the ledge of the vault doors and gazed at the sunbaked cemetery. "If we had been born into poverty, we would think that we deserved nothing better."

"What's all this about?" Domenico sat down next to his sister. "I hope you're not going to preach a sermon at the funeral."

"There was a box stuffed with gold and silver in Paglio's office."

"What?"

"Papa had been losing his grip on the business for a long time. Paglio saw it, and quietly kept everything running smoothly. Don't worry, all the money is accounted for."

"Paglio is a good foreman. I'm sure Mother will reward him."

"You're missing the point, Domenico. At any time in the last year, Paglio could have stolen enough money to set him and his family up in luxury."

"Until he was hanged."

"He could have fled across the Alps to Switzerland, vanished in Bohemia. He had enough money to put his family beyond the reach of the law, and he could have justified it all with scripture. *We are equally made in God's image.* But he didn't. You know why?"

"Because he's a moral man."

"No. Because deep in his soul, he believes that his place in society is lower than ours. That he is less deserving than us. And the only reason he thinks that is because he was born poor, and we were born rich. Regardless of what the Bible says, his heart tells him that we are more worthy than his own flesh and blood. But in truth, wealth is not based on talent or skill, it is down to luck." She pointed to the rows of silent tombs. "The luck of having the right ancestors."

Domenico felt uncomfortable at the challenge to his status. "Maybe God made us lucky because he favours us."

"You really think he favours us more than Paglio, the most honest man I've ever met? You think he favours me above the foreman's daughter, a skilled weaver and a devoted mother?"

"Cristina, I cannot read the mind of God," Domenico replied testily. "None of us can."

"The mind of God is clear. It's written in the New Testament. 'For the love of money is the root of all evil.' But in the minds of men, money vindicates inequality, and the exhortations of priests are powerless against it."

Domenico stood up and shook his head. "You really do choose your moments."

He started to walk away, but Cristina grabbed his arm. "This is not just philosophy, Domenico. It is the key to finally catching the people-traffickers."

Her brother blinked in the harsh sun, trying to follow the logic.

"This is why we have been unable to outwit Spiro and Orsini. I have been trying to outthink them without truly understanding them. I believed that in their hearts, they knew that one day they would have to account for their actions before God. However dark their desires, I thought their behaviour would still be constrained by some form of morality. But I was wrong. I can see now that Spiro and Orsini believe money is the most powerful force on Earth and in Heaven, and that determines everything they do. There are no moral constraints on their actions; there is just money. So to catch them, I need to think like them. And to think like them, I need to imagine that gold is God. If the *only* thing that matters is money, what would I do?"

"What about mourning?" Domenico asked. "Shouldn't you take time to grieve for our father, rather than rushing back into the investigation?"

"The best way for me to heal is to keep busy. And if I can reexamine all the evidence from the singular perspective that gold is God, I think I can finally solve these terrible crimes and bring Spiro to justice."

"By following the money, rather than the clues?"

"I won't just follow the money; I will *become* the money."

50: CONSORTIA

Cristina sat in the office of the art dealer Ludovico Labirinto and gently dabbed a lace handkerchief to her eyes. With the help of Isra, she had dressed the part of a grieving daughter perfectly: her mourning veil merged with her long black dress, which touched the floor as she walked, making her resemble a floating spectre of death. The effect was so striking, it silenced even Labirinto's glib cynicism.

"I appreciate that you and I have not always seen eye to eye," Cristina confessed, "but the untimely death of my father has given me a new appreciation of the pressures that so many men must manage."

Labirinto nodded. "It is a heavy burden."

"As you know, I have often been scornful of those who devote their lives to the pursuit of money, but this sudden change in my family's circumstances means that I too must focus on financial matters." She pulled her veil aside so that she could lock eyes with the art dealer. "Put simply, if my mother is to enjoy financial security, I must find more innovative ways of investing my father's legacy. And that is why I am here, Signor Labirinto. To ask for help."

Cristina realised the art dealer was trying hard to look sombre, yet there was a sparkle in his eyes that betrayed his enjoyment of this moment.

"Ah, the changeable woman," he mused. "As Catullus wrote, '*In vento et rapida scribere oportet aqua.*' What a woman says might as well be written on the wind or etched on running water."

"I confess, now I can see the wisdom of the poet's words."

"And now also, perhaps, you understand the pressures of providing for a family?"

"Indeed."

"The daily challenges men must rise to as they protect and nurture the next generation?"

"And when one reflects on how rarely we hear men complain about their burden … such forbearance." Cristina was enjoying this, and it was so easy to fluff Labirinto's feathers.

"Welcome to my world, signorina. Or may I call you Cristina?"

"Of course, Ludovico. And if on this matter of financial acuity, you could take me under your protective wing, I would forever be in your debt."

"You have done the right thing coming to see me, Cristina, and your timing is perfect. I have a new shipment of paintings coming from various masters in the Low Countries which will be the perfect vehicle for your investment needs."

Cristina frowned. "I don't think art is going to be suitable."

Labirinto was irked. "Frankly, I had expected more enthusiasm from you. This is a rare opportunity."

"I meant no disrespect. But after the debacle with Visconti, my mother is wary of investing in art. Instead, she was thinking about speculating in some of those new trading routes that are being established."

There was a sharp, disapproving intake of breath from Labirinto.

"I hear there are expeditions being mounted to find the Spice Islands. And what about opening up the sea routes to China?"

"Very risky."

"But only last year Mauritius was discovered. How many more pearls are waiting to be plucked from the ocean?"

"Cristina, Rome's taverns are full of drunkards who have lost everything on such foolish speculations. For every success, there are a hundred disasters."

"But the rewards —"

"Are elusive. Your mother would not thank you for putting your family's money into such reckless speculation."

Cristina fell silent, giving the impression that she had run out of ideas. Then after a suitable pause, she asked, "What about investing closer to home?"

"With one of the Florentine banks?"

Cristina lowered her voice to a whisper. "I hear that fortunes are to be made from the consortia building St Peter's."

Labirinto eyed her warily. "I thought you didn't approve of that sort of thing?"

"As I explained, my family's predicament no longer affords me the luxury of moral judgement."

"You are not a builder, signorina. What could you possibly offer the basilica?"

"Come now, Ludovico, we both know there are men in Rome getting rich from St Peter's without knowing one end of a nail from the other."

Labirinto rocked back on his chair. "We know that, do we?"

"Naturally, in my position I could not get involved in anything illegal. And I cannot be seen to have conflicting interests. But I appreciate that the hunt for high returns is not for the fainthearted."

"What would the Holy Father say if he knew you were dabbling in these waters?"

"The Holy Father will never know, because discretion is paramount. That is why I have come to you, Ludovico. And that is why I am offering you such a generous commission on any investments I make."

Cristina watched as Labirinto's mind danced around the possibility of easy money.

"Nothing less than … a forty per cent commission would be considered generous, would it?"

"Absolutely. And to show my goodwill…" Cristina reached into the folds of her mourning dress, pulled out a purse stuffed with gold and pressed it into Labirinto's hand. "A small gift."

The art dealer loosened the drawstring on the purse and studied the contents. "Very nice." He unlocked the drawer of his desk, secured the purse inside, then beamed an endearing smile. "'And the Lord opened a door of opportunity for me.' Two Corinthians."

The basilica consortia had taken over one of Rome's most eminent gaming houses for 'an evening of contract brokerage'. As Labirinto ushered Cristina inside, she was stunned by the enormous frescoes that covered the walls and ceilings: on the far wall, the gods of classical mythology were playing dice, but as you moved across the room, the gambling turned into a feast, then a full-on orgy; no wonder the ceiling was painted with vivid depictions of the torments of Hell.

The gaming floor itself was crowded with hundreds of people, mostly men, who huddled around repurposed card tables that had been set in three lines running the length of the chamber. Investors moved from table to table, persuading, haggling and arguing; everyone seemed to have been galvanised by a greed-fuelled energy.

"How does this work?" Cristina had to shout to make herself heard above the frenzy. "Where do we begin?"

"These are highly specialised financial instruments," Labirinto replied. "You should spend some time observing before you commit." He pointed to the rows of gaming tables.

"Each consortium has its own table. You and I cannot bid for contracts to build St Peter's itself. Only approved consortia can bid. But it is possible to buy your way into those consortia."

"With a bribe?"

"With an investment." He led her to the nearest table. "So, for example, this consortium is currently bidding for the contract to supply all the rope to the main construction site for the next two years. You can give them money to invest in that bid. If they win the contract, they will get rich, and you will get rich as the profits are shared out. But if they fail to win the contract —"

"I get my money back?"

"No. You lose it. And there's the risk."

Cristina looked worried. "That doesn't sound fair. The consortium keeps my money, win or lose?"

"Because they have invested heavily in putting the bid together. They have sourced raw hemp and paid an option on supplies; they have had to secure capacity in at least six ropemaking factories. They have paid out a lot of money which they will lose if they don't win the contract. The money you invest helps to mitigate their losses."

Cristina frowned. "So, this whole thing is a reckless gamble?"

"But the rewards are extremely high. Where else could you get such a handsome return over several years?"

"What if you keep investing in consortia that fail to win contracts?"

"You need deep pockets to play this game, Cristina. You have to ride out the spells of bad luck, because when you win a contract, it more than compensates. Just this year the Vatican will be spending eighty-seven thousand ducats on St Peter's, so there's a lot of money swilling around Rome."

"But there is no guarantee you'll ever win. You could be ruined."

Labirinto shrugged. "If you can't afford the losses, you shouldn't be in this room."

Slowly, Cristina turned on the spot, soaking in the frenzy of activity. She could never have imagined that her vision of a great Christian monument would only be realised through such ravenous dealings.

"What do you fancy?" Labirinto asked.

"Well … what's here?"

The art dealer consulted a sheet that had been circulated beforehand. "Tonight there's rope, leather buckets, cranes and hoists, removal of donkey dung from the building site, renewal of barges for soil transportation, renewal of barges for stone shipments … all sorts." He offered her the sheet. "See for yourself."

"What are you going for?"

"I've had my eye on a consortium that is bidding for the contract to demolish buildings between the Vatican and the Tiber. Lots of possibilities there."

"I think I'll look around first," Cristina said.

"As you wish. But you need to be quick or you'll miss out on everything." With that, Labirinto hurried to the far end of the gaming room.

Left alone, Cristina could feel the full horror of this place. Fat, middle-aged men sweated and grunted like hogs as they crowded round the consortia's tables. But it wasn't just the lure of profits that galvanised them; the risk of losing also thrilled them. Pitting their wits against fate seemed to make these men feel virile again; perhaps that was why gambling was as old as civilisation itself.

Suddenly a fight broke out at the cement consortium's table — there was only one slot left for investors, but Count Panzutti and the Marquis of Apulia both wanted it.

Encouraged by their friends, the elderly men tried to throw punches at each other, but neither had the strength to land a proper blow, and they ended up tugging at each other's clothes as they collapsed on the floor in a humiliating tangle.

"*Testa di cazzo!*"

"*Vaffanculo!*"

A crowd of jeering aristocrats encircled the men as if they were schoolboys brawling in the playground, and for a few moments everyone seemed to forget about business.

Or nearly everyone.

In a corner of the room, Cristina saw a man crouched on the floor, weeping as he tore a contract into little pieces. She walked over and held out her hand. "Are you all right?"

He recoiled like a wounded animal and looked up at Cristina with bloodshot eyes. "All is lost!" he cried. "Everything! Gone! Everything!"

"Come now. Don't let people see you like this."

The man closed his eyes and uttered a strange, heartbroken wail. Then he slumped forward like the most desperate of beggars. "Lost! Lost! Lost!"

And suddenly Cristina realised where she had seen this desperation before.

51: REDACTIONS

Tomasso unbolted the metal gates that led down to the network of cellars under the Vatican and swung them open.

"These never used to be locked," Cristina said as she plucked a flaming torch from a sconce on the wall and walked towards the steps.

"After the murder of those priests in the shadow of the Sistine Chapel, they put in extra security. Didn't want any more bodies being discovered in the Vatican cellars." Tomasso closed the gates behind them. "Which is why I'd feel much better if we had Domenico's permission to be down here."

Cristina waved his concerns away. "He'll be in Frascati for another couple of days, sorting out notaries and paperwork. But I'm sure he'd approve."

"Right." Tomasso knew she was bluffing, but if things went wrong, it was now squarely on Cristina's shoulders.

They made their way down two flights of stone steps and emerged into a labyrinth of corridors and cellars. Small skylights high in the walls allowed in a trickle of light which puddled at regular intervals on the floor.

"According to the schematic, Building Committee paperwork is archived in the eastern corridor, cellar fifty-seven." Cristina held up the torch to read the numbers etched above one of the brick arches, then led the way deeper into the gloom.

"Didn't you already ask to see these records?" Tomasso said. "I thought they refused."

"The mistake we made was asking to see contracts for the successful bids, but what we're really interested in are the failures."

Tomasso frowned in confusion. "Surely, by definition, a failed contract can't be anything to do with the people-trafficking that is actually happening."

"That was what I assumed. But I was wrong. Last night I saw a proud, respectable man reduced to humiliating desperation because he had lost all his money investing in failed contracts. He had gambled too much and lost everything, including his mind. A few weeks ago, he would have been mortified at the thought of demeaning himself in front of his peers. But financial ruin has cut him adrift from all the bonds that held him in check. Now, imagine if someone offered him a chance to save himself by committing a terrible, barbarous act; I think he would take it." Cristina turned hard right, led them through a bridging tunnel, then turned left into the eastern corridor. "What if destroying the *Speranza* had been someone else's escape from shame and financial ruin?"

"Sacrifice everyone to save yourself?"

"The *Speranza* tragedy smacks of desperation, doesn't it? And desperation starts here, with failed bids." Cristina stopped outside an arched vault and held the torch up to reveal number fifty-seven.

Tomasso peered into the gloom. The space was stacked high with wooden crates, each one stuffed with papers. "This could take weeks."

"We don't need to check every crate." Cristina clipped the burning torch into a sconce on the wall. "Theory: the *Speranza* was abandoned as a desperate act to mitigate losses following a failed contract bid. Which means the bid must have been rejected shortly before the ship was found drifting. Which means we're only interested in crates with paperwork around that date."

Tomasso unsheathed the dagger from his belt and prised the lids off a dozen of the least dusty crates, then he and Cristina started checking the documents inside.

As they searched, Tomasso couldn't resist asking a question that had been burning inside him. "Does he miss me?"

"What?"

"Alnaaji. Does he miss spending time with me?"

Cristina looked at Tomasso, who suddenly felt awkward.

"It doesn't matter. I was just…" Tomasso mumbled.

"No, no. It does matter. And yes, I think he does. He's always telling Isra stories about what the two of you got up to."

Tomasso allowed himself a chuckle. "He's a good boy."

"Nothing in here." Cristina moved to the next crate.

"Did you find out if his family is still alive? His mother?"

"We never made it to his village. That would have been another day's travel across the desert. The massacre changed everything."

"A child belongs with his family, of course. But it will be difficult to say goodbye."

"I know. It will."

They lapsed into silence, their eyes scanning the dates on the documents, their minds haunted by the knowledge that one day Alnaaji would vanish from their lives forever.

Finally, Tomasso pulled out a sheaf of documents that had been bound with a red ribbon and checked the date on the front. "This looks promising." He flicked through the first couple of pages. "It's a bid for the contracts to supply labour to the stone quarries at Tivoli. But it's not from Orsini, it's from Fabrizio Colonna."

Cristina took the papers and studied them. "So, Colonna was trying to muscle in on Orsini's operation, undercut the labour costs, win that contract, then probably make a move on the quarrying itself." She flicked through the pages, picking out details of the bid. "They claim here to be able to source men at two thirds the price. And it sets out details of how they're going to do it. They have chartered the *Speranza* ... secured a deal with the Hafsid rulers."

"It's exactly the same as Orsini's operation."

"But it looks like Colonna was planning on paying fatter bribes and giving virtually nothing to the workers except false promises." She leafed through some more pages and came across a section that had been heavily redacted — entire paragraphs had been blotted out with ink. "What do you think that's about?"

She handed the pages to Tomasso, who held them up to the light to try and see through the blocks of ink. "Do you think the Buildings Committee made these redactions?" he asked.

"Who else could it be?"

"But why would they do that? Why change the bid when you can just reject it?"

"Unless..." Cristina sat down on the crate and tried to shuffle the pieces of the puzzle in her mind. "Unless Colonna's bid was going to win. But politics got in the way. Remember, Orsini and Colonna hate each other. So, what if Orsini bribed the Buildings Committee to reject the rival bid? But to cover their tracks, the committee had to destroy evidence that proved Colonna had the cheaper proposal."

"Hence the redactions."

"But it must have happened very late in the day." Cristina pointed to the paragraph about the *Speranza*. "So late, the ship had already been chartered."

"Wait, let me get this clear. Colonna was so convinced he was going to win, he'd already chartered the ship and collected the first load of workers from North Africa?"

"Then at the last minute, his bid was rejected. But he was left with a shipload of men and a huge loss." Cristina and Tomasso looked at each other in disbelief as the terrible truth dawned on them.

"That would mean the *Speranza* wasn't an accident," Tomasso whispered. "It wasn't negligence, and it wasn't some mysterious plague. It was mass murder. For profit."

52: EXHUME

By the time Domenico arrived with the Vatican's Licence to Exhume, Tomasso and two Apostolic Guards had already started digging up the mass grave.

They were back on the stark clifftop overlooking the Tyrrhenian Sea, only this time there were no prayers, no imam, and no readings from the Quran. Aware of the religious sensitivities, Cristina wanted as few people as possible to know that they were digging up the corpses of Muslims.

She and Domenico watched the men toil in the early morning light. "You'll probably need to cover your faces," Cristina said. "The bodies have been down there for a couple of months."

"We've still got a few feet to go," Tomasso replied, wiping the sweat from his forehead.

Cristina looked up at the sky — billowing dark clouds heralded an incoming storm, but that was better than digging in the heat of the day.

"Are you sure this is absolutely necessary?" Domenico asked.

"The Pope wants evidence —" Cristina patted a leather satchel that was slung around her shoulder — "and these tests will provide it."

"If there's much left to test. I've seen bodies decay on the battlefield. They don't last long."

"This is different." Cristina was adamant. "Burial slows decomposition because blowflies can't lay their eggs on the corpse. And this ground is quite dry, which also helps."

"It still seems a leap of logic to go from reading a failed contract bid to exhuming a mass grave."

"I didn't just read those documents, Domenico. I went through them in detail. A syndicate run by a man called Prospero Filippo and backed by Fabrizio Colonna wanted to copy the slave labour scheme set up by Caposquadra Spiro. The difference is, they were going to slash the cost to the Vatican by over a third, making their bid really tempting."

"How can you cut costs when you've already enslaved the workers?"

"Colonna would give the men minimal payments up front. They would cut the cost of crewing the ship by using newly released convicts, and provisions on board would be slashed to the bone. The only thing that was going to increase was the budget for bribing the Hafsid rulers in Tunis."

"And the Building Committee didn't care about the morality of all this?"

"They're only interested in the bottom line on the ledgers. Keeping the cost of St Peter's down holds them in the Pope's favour. Prospero and Colonna were so confident they were going to steal the contract from Orsini, they chartered the *Speranza* and shipped the first load of workers from Ifriqiya. When Orsini found out, he was furious, because he knew that once he lost the contract for the workers, he risked losing the whole of the quarrying operation. So he bribed the Building Committee to reject Colonna's bid. But that left Colonna and Prospero with a ship full of men still at sea, but no contract from which to recoup their costs."

"Couldn't they have sold the men to Orsini?"

"Not that simple. All the bills for the *Speranza* became due the moment it docked — crew wages, balance of the charter costs, customs duties if they went anywhere near a proper port. And even then, Orsini was more interested in hurting his rival, so he would probably have refused to buy the men even at a knockdown price."

"And if the ship *never* docked, Colonna and Prospero could just walk away from the bills?"

Cristina nodded. "If the journey is never completed, the contracts have not been fulfilled, and payment cannot be enforced. The ruthless logic pits human lives against money, and in a contest like that, money invariably wins."

Suddenly Tomasso called out, "HOLD!"

Everyone stopped digging. Tomasso crouched down and studied the freshly turned earth. He brushed some dirt aside to reveal the folds of a winding sheet. "Cover up!"

Cristina, Domenico and the Apostolic Guards all wrapped scarves around their faces.

"Ready?"

Cristina nodded.

Using his hands, Tomasso gently scooped away enough soil to reveal the full shape of a shrouded corpse. "How many do you need to see?"

"Three, to be certain," Cristina replied.

The other guards set about uncovering two more bodies; when they had done that, Tomasso pulled a knife from his belt and carefully cut the three shrouds open, revealing the dark skin of the victims inside. "They're all yours."

Clutching her leather satchel, Cristina knelt down next to the first corpse and teased back the winding sheet until she found a piece of flesh that was covered with blisters. "You remember these?"

Domenico peered over her shoulder. "They were there when we first inspected the bodies. We thought it might be the plague."

"I made a careful sketch of the shape and colour, but it didn't tally with any plague symptoms. But last night I cross-checked it with an encyclopaedia of toxins. These blisters look just like the symptoms you get from cantharidin poisoning."

"I've never heard of that."

"It's secreted by beetles, and it's extremely dangerous. It causes vomiting, agonising pain and internal bleeding." Cristina unbuckled her satchel and took out three phials containing different coloured powders, a small spoon, and a mixing beaker. Everyone watched closely as she measured out and mixed the powders, then added some drops of water to create a green paste. Carefully she used a brush to apply the paste directly onto the corpse's blisters, then she started counting. By the time she had reached one hundred, the paste had turned a reddish-brown.

"What does that mean?" Domenico asked.

Cristina didn't reply, but patiently repeated the procedure on the other two corpses. Only when she had got identical results did she turn to her brother. "These men were all poisoned with cantharidin."

"Are you sure?"

Cristina nodded. "We saw blisters on all of the bodies. They were all murdered."

"How do you poison two hundred and ninety-three men at the same time?"

"We'll never know for sure, but most likely through the water. When Colonna discovered that his bid had failed, Prospero could have sent out a tender to the *Speranza* to resupply them with fresh water. But the barrels would all have been poisoned."

"And the crew would have used different barrels of water," Tomasso added. "Which explains why they survived."

"What about Alnaaji?" Domenico asked. "How did he survive?"

"That's a very good question," Cristina said. "I don't know."

"He told me that he'd been seasick for the whole journey," Tomasso suggested. "If he couldn't keep anything down, he wouldn't have drunk from the poisoned barrels."

"Possibly," Domenico said. "Either way, he had a lucky escape."

"This crime is now beyond doubt." Cristina looked at the grave. "We have hard evidence of mass murder. Fabrizio Colonna and Prospero Filippo are named on the failed bid, and these victims were deliberately poisoned to cut the consortium's losses. Now the Pope must act."

53: JUSTICE

Pope Julius II cradled his head in his hands and cried out in sorrow.

He sat motionless for a long time, immersed in grief. Cristina and Domenico weren't sure what to do, for the Holy Father had dismissed all his attendants, leaving just the three of them in his private study.

"I do not want to believe that men are capable of such calculated evil," he said at last. "I do not want to live in such a world."

"Forgive us for the pain we have caused you, Holy Father, but this is the truth," Cristina replied.

Pope Julius stared at her. "You are sure? You have no doubts?"

"Logic does not lie."

"But it can be misled."

"Not in this case, Holy Father. It has taken us a long time to reach this point, but we are convinced of Colonna's guilt."

"Bad enough to treat St Peter's as an object of speculation and profiteering, but to murder in cold blood simply to protect the ducats in your purse..." Pope Julius sipped from a goblet of wine in a vain attempt to numb the pain. "Nearly three hundred souls, wilfully destroyed. What monsters walk among us?"

Domenico was keen to move from outrage to action. "I cannot explain their evil, Holy Father, but I know who these men are and where to find them. Fabrizio Colonna and Prospero Filippo masterminded this terrible scheme. We should start by arresting them."

Pope Julius nodded thoughtfully.

Cristina had expected immediate assent, but the silence dragged on. Surely, he could not be considering forgiveness?

"Colonna and Prospero's names are on the bid documents, Holy Father. It is as good as a confession. Of course, their arrests will only be the first of many."

"Arresting them will shake the foundations of this city."

"And so it should!" Cristina tried to control her anger. "This goes far beyond one consortium. All the dynastic families have blood on their hands. The entire construction project is being used to divert Church funds into private pockets. St Peter's has become a lightning conductor for greed, and greed is a monster that can never be sated. It can only be slayed."

Julius stood up and crossed the room to gaze out of the window at the turbulence of the construction site. "And yet, the system we have in place, however flawed, is working. A new basilica is rising."

Cristina couldn't believe the Pope was following this line of thought. "Holy Father, if you surrender to the forces of greed, St Peter's will never be finished."

"That does not follow."

"When the basilica is finished, the lucrative contracts will dry up, which is the last thing the oligarchs want. So, they will find a way to make the construction last until the end of time. This is the perverse logic of free enterprise."

Pope Julius watched a massive block of stone being hoisted up to one of the barrel vaults, and suddenly he felt nauseous at the sheer scale of what he had undertaken.

"Holy Father," Cristina pressed, "you decreed that whoever was guilty would be banned from all future building contracts. You warned the oligarchs, yet they continued with their corrupt practices. I witnessed Caposquadra Spiro massacre innocents on behalf of Orsini —"

"That was on foreign soil," Pope Julius interrupted. "I have no jurisdiction there."

"I have witnessed slave labour camps in the travertine quarries east of Rome. And we have seen bribery and corruption taint the Building Committee of St Peter's. In one way or another, all the oligarchs are guilty."

"But who else can I turn to?" Pope Julius exclaimed. "Who else is left to build this great symbol of light? Idealism does not move mountains!"

Cristina let the fierce echo of his voice decay to silence. "Holy Father, do you want St Peter's to be built on foundations of greed, or of justice?"

"I want it built. Just that. Or I will be remembered as the fool who destroyed one great basilica but was unable to raise another."

Domenico could see they were hurtling towards deadlock. "Might I make a suggestion, Holy Father? We move against the Colonna dynasty with the full force of the law and pray that the other oligarchs will be scared into obedience. Break one, and they will all tremble."

Pope Julius considered the idea, then slowly nodded his assent.

Casa della Mobilita was not one of the newer charitable foundations in Rome. For nearly fifty years it had been quietly helping amputees and the lame by supplying crutches and hand-crafted walking aids, mainly to ex-soldiers. But at the start of the year, Fabrizio Colonna had chosen to favour the charity with his generous patronage, and since then things had moved quickly.

Today the great and the good had gathered to celebrate the opening of a new, beautifully equipped carpentry workshop. The family's coat of arms adorned the front of the building in vibrant, freshly painted colours, while inside various members of the Colonna clan were squeezed between workbenches where carpenters stood in crisp new overalls. A carefully curated selection of beneficiaries waited to receive their mobility aids at the appropriate moment.

Domenico and Tomasso entered the workshop discreetly, to find Fabrizio Colonna standing on a dais at one end of the room, delivering a worthy speech.

"...which is why this cause is so close to my heart. Victims of war, disease and accidents are among those who reach out to us for help." Colonna took a moment to smooth his upturned moustache. "Bad enough to lose a limb, but invariably the loss of livelihood follows, and that is where my House of Mobility steps in. By generously providing free crutches, walking sticks and custom-made devices, the House of Colonna helps these poor people to help themselves!" He raised his arms in triumph, and everyone in the workshop dutifully applauded.

Carried away by his own humanity, Colonna picked up a pair of crutches from one of the benches and started swinging himself around the workshop at high speed. "See how well they work!" he called out with a laugh.

The beneficiaries waiting to receive their walking aids watched in bemusement, unsure whether Colonna was mocking them or celebrating their resilience.

Domenico, however, had seen enough. As Colonna swung past, he stuck out his foot, caught one of the crutches and sent the oligarch clattering to the floor.

A gasp of shock echoed around the workshop. As Colonna picked himself up, his face was flushed with rage. "Who did that?" he roared. "Who tripped me?" His gaze flashed angrily at the crowd. "Speak up! Who was it?"

Domenico stepped forward. "Perhaps your charitable gestures would be more moving if you were not also murdering the most vulnerable for your own profits."

A moment of stunned silence. No-one could believe what they'd just heard.

Then Colonna raised one of the crutches and prodded Domenico in the chest. "I'll have you flogged for such impertinence."

Domenico grabbed the crutch and yanked it from the oligarch's hand. "Fabrizio Colonna, you are under arrest for conspiring to murder two hundred and ninety-three migrant workers on board the *Speranza*."

"Get this insolent dog out of my sight!" Colonna thundered.

Colonna's servants moved forward, but at that moment a dozen Apostolic Guards surged into the workshop, swords drawn, and lined up behind Domenico.

Realising that he was outnumbered, Fabrizio Colonna drew himself up to his full height and lifted his chin. "How dare you barge in here making wild and defamatory accusations? We are here to help the most downtrodden among us, to raise them up with Christian charity."

"Don't try and play the innocent." Domenico brandished the bid documents. "Your name is on this paperwork."

"I have nothing to do with paperwork. All that is delegated. I am far too busy to be aware of everything that is done in my name."

"We have already arrested Prospero Filippo. And he has confessed that he took orders directly from you." Domenico nodded to Tomasso, who unclipped a pair of manacles from his belt and moved towards Colonna.

"Don't even think about it!" the oligarch hissed.

Calmly, Domenico took the manacles from Tomasso and grabbed hold of Colonna's hands. "Keep still."

Colonna yanked his hands away petulantly. "You are ending your career. You are destroying any chance of a future in Rome. You will be begging on the streets by the time I have finished with you."

Domenico snapped the manacles around Colonna's wrists. "I'll take my chances."

54: BLAME

The hearing took place in the same courtroom Cristina had found herself in five years earlier — an imposing wood-panelled chamber bustling with uniformed officials, the walls lined with enormous bookshelves which creaked under the weight of hundreds of volumes of city statutes. Only this time, Cristina wasn't the accused — now she was a special adviser to the prosecutor.

"When will the cross-examinations start?" Cristina asked as she laid out her documents on the large, polished desk.

The prosecutor gave a shrug. "The first stage is investigation. The magistrate will question all parties to build up a picture of what actually happened. After that, things will get heated. But this morning will be mainly procedural."

Fabrizio Colonna was taking no chances. His arrival at the courtroom was designed to intimidate. He strode into the chamber flanked by his defence lawyer and a team of assistants; in his wake strode Prospero Filippo, and behind him came a dozen of the most senior members of the Colonna family. Everyone was dressed to impress — luscious fur cloaks, saffron-dyed silks laced with gold thread, rich velvet doublets studded with pearls, elaborate hairstyles dressed in veils, and more ceremonial gold chains than you could shake a stick at. The spectacle silenced the court officials, who gazed in wonder as Colonna's entourage colonised one half of the chamber.

Cristina glanced at the magistrate, who seemed irked at being upstaged in his own courtroom.

"When you've quite finished," he said sourly.

Immediately the defence lawyer sprang to his feet. "Actually, Your Honour, before you start the questioning, we do have a procedural matter to raise."

"Which is?"

"My clients have been held in custody for six days. Given the status of Fabrizio Colonna, his generous patronage of Rome, and the four centuries of service the Colonna family have given to the Italian states, this is an outrageous insult to his dignity and station. To be incarcerated alongside common thieves and cutthroats is vindictive and unnecessary, and we petition the court to grant immediate bail to the defendants."

The magistrate looked at the Colonna delegation. He disliked people parading their power in his courtroom, because there was only one master here — the Law. And yet, when he cast his eye along the rows of aristocrats, the magistrate's resolve wavered. They looked back at him with haughty determination, silently daring him to defy their money and connections. Did he really have the stomach to take on the Colonna dynasty?

"Very well." The magistrate cleared his throat as if this was nothing more than a routine point of order. "The defendants are to be released from custody but must remain within the city limits for the duration of the trial."

"Thank you, Your Honour," said the defence lawyer, bowing appreciatively.

The court notaries scribbled down the exchange in their ledgers, and an official Notice of Temporary Release was passed to the summoner.

The magistrate banged his gavel decisively. "This court is now in session. We are to consider the guilt or innocence of Fabrizio Colonna and Prospero Filippo in the matter of the abandonment of the *Speranza* and the death of two hundred and ninety-three men on board."

"Forgive me, Your Honour." The defence lawyer sprang to his feet once more.

The magistrate scowled. "What now?"

"The defence submits that in order to consider this case, all the defendants need to be present in court."

A moment of confusion. Notaries checked their paperwork, and the magistrate glanced at Colonna and Prospero.

"Enough obfuscation! Speak your mind," the magistrate snapped.

"Your Honour, new evidence has come to light which exonerates my clients —"

"And you will have the opportunity to present it."

"But this evidence proves that the person who is actually responsible for the tragic deaths on the *Speranza* is one Caposquadra Spiro. This trial will make a mockery of justice if Spiro is not present in court to face the charges."

There was a flurry of panic in the courtroom as notaries referred to precedent and procedure.

The prosecution lawyer turned to Cristina and whispered, "Did you know about this?"

"No. But if it's true, it changes everything."

"What could this evidence be?" The prosecutor tapped his finger on the dossier in front of Cristina. "I thought everything we had was in there."

"Maybe this is all part of the ongoing feud between Orsini and Colonna."

The magistrate rapped his gavel to restore silence, then turned to the defence lawyer. "Anyone can concoct fanciful stories to deflect blame and confuse the court. Clarify your assertion."

"Your Honour, we have sworn testimony that proves Caposquadra Spiro sabotaged the *Speranza* to benefit his master, Giulio Orsini. We can prove that he took barrels of poisoned water out to the ship shortly after it passed Naples."

"And you have a motive for this fanciful theory?"

"An act of intimidation, Your Honour, to scare off the Colonna family from bidding for labour contracts that Orsini holds."

The magistrate glanced at the prosecutor. "You know this man, Caposquadra Spiro?"

The prosecutor and Cristina went into a huddle to discuss their response, then Cristina stood up. "We do, Your Honour. Although he is not implicated in this crime, Spiro is linked to others, and he is a person of interest. We have no objection to him being arrested."

"And I thought this was going to be a straightforward case," the magistrate muttered to himself. He held out his hand to the notaries. "Warrant."

One of the court officials thrust a warrant into his hand, which the magistrate signed with a flourish.

The summoners decided to arrest Spiro shortly after he entered a notorious bordello in the Trastevere district of the city. They had received a tip-off about his movements and could easily have seized him on the way in, but this way, a courtesan would get paid without having to work and Spiro would be humiliated.

So they waited until they heard the bells in the old Basilica di Santa Maria chime the quarter, then stormed into the brothel.

Scantily clad women screamed and tried to cover themselves, respectable-looking men hid their faces and ran for the doors, while the boys serving wine just sniggered.

"Spiro! Which room?" the lead summoner demanded.

"This is a private —" the brothelkeeper began.

The summoner slammed her against the wall. "Which room?"

She saw the fierce expression on his face. "Five."

The summoner led his men up the stairs, enjoying titillating glimpses of flesh that rushed past in the opposite direction. When they arrived outside room five, the summoner kicked open the door to reveal a half-naked Caposquadra Spiro on the bed.

"Just in time," the summoner smiled.

Spiro tried to scramble away but he was no match for the summoners, who took immense pleasure in hauling him down the stairs.

"You have no idea who you are dealing with!" Spiro yelled.

"Tell it to the judge."

With that, the summoners threw Spiro into the back of the prison cart that was waiting in the square, and snapped the locks shut.

55: SCAPEGOAT

As his rage subsided, Caposquadra Spiro realised that he had nothing to worry about. When you wielded power such as his, you made enemies who were constantly trying to drag you down. But he had served Giulio Orsini well, and that would guarantee his protection now. The more he thought about it, the more Spiro realised that his arrest was just political theatre, designed to intimidate; no doubt urgent discussions were being held even now to secure his release.

Spiro sat back against the dank prison walls, adjusted the iron manacles around his wrists so that they didn't cut into his skin, and waited.

And waited.

But nothing happened. No one rushed to see him; there was no delegation from Orsini, no lawyers posted applications for bail, and no-one bribed the guards to secure him a better cell.

As the hours passed, surprise soured into disappointment; then just as panic was starting to take hold, Spiro heard keys jangling in the corridor outside and footsteps approaching.

Finally, they were going to get him out of here. Spiro stood up and held out his hands ready for the gaoler to remove the manacles.

But as the door swung open, crushing disappointment filled Spiro's heart. "What are *you* doing here?"

Cristina smiled. "I thought you might like a visitor."

Spiro waved her away and slumped back against the wall.

Cristina looked down at him. This tyrant who had abused workers, this monster who had massacred a whole tribe to appease his anger, was now just a man in chains. Yet his incarceration had brought no humility.

"Have they told you the charges you're facing?"

"I know nothing about the *Speranza*. That's nothing to do with me."

Cristina pulled a small wooden stool into the centre of the cell and sat down opposite Spiro. "It's your word against that of a very rich and powerful man."

"I have a rich and powerful man on my side as well."

"Really? Has he been down here to see you? Has he appointed lawyers to represent you? Has he even arranged for better food?"

Spiro remained silent.

"I thought not."

"He's a busy man."

"Right now, he is busy betraying you."

"You know nothing about Giulio Orsini!"

"Take his silence as a warning. He will only stick by you as long as it serves his own ends." Cristina pulled a leather satchel from her shoulder, undid the buckles and took out a loaf of bread, a chunk of Grana Padano, and a small flask of wine. She set the food on the stone floor in front of Spiro. "What has the world come to when your friends ignore you, but your enemies bring food?"

Spiro looked hungrily at the food, but he refused to reach out and take it.

"You have done many terrible things, Spiro, yet there is still a chance you can find redemption."

"If I'd wanted a priest, I would have called for one."

"Switch sides. Come over to the side of justice and give evidence about the crimes and fraud you have witnessed in the Orsini family. Some of your own crimes could yet be pardoned if you provide evidence that brings down the entire machinery of exploitation."

Spiro looked bewildered, as if he was struggling to understand what she was offering.

"The people we're really after are the oligarchs," Cristina pressed. "They are the architects of profiteering in this city. If you turn Pope's evidence, you will not only save your soul, but you will minimise your own punishment. It's the right thing to do."

Caposquadra Spiro blinked, then roared with laughter. "Are you insane, woman? I will not turn against my own family!"

"You seriously think Orsini considers you to be family? Can't you see what's going on here? The two dynasties have done a deal, and you are the scapegoat, Spiro. You will take all the blame."

"No! Orsini and Colonna are sworn enemies. They would never do a deal."

"But the one thing they hate more than each other, are the classes beneath them. They have aristocracy in common, and class loyalty is more powerful than any duty of care they pretend to have for those who work for them."

"I am different!" Spiro stood up. "I am special!" He yanked on the chains that held him to the wall, making them rattle. "I have made Giulio Orsini a fortune from his basilica contracts, and he will not abandon me."

Cristina looked up at Spiro and shook her head. "You will never be one of them."

"But I have something Orsini does not." Spiro tapped a finger to his forehead. "Using just the power of my mind, I can conjure schemes to make the nobility rich. Orsini has culture and breeding; he is a polished man. But when you dig down, he's actually quite stupid. They all are. Aristocrats have little imagination, which is why they need men like me."

"And would these clever schemes of yours include slaughtering a Bedouin tribe?"

"I know nothing of that."

"Or perhaps having Imam Sufian beaten to death?"

"You are confused. Sufian took his own life while in prison."

"I was there! I saw it with my own eyes. The life was beaten out of him because he was going to expose your corruption."

Spiro shrugged. "That is not how I remember it."

Cristina studied him, amazed at his unshakeable belief in his masters. "It is not clever to be flippant with the truth."

"Truth is overrated. Power is all that matters."

"But power carries responsibility. Which is why you will take the blame."

"I have served my master well. He will protect me."

"As you wish." Cristina picked up the wine, the bread and the cheese and packed it all neatly back into her satchel. Then she stood up and banged on the door to call the guard. As she left, she turned back to Spiro one last time. "You have much to learn about the aristocracy. And that lesson will cost you dearly."

56: TRIAL

The hearing resumed the following day. Once again, the court was treated to the spectacle of Colonna wealth, only this time the whole family made a point of wearing completely different clothes. Not one item that had been paraded the previous day was on show again; in a city where most people lived in the same clothes seven days a week, it was an arrogant assertion of privilege.

Yet that was nothing compared to the audacity of their defence, as became clear when their lawyer stood to make his opening remarks to the magistrate.

"Justice without mercy is cruelty. The words of St Thomas Aquinas, Your Honour, and never were they more appropriate than today. No-one in this courtroom denies that a terrible tragedy occurred at sea. A dreadful loss of life. But rather than praying earnestly for the two hundred and ninety-three souls that perished on the waves, the prosecution has set about looking for scapegoats to punish. Rather than investigating the competence of the captain and crew, the prosecution and their 'special adviser' have launched this vengeful and vindictive case against my clients. We all know where this originates: guilt. The Vatican's guilt that the full cost of St Peter's will be measured not just in millions of ducats, but in countless human lives as well. And to assuage their guilt, they are now persecuting my client, Fabrizio Colonna, a noble and philanthropic man from a great and ancient family. What the prosecution are doing is not simply wrong, it is unchristian. Rather than read from the angry pages of the Old Testament, they should study the pages of the Gospels. Pain, grief and guilt are not healed by revenge,

but by mercy. Exactly as Aquinas writes: *justice without mercy is cruelty*. Your Honour, I move to have this case dismissed. It is a malicious prosecution that should never have come before you, and it demeans the dignity of this court."

Cristina couldn't believe the audacity of their argument. "He's mocking us!" she whispered to the prosecutor.

"All we have to do is focus on the evidence —"

Too late. Cristina was on her feet and addressing the magistrate. "Your Honour, do I have permission to address the court directly?"

"I'll allow it."

She turned to the defence lawyer. "You talk about forgiveness and mercy and philanthropy only because at this precise moment they serve your purpose. But if you can wrap yourself in Christian values like a piece of clothing, allow me to hang mine in the wardrobe for a few moments." Cristina focussed her indignation on Fabrizio Colonna. "There can be no forgiveness because the blood of hundreds of innocent lives is on your hands. You deserve no mercy because you have shown no mercy. It is not wrath that motivates this prosecution, but anger — the rage of the righteous that vanquishes evil. And that is what you will face in this courtroom."

"Objection, Your Honour!" The defence lawyer stood up. "We expect justice, not cruelty. And that woman —" he pointed at Cristina — "is clearly motived by nothing but malice."

The magistrate sat back in his chair, his eyes darting between Colonna and Cristina. Perhaps if the oligarch had shown a little more humility and not paraded his wardrobe before the court, things may have gone his way.

"Swear Fabrizio Colonna in," the magistrate ordered. "I wish to question him."

Reluctantly, Colonna took the stand and gave a passable impression of humility before the magistrate. Under questioning, he held firm to his line of defence: Giulio Orsini was terrified of losing his contract to Colonna's more competitive bid; they tried to bribe him to withdraw but he refused, so Orsini pulled strings to get Colonna's bid cancelled at the last minute.

"Yet still you shipped workers from Ifriqiya?" the magistrate pressed.

"We were determined to prove how well our system worked. How lean and efficient it was. So we chartered the *Speranza*. When Orsini found out, he was determined to sabotage our operation, and that is when this tragedy unfolded; Caposquadra Spiro was despatched to deliver poisoned water to the ship."

"An explanation can be coherent without being true," the prosecutor interrupted. "They could just as easily have claimed a many-headed Hydra rose from the depths and destroyed the *Speranza* with its poisoned breath. Where is the evidence for their claims, Your Honour?"

"We have a witness waiting outside," the defence lawyer countered. "A man of unimpeachable integrity."

"Then bring him in." The magistrate waved Colonna to clear the witness stand, and all eyes turned to the courtroom doors. A few moments later, one of the clerks of the court led in the harbourmaster from Civitavecchia.

"Should I be worried?" the prosecutor whispered to Cristina.

"We have already taken his testimony. He was with Tomasso when they discovered the ship. That was the first he knew about the *Speranza*."

But as Cristina watched the harbourmaster make his way across the courtroom, she started to feel anxious. She remembered him as an authoritative man who strode with the confident gait of someone who had spent a lifetime on the water, yet now he walked timidly towards the witness stand, head down, refusing to make eye contact. Under oath, he gave an account of how he had seen Caposquadra Spiro charter a caravel two days before the *Speranza* was discovered drifting.

"What was on board this boat?" the magistrate asked.

"I saw men loading barrels onto it, Your Honour."

"Barrels of what?"

"I cannot say for sure. Wine or water, I cannot say."

"And you saw this with your own eyes?"

"Yes, Your Honour."

The magistrate looked towards the prosecutor, but it was Cristina who answered. "He's lying, Your Honour."

"That is not for you to judge."

"Apologies, Your Honour. But this man was with Deputy Tomasso when they discovered the *Speranza*, yet he made no mention of this caravel at the time. We questioned the harbourmaster in detail, and he said nothing about Spiro because the incident never happened."

"I was too frightened to tell the truth!" the harbourmaster snapped.

"Frightened of whom?" the magistrate pressed.

"Your Honour, Spiro had threatened to harm my family if I breathed a word of what I witnessed. I could not put my family in danger, but I swear I am telling the truth now."

Cristina glared intently at the harbourmaster, but still he averted his gaze.

"He's been bought," she whispered to the prosecutor. "He can't even look at me."

Now the prosecutor was worried. "He's a credible witness. A trusted official."

Cristina looked at Fabrizio Colonna and saw the smug contempt in his eyes. This was a man who knew how to use the corrupting power of money to get whatever he wanted.

57: SACRIFICED

Caposquadra Spiro strode into the courtroom, confident that his voice would be heard and that justice would be done.

Despite the intensity of the magistrate's questioning, Spiro kept his temper. He vigorously denied any involvement in the *Speranza* disaster, and although he claimed to have no knowledge of the individual who did actually deliver poisoned water to the ship, he was convinced that Fabrizio Colonna was behind it.

"By what reasoning?" the magistrate asked.

"They were so confident of winning the contract to supply labourers, they started shipping men across the Mediterranean. When their bid failed at the last minute, they had to cut their losses. And the most efficient way of doing that was to…" He tried to find the right word. "Cancel the cargo."

"Cancel? You mean murder two hundred and ninety-three men and boys?"

"Either way, Your Honour, it was nothing to do with me."

Cristina studied Spiro's face. She hated this man, she had seen the evil he was capable of, and yet on this one point she agreed with him; the *Speranza* was not his crime.

The magistrate was less convinced. He consulted his notes, then stared intently at Spiro. "We have compelling testimony that says otherwise."

Spiro shook his head. "Whoever gave that testimony is lying."

"You are calling the harbourmaster of the port of Civitavecchia a liar?"

"Yes."

"The man is a trusted public official, responsible for the largest harbour in the Papal States. He oversees the collection of customs duties on countless thousands of tons of cargo every year, and the safety of every sailor who passes through that port is in his hands."

"The harbourmaster is a liar, Your Honour."

The magistrate raised his eyebrows. "Why should I believe you?"

"Because Giulio Orsini will vouch for me."

The name sent a ripple of excitement through the court officials, who realised they now had ringside seats for the next round of the Colonna-Orsini feud.

"My master, Giulio Orsini, knows the truth," Spiro insisted. "The *Speranza* was nothing to do with us. My innocence will be proved by his testimony."

The magistrate went into a huddle with the clerks and instructed them to issue a summons for Orsini to appear in court without delay. Cristina glanced at Colonna — this development should have worried him, as the word of a powerful noble like Orsini would carry far more weight than the harbourmaster's testimony, but strangely, Colonna seemed unflustered.

The court adjourned for lunch, and by the time everyone returned, Orsini had arrived to give evidence. He was clearly trying to play the same game of dressing for power as his rival, but not having had as much time to prepare, he did not cut quite such an impressive figure.

The magistrate put him directly onto the witness stand. "The claim before this court is that Caposquadra Spiro, a foreman in your service, conspired to poison nearly three hundred migrant workers on the *Speranza*, in order to send a warning to anyone who dared challenge the Orsini family's grip on labour contracts. It is a profoundly serious allegation."

Orsini shook his head gravely. "Your Honour, let me reassure you and this court that I would never dream of intimidating a business rival. That would be counter to my whole philosophy."

"Which is?"

"The most competitive contract should always win. The playing field should always be fair and true. In that way, the greatest glory goes to St Peter's Basilica and the Supreme Pontiff, Julius II."

"So you refute Colonna's claims?"

From his seat across the courtroom, Spiro looked at his master expectantly.

But Orsini hesitated before speaking. "Sadly, there is some truth in the claims."

Confusion rippled through the chamber.

"Please explain," the magistrate said irritably.

"Although I maintain the highest ethical standards in my own life, sadly the same cannot be said for Caposquadra Spiro."

"But he works to your orders."

"Over the past six months, there has been a regrettable tendency for Spiro to take actions which are at best unorthodox, at worst, criminal. Which is why I have been forced to sever all dealings with the man."

"Since when?"

"Since just now, Your Honour."

The courtroom bristled with excitement. Cristina looked at Spiro, who had gone very pale.

The magistrate banged his gavel to restore calm, then focussed again on Orsini. "Are you telling this court that Caposquadra Spiro poisoned the *Speranza* of his own volition?"

Orsini looked thoughtful. "I have no direct knowledge of that, but I would not be in the least surprised if he did."

"I don't understand. If he was not working to your orders, what was his motivation?"

"Spiro has always run the labour contracts for our quarrying operation. If Colonna were to win those, Spiro would lose his power and a considerable amount of money."

"Considerable enough to commit mass murder?"

Orsini shrugged. "Spiro is a sadistic man. I'm ashamed to confess I have witnessed it with my own eyes. Numerous times he has been reprimanded for the way he treats workers, but to no avail. There is a side to him that seems to relish cruelty."

"That is a lie!" Spiro finally found his voice. He lunged towards the witness stand, but immediately the court guards rushed to intercept him.

"Enough!" the magistrate bellowed, banging his gavel on the desk. "You will respect this court or be sent back to the cells for contempt."

"What happened to justice?" Spiro shouted, struggling with the guards. "What happened to telling the truth before God?"

"Sit down and be silent!" the magistrate warned.

"I have given you loyal service my entire life!" Spiro screamed at Orsini. "I have gone beyond what any man should do, just to please you. And now you throw me to the dogs? *Vaffanculo! Cornuto!*"

"You will be silent!" the magistrate shouted.

"While they blame me for everything?" Spiro's face was pulsing with rage. "I must be silent while they walk away as innocent men, when we all know where the real villainy lies?"

Orsini turned his head away to shield himself from the outburst and appealed to the magistrate. "Your Honour, do I really have to be subjected to this vile abuse?"

The magistrate's patience snapped. "Take him away." Two more guards joined the ruckus and wrestled the distraught Spiro towards the doors.

"Betrayal! This is betrayal! You Judas!"

The guards bundled Spiro through the doors and down the corridor, until the sound of his cursing could no longer be heard.

In the silence, Orsini turned to the magistrate and quietly asked, "Is that how an innocent man behaves?"

Cristina looked from Orsini to Colonna and saw the two oligarchs exchange the briefest of smiles. It was a look of acknowledgement, of supremacy, of triumph at outwitting the authorities. At the end of the day, these two men would always end up on the same side because aristocratic solidarity served them both so well.

By the end of the week, Caposquadra Spiro had been found guilty of causing the deaths of two hundred and ninety-three men on the *Speranza*. He was sentenced to be hanged the following week.

58: KARMA

Cristina saw Spiro one last time, on the morning of his execution. He had undergone a considerable change.

Gone was the overseer who once rode through the travertine quarries terrorising workers; gone too was the arrogant, entitled man who struck down anyone who stood in his way. The figure who now crouched before Cristina in the dank cell seemed to have shrunk into a frightened old man with grey stubble and matted hair.

Spiro squinted, momentarily blinded by the light coming through the cell door. As he recognised Cristina, he prostrated himself on the ground, arms outstretched in supplication. "For the love of God, help me!" His voice was hoarse from the hours he had spent protesting his innocence to the prison guards. "Do I not deserve justice?"

Cristina edged back to keep her feet beyond Spiro's grasp. "It is too late."

"Have I not done St Peter's noble service? The stones that pilgrims will gaze on for a thousand years were quarried under my supervision. Does that count for nothing?"

"You were given your chance. In this very cell, I offered you a deal. You said no."

Spiro's shoulders trembled as he started to sob. "How could they turn on me? After everything I've done for them."

"I told you. I warned you."

Spiro scrambled to his knees. "You know I am innocent of the *Speranza* slaughter. You know it!" He lunged towards Cristina until his chains yanked him back to the wall. "How can you stand there and allow this miscarriage of justice?"

"You may not be guilty of the *Speranza*, but you are a guilty man, Spiro. Guilty of the massacre in Tunis. Guilty of trafficking people into slavery. Guilty of extreme cruelty over many years."

"I was only following orders!" he protested. "Giulio Orsini was my master; I had to do his bidding. I had no choice! Do you think any of these things happened without his knowledge?"

"That does not absolve you, Spiro."

He yanked his chains in frustration. "It is all Orsini's fault. He is the master. He commanded it. He is the traitor!"

Cristina looked Spiro in the eye, refusing to be intimidated by his rage. She waited for the wave of anger to subside. "Do you know what evil is? True evil?" she asked quietly. "It is not just the beating and torture of your fellow humans, nor is it simply the abuse of the power and trust placed in you. No, Spiro, true evil is when you divide the world into compartments and focus only on what is within your own little sphere. Because when you detach yourself from the rest of humanity, there is no limit to the horrors that can unfold. Following orders does not absolve you of guilt, it just reveals what a weak man you are."

"I beg you! Save me!" Spiro wailed. He had tried anger and persuasion, but neither had worked, so now he relinquished all pride and cried like a child. Tears ran down his unshaven face as he howled for forgiveness.

It was desperate to watch, and Cristina felt her heart flutter as if it was urging her to allow mercy to enter. But she had learnt her lesson. "Let me put it in terms you understand, Spiro. You have committed many cruel and unlawful acts. Each of those incurred a cost. Now the debts are due, so you must pay the bills. There can be no exceptions, because people like you believe that gold is more powerful than God. That is the logic you have lived by, and that is the logic by which you will die."

There was a rattle of keys in the cell door as it swung open. "It's time," the guard said.

Cristina nodded. "Good luck in the next life, Spiro. You'll need it." Then she turned and left.

As part of the prosecution team, Cristina was expected to witness the execution from the public viewing platform, but she had seen so much death recently that she could not face another one. In any case, there would be plenty of other witnesses. Instead, she waited under the giant horse chestnut tree in the courtyard outside the prison governor's office. The sounds alone painted a ghastly picture.

Cristina heard the crunch of the guards' boots on gravel, along with the dragging sound of Spiro's feet as he tried to resist. She heard his angry, sobbing cries and his desperate appeals for justice.

Moments later, she heard the thump of feet on the scaffold steps as the guards dragged Spiro up to the platform, then the mumbled prayers of the priest, who raced through the formalities as quickly as possible.

Nothing could stop this process now. The priest fell silent … then there was a violent clatter as the trapdoor opened and Spiro's body fell.

Cristina knew this should feel like success, but it didn't. Because although the man who had been punished was guilty, not all the guilty had been punished. They had got away with their crimes.

59: REFORM

The Sistine Chapel was something to behold. A giant wooden cradle now dangled on a web of ropes that dropped down through the ceiling, creating a floating platform sixty feet in the air.

Cristina craned her neck to study the structural details. "So, when does Michelangelo start painting?"

Chief Architect Bramante sniffed. "Whenever his 'creative sensibilities' decide the time is right."

"I take it you don't like the man."

"He's so unprofessional," Bramante replied, scowling. "Many artists would kill for a chance to paint this ceiling, but all he can do is complain."

"Perhaps because he knows he's a genius. But at least he can't complain about the cradle you've built for him to work on."

"He's refused to use it."

"What?"

"He won't even try it out."

"Why not?"

"He took one look at it and accused me of trying to kill him out of jealousy."

"That's absurd." Cristina sat down on one of the pews next to Bramante. "If you can build a great basilica, you can certainly build a scaffold."

"That is exactly what I said. But the 'maestro' insisted it needed more rope." Bramante looked up at his redundant creation. "In truth, it has precisely the amount of rope it needs."

"So what happens now?"

"He's going to build his own scaffold from the floor up and move it around the chapel as he finishes each section."

"Not a very elegant solution."

Bramante sighed. "Yet the Pope indulges him."

Suddenly the southwest doors swung open, and Cardinal Riario strode in carrying four folios stuffed with documents. He glanced at Bramante. "Let me guess, you were complaining about Michelangelo?"

"Isn't everyone?"

Cristina hurried across the chapel to take the folios from the cardinal. "Did you secure the backing of the Holy Father?"

"He was impressed by your work. And yes, he has sanctioned it." Riario arranged the folios in a line on a small table. "Now all we need is for the oligarchs to sign up to it."

"Good luck with that," Bramante muttered.

"Show a little faith in me," Riario said.

"Trust me, the oligarchs will not sign."

They didn't have to wait long to find out, as a few moments later the heads of the four most powerful dynastic families in the Italian peninsula were led into the chapel: Orsini, Colonna, Medici and Sforza.

Cardinal Riario indulged them with some small talk, then picked up one of the folios. "Gentlemen, I have summoned you here to announce that the construction of St Peter's is entering a new phase of civilised building."

The oligarchs looked bemused.

"The Holy Father has decreed that change must come from tragedy. If we want to honour the victims of the *Speranza*, we must use this moment to introduce sweeping reforms." He started handing out the folios, one to each oligarch. "We have drawn up a code of conduct which all parties bidding for contracts must adhere to. The code sets out minimum rates of pay for workers, as well as directives on working conditions. It sets a cap on profit margins and bans the use of cheap imported labour. With immediate effect, contracts must fulfil transparency clauses, declaring the interests of all parties and any conflicts of interest. This code will ensure that St Peter's won't just be a beacon of spirituality, it will also be the most moral building in the world."

The oligarchs said nothing as they leafed through the folios, glancing at page after page of new regulations.

"You can study the details in your own time, but the headline points are exactly as I've outlined. So, gentlemen, can I assume that you will all sign up to this code?"

Colonna scratched his beard, Medici stroked the top of his bald head, and Orsini gave a muted belch. None of them seemed impressed, but no-one wanted to be the first to start an argument with the cardinal.

Suddenly another voice spoke behind them. "I recognise that silence."

The oligarchs turned and saw Pope Julius II striding towards them across the chapel.

"I recognise it, but I do not accept it."

The oligarchs bowed their heads respectfully as Julius walked down the line, offering his heavy gold ring for each of them to kiss. "The simple truth is, if you do not sign up to this code, you will not be able to bid for construction contracts, either directly or through subsidiaries."

The oligarchs exchanged uneasy glances, then finally Orsini plucked up the courage to speak. "Holy Father, while we applaud this initiative, the code does create some technical difficulties."

"Namely?"

Colonna took up the baton of deferential defiance. "We are fully committed to humane working conditions, but these regulations…" He ran his fingers over the folio. "They are so onerous; they would make it impossible to continue with any construction work at all."

"It would involve an enormous amount of paperwork," Sforza added. "Which would introduce inefficiencies and erode profit margins."

"As well as making the final cost of St Peter's considerably greater." Medici gestured to his colleagues. "The great families disagree on many things, Holy Father, but on this point we are as one: if you force us to adhere to this new code of conduct, we shall all be forced to withdraw from the basilica project."

The other three oligarchs nodded their agreement.

Pope Julius turned away so that they couldn't see his face, but not before Cristina glimpsed the emotions etched there: anger that these men dared to defy his authority, and fear that the entire construction project was about to collapse. Without the oligarchs, nothing could move forward. Although they had all spoken separately, it was clear that someone had leaked news of the code to the oligarchs in advance, giving them a chance to collude. It had turned the issue into a dangerous test of the Vatican's authority.

The silence dragged on until Cristina cleared her throat. "May I speak, Holy Father?"

"I wish somebody would."

"If the new building code is too complicated, perhaps there is a simpler solution that these great nobles will understand. A tax. A stone tax."

The oligarchs looked anxious — tax was a word they hated even more than regulation.

But Pope Julius glimpsed a way out of the deadlock. "How would it work?"

"Every successful contract will be taxed with a levy. The money raised from that will be used to establish a mission in Ifriqiya, dedicated to helping the poorest Bedouin tribes and the remote Berber villages, so they are no longer forced to place their lives in the hands of people-traffickers."

"A charming but naïve idea," Orsini scoffed. "All the money will simply end up in the pockets of the rulers. That's how it works in Ifriqiya."

"Not if the mission is established by the Church, and run under the direct governance of Rome," Cristina replied.

Colonna looked indignant. "So, as well as maintaining our own households and looking after all the workers on our estates in Italy, we now have to support those in some far-flung land?"

"You were happy enough to exploit them," Cristina replied, "so why is it a problem to help them?"

"Because charity, for that's what this is, should begin at home," Giulio Orsini pronounced. The oligarchs stared at Julius, united in their defiance, confident that they could kill this latest suggestion as well.

But the Pope's face darkened as anger took hold. "Gentlemen, let me make this perfectly clear," he said with quiet menace. "If you refuse to sign the code of conduct, *and* you refuse to pay a Stone Tax, then you may as well sell your palazzos on the Tiber and leave Rome for good, because I will have no further use for you. Not only that, but the Church itself will no longer favour your families or protect your interests. You will be on your own, and I will make it my personal mission to court a new generation of powerful men who will appreciate the patronage of the Pope."

The oligarchs realised they had pushed this as far as they dared — the golden goose was about to bite their fingers off.

Giulio Orsini beamed a charming smile. "Holy Father, once again your wisdom has shown us the way. A mission in Ifriqiya, funded by the construction contracts for St Peter's is not only inspired, it is a testament to your own humanity and wisdom. You have my full support for the levy."

And once one oligarch had cracked, they all crumbled.

Hoping to capitalise on their retreat, Cristina turned to Pope Julius. "Holy Father, there is still the matter of Paolo Bottero to be resolved."

Julius blinked, struggling to place the name.

"The Apostolic Guard who was murdered in your service?" Cristina prompted.

"Ah, yes." Julius turned to the oligarchs. "Do I need to order a fresh investigation? Or does one of you have a conscience that is crying out to be cleansed?"

The oligarchs looked bemused. In truth, the deaths of ordinary people meant very little to them, but they could see that Pope Julius needed to be given something.

Orsini decided to seize the nettle. "Holy Father, I fear the truth behind that tragedy was silenced when you executed Caposquadra Spiro."

"He was guilty of the murder?"

"He was certainly capable of it. How can we know for sure what depravities lurked in the man's black heart?"

"How convenient for you that Spiro is unable to defend himself."

Orsini frowned. "My only thoughts are for the grieving family of the Apostolic Guard. Perhaps having someone to blame may ease their suffering."

"Perhaps." The Pope's eyes narrowed. "But remember, in the Final Judgement, we will all face God's justice. And then there will be nowhere to hide."

60: REPARATIONS

The north coast of Ifriqiya emerged through the sea mist as a thin grey line. Alnaaji stood on the quarterdeck clutching the railings, watching his home creep closer. Cristina, Tomasso and Isra took turns to keep the boy company, but there were many other tasks that had to be completed before they docked in Tunis.

Pope Julius had proved as good as his word. Within days of the meeting in the Sistine Chapel, he had confiscated Father Volpe's palazzo on the Tiber and ordered its mysterious underground rooms to be put at the disposal of the Vatican archivists for the storage of holy relics that were too fragile to be displayed. The sequestration was a warning to all members of the Building Committee of St Peter's to curb their venality.

Three days later, the Holy Father released enough money to establish the new mission in Ifriqiya, although it took another month to find a suitable galley, then recruit and equip a team of experts. It made for an eclectic mix of people on board: two Vatican diplomats to smooth the way and charm the Hafsid rulers; five young academics from Sapienza University, who would both teach and learn from the Berber peoples; a dozen merchants who had identified trading opportunities between Ifriqiya and Europe that could create lucrative new businesses and bring Italian wealth into the country; and a small squad of Apostolic Guards to protect the mission.

Cristina knew that establishing a base would be the easy part; the challenge was to make sure that the wealth spread far beyond the capital and reached the remotest settlements that were most vulnerable to the predations of the people-traffickers. Perhaps that was why her excitement was tempered by trepidation.

"It's hard to grasp the scale of Africa," Tomasso said as he approached the deck rail and stood next to Cristina. "Just imagine the vast wealth hidden in all those jungles and mountains. And how far south it stretches."

"God forbid the European powers ever stop fighting each other long enough to turn their attention to this continent," Cristina replied. "The people-trafficking scandal will look tame compared to what will happen then."

"Not necessarily," Tomasso objected. "Look at this mission — we're coming to help, not steal."

But Cristina shook her head. "Once Europeans taste the wealth of Africa, they will loot it without mercy and leave behind a desiccated husk, because greed unleashes the other evils. It is the father of all sins."

"Well, I'm glad Alnaaji doesn't share your outlook," Tomasso said, looking along the rail to where Isra and the boy were picking out features on the approaching coastline. "He can barely contain his excitement. Will his mother really be waiting for him in Tunis?"

"We sent messages via all the camel trains. One of them must have got through."

"Let's hope." Tomasso listened to Alnaaji's excited laughter as he tried to touch a seagull that was chasing the galley. "I'll miss him."

"We all will. But this is the right thing to do." Cristina thought of her own father, now lying cold in the family vault. "Children never stop needing their parents."

They walked over and joined Isra and Alnaaji on the other side of the deck. Tomasso found some pieces of hardtack in his pocket, and after a little trial and error, they were able to lure one of the seagulls down onto the rail. But its affections were fickle — the moment it had eaten the biscuit, it swooped back up into the sky and was gone.

In the moment of sadness that followed the bird's departure, Cristina put her arm around Alnaaji's shoulder. "I have a present for you."

"A present?" The boy looked up at her with an expectant smile.

Cristina reached into her pocket and pulled out a silver chain; dangling on the end of it was one of the winding keys for the verge-and-foliot clock in her library.

"Really?" Alnaaji looked at the key with reverence. "But you need this."

"I have two. And now we have one each." She put the key into his hands; he clutched it like a precious jewel.

"Thank you," he whispered. "I will keep it always."

"Whenever you look at it, you can remember the months you spent in Rome, learning about different people, and a different way of life."

Alnaaji considered her words, then shook his head. "No. When I look at this, I will think of you, and Isra and Tomasso. And the kindness you have shown me. That is what I will think of."

Then he turned his gaze back to the approaching coastline, waiting to catch the first glimpse of his mother.

A NOTE TO THE READER

In January 1939, my father, who was then just sixteen years old, escaped from Nazi-occupied Vienna as a refugee. Three years later, his life was again hanging by a thread — he was serving as an engine boy on a cargo ship in the Mediterranean, when they ran into a terrible storm.

The ship started leaking, the bilge pumps couldn't cope, and eventually the engine fires were flooded. With no power, it was impossible to control the vessel, which drifted broadside to the high waves and started listing badly. As the ship sank and the lifeboats were overwhelmed, my father found himself in the sea, desperately swimming for his life. He wrote in his diary:

...nearer to the shore we suddenly came face to face with a new menace: huge, ugly rocks between us and the beach. I was thrown up against one but managed to protect myself against the impact with outstretched hands, only to be pulled off again by the backwash. This happened about three times until I was able to climb high enough not to be dragged back into the sea again. By that time, the local Arabs from a nearby village, who had witnessed our shipwreck, came down to the beach and helped us to the shore. They showed courage, compassion and great hospitality, immediately lit fires on the beach to give us some warmth, and treated us wonderfully. I know I owe my life to them, because without their help we could easily have died from exposure on the beach. They took us into their humble houses, bathed our feet, dried our clothes and fed us. It was most touching to see the kindness with which they treated us.

Reading this made a lasting impression on me and fed directly into the opening chapter of this novel. It wasn't just the drama of the near-death experience that affected me, but the kindness of the local people who reached out to help complete strangers.

In today's world, strangers who are washed up on the shores of Europe are frequently met with hostility and suspicion. But the veneer of security that we enjoy is gossamer-thin, and a small shift in fortunes could see any of us plunged into a hostile world as refugees seeking safety, or migrants trying to escape poverty. What better way to explore some of these issues than through the lens of sixteenth-century Rome?

When you stand in the middle of St Peter's Basilica, the incredible thing is not that it took 120 years to build, but that it *only* took 120 years to build. Even to modern eyes that are accustomed to skyscrapers and mega-structures, St Peter's is breathtaking. It is the largest church in the world, situated in the smallest country in the world. It can hold 60,000 people inside, with another 300,000 in the square outside. Yet the whole structure is so brilliantly designed that it seems perfectly balanced and in proportion. Look up at the beautiful paintings on the walls and inside the dome … then realise that they are not paintings at all, but incredibly detailed mosaics made with tens of thousands of pieces of stone, glass and ceramic that will never fade.

You could be forgiven for thinking that this could only have been achieved with slave labour, and it is one of the most frequent questions asked of tour guides. The answer is no, St Peter's was not built by slaves, but by skilled craftsmen. Yet while the Catholic Church condemned slavery in the fifteenth and sixteenth centuries, it often turned a blind eye to Catholic countries which participated in the slave trade, and the Vatican was happy to use captured Muslim galley slaves in the Papal fleet.

Pull all these strands together, and you have an interesting set of ideas on which to build a story that resonates both with the sixteenth and twenty-first century: a Pope who condemns slavery, yet whose ambitions create a situation that encourages it; ordinary people trying to escape the poverty of developing countries by travelling to wealthy nations to work; an economy controlled by powerful men who are driven by greed. And yet, out of all this, comes an achievement of astounding beauty and brilliance, executed by some of the greatest artists of the day.

Thank you for joining me on this fourth journey in *The Basilica Diaries* series; I hope you enjoyed reading it as much as I enjoyed writing it. I am always fascinated to hear feedback from readers, either through **Amazon** or **Goodreads**, or if you'd rather give me feedback through social media, here are the links:

Website: www.RichardKurti.com

Instagram: RichardKurtiWriter

X (Twitter): @Richard_Kurti

If you get the chance to post a rating or review, or just to drop me a line with your thoughts, that would be great! In the meantime, I'm rolling up my sleeves to start plotting Book Five!

Sapere Books is an exciting new publisher of brilliant fiction and popular history.

To find out more about our latest releases and our monthly bargain books visit our website:
saperebooks.com